ATTA BOY

T0030776

ATTA BOY

Cally Fiedorek

UNIVERSITY OF IOWA PRESS | IOWA CITY

University of Iowa Press, Iowa City 52242
Copyright © 2024 by Cally Fiedorek
uipress.uiowa.edu

Printed in the United States of America

ISBN 978-1-60938-941-3 (pbk)
ISBN 978-1-60938-942-0 (ebk)

Text design and typesetting by April Leidig

No part of this book may be reproduced or used in any form or by any means without permission in writing from the publisher. All reasonable steps have been taken to contact copyright holders of material used in this book. The publisher would be pleased to make suitable arrangements with any whom it has not been possible to reach.

Printed on acid-free paper

Cataloging-in-Publication data is on file with the Library of Congress.

Portions of this novel originally appeared in *Narrative* magazine, and in the *Sewanee Review* 130.1.

For my parents

HE HAD TATTOOS up and down his arms that this morning, getting up, in the seconds before pride arose seemed very stupid to him. Aces, shamrocks. Lurid glyphs. A crouching panther on his shoulder, 'cause why not. A hula girl he might've gotten on a naval ship in Polynesia, when he'd hardly ever left the tri-state. Some Latin phrases on his wrists—*Honoris et Virtus et Something-or-Other*, which . . . honor? Virtue? Whose? *His?* At least he'd stopped himself before that *Stephanie Forever* bit.

Rudy turned on Broadway. He was due to open at the bar. There was Christmas crap in windows, bells ringing—not for him, though. 'Twas the season to be robbed, dumped, jumped, kicked out of love. Threatened eviction by his landlady, a Russian ogress in Bulgari shades, paid for with a blind old tenant's stolen disability checks. It was the season to be sick with drink, and bursting with regrets, no less real and wretched for how fictional the world seemed. This pasteboard town, its codes and quotas, madly ticking clocks. . . . Maybe *that* was it. Maybe the city was the problem.

New York. He was sick of it. He was fed up with the myth of it. Everybody always telling him how great it was . . . helluva town, New York! So *vibrant*. . . . He thought of some talking head in a PBS doc they'd shown in school once, years ago, some midlife virgin in a bowtie and suspenders losing his shit over Walt Whitman. The Bridge, *ooh!* Central Park! The park was the least Manhattan could do to keep you from despair. To him it was all fin de siècle, like Rome before the sack. Weimar Berlin.

Glitter and doom, not even—Pret and doom. It was scaffolding and pigeon shit and when he'd walked just now into the soup 'n' sandwich place near Macy's for his egg-and-cheese, no bacon—you had to try and be good, some days, keep the death away—he was spooked by every face he saw in there, the bearded ladies, their piehole eyes, and he knew for sure that God had pulled the pin. Never had the city felt so tuneless to him, so jagged, so uncharmed. The palimpsest so worn and muddled. . . . Lotto shops and lash extensions, gleaming plazas out of Dallas. It's not that it was ugly—though there was plenty of *that*—it's that he didn't even know what he was *looking at* no more. What *was* it? Whose *idea* was it?

He opened the metal gates. Just the sight of Liffey's empty in the daytime gave him heavy, deep-in-childhood creeps. It was filthy in here. It stank like rum and dirty pants. He checked the register and changed the kegs and filled the ice and put the TVs on. There was memorabilia caked to the rafters. It would bury you alive. They wouldn't find you 'til the spring. Corncob pipes and top hats from Tammany Hall days, and Jimmy Coonan's holster, and Dean Martin's fedora, and some mangled rebar from Ground Zero, and keepsakes left behind on loan by soldiers shipping out—to France, Korea, Vietnam—hankies and harmonicas like collateral to fate. On the walls were signed glamour shots of random-ass celebrities, and pictures of his dad—he owned the place—with Bono and The Edge, and with Connie Chung, for some reason, and one photo Rudy liked of his cousins once removed, known hatchet men for the IRA: deep in the '70s, groovy-shirted, mutton-chopped, smoking away on some farty-looking mustard couch in County Clare, their eyes abrim with murder. All this New *Yawk*-Irish crap, the stuff that pinned his world to space, and today he didn't know whether to retch or weep or tear it down. It was all just so . . . so *over*. It was *junk*. Bone dust. A bum replacement for a life.

She had a life. Allison. She was moving west to go to law school, out in Colorado, and he was not invited anymore. She had canceled the party on him—at *nine*—when he'd just arrived, with bells on his boots, ready for love. They'd been playing "Take My Breath Away" from *Top Gun* in the Duane Reade earlier and he'd had to leave. Just left his basket with his milk and Preparation H and shit he really needed and *vamoosed*. That beautiful song, it—stop it. Not now with the tears again. He would not cry today. He had his shift to get through. Saturday night. There was a UFC fight on down the street at MSG, plus some basketball games he had more than casual money riding on. It was the longest night of the year, the solstice—big spenders coming out. Something would get shaken loose before the night was through. He should fix himself a nip, get in the spirit of things. That'd help.

Why was he in such a tizzy? Why these vicious, hopeless, no-good thoughts? It was Christmastime—he *loved* Christmas—and he was still young and healthy, kind of, with a steady job. And *friends*. Friends, friends . . .

He'd gone to see one friend from high school last week, Matt Galapo, trying to get back out there from his love hole, reconnect with people. All nervous on the subway to go see him. *Nervous* to go get a drink with *Matty Galapo*, the least intimidating biggest goober individual on the face of planet Earth. Rudy thinking he was gonna have a heart attack just walking in the restaurant, and his voice all weird and shaky saying hi, and then pretending he had to take a piss just to go to the bathroom and catch his breath a second—what the fuck was *that* about?

He used to be the most sociable, most natural guy around. Life of the party. Leader of the pack. But it was one thing to just listen to folks talk, like behind the bar—Rudy had no problem with that, he liked it sometimes, even—but *friends*, friends had to put you on the spot. To be *polite*. "Enough about me, I'll shut up now! What about *you*? What's new with *you*, man?" And then, oh . . . then you saw it. That dull look in their eyes as you trotted out your little spiels, your crackpot plans, your stupid-ass ideas for start-ups. Walking home fifty bucks poorer on some crappy tapas, running back the tapes of conversation like a crazy person, feeling so . . . so trapped in their perception of you, like you'd just let some ersatz self out of the bottle for them, some holographic undead Tupac-at-Coachella self out and now it was just . . . out there with them, unauthorized, doing God knows what, and when mutual friends asked Matt Galapo, "Oh, you saw *Rudy?* How's *he* doing?" Matt Galapo would say, "Well, you know . . . he's . . . *weelll*, let's just say he's Rudy. He's still Rudy." Meaning *what?* Meaning *who?!* Your life, your blood, your dreams, your name, the chambers of your beating heart, just another bit of chump change in another *nothing* conversation.

Were other people . . . worth it? Rudy wasn't sure today.

"OH FUCK THAAAT. Fuck thaaaat," said Gary.

Soon the regulars were all assembled, holding court around the bar, Gary in the middle in his Santa hat, his big potato face already swollen.

"I'm so fuckin' sick of hearing that response to everything," he said. "Oh, well in *Canada* they've got this, and the social safety net, and if so-and-so's elected, *I'm* moving to *Canada.* Bye! And that . . . what is it . . . the Netherlands. Yeah, yeah, they're so great, and their major industry is fuckin'—what's that—Muenster *cheese.* This is New York City, *bitch!* We didn't get to be the greatest city in the world, in the greatest *country* in the world, by letting—"

Rudy had grown up around men like Gary, friends of his father's and his uncle's. Big-city bumpkins. Meant well—maybe—but never stopped talking for one second. Scour the shacks and shantytowns, the monster truck expos, you'd be hard-pressed to find hickdom half as rabid as a certain breed of near-Queens knuckle-dragger. This man had seen Billy Joel at the Garden *thirty-one times.* No disrespect to Mr. Joel of course. . . . Lots of it to Gary, though.

"—but what we've got now, this is what happens when you let lame-duck pussyfooting liberal mayors run the show. He's emptying the *jails*, he's kowtowing to special *interests*, he's—"

"What do you mean, 'special interests'?" Hector said. Hector was a super in a building down the block. "You mean interests that aren't yours?" They did this all the time, these two. They loved each other.

"I mean I see a guy passed out right outside here yesterday, with shit in his pants. This was a bar for working people. Not hoboes. Not addicts. Not—"

"Who here's not an addict?" Elaine said. She used to be a Rockette in the '80s, Elaine. Never recovered from retirement, and now she lived in her Sambuca and her crosswords. "And I've seen you poop your pants before, Gary. Two years ago, on Halloween. Betcha don't remember, do you?"

Liffey's used to be a dime a dozen in this neighborhood, pool and darts and potpies, a place for union hard hats to cash their checks. Assailed on both sides now: from on high, by the powerful, trying to raise the rent and tear it down for retail space, and on the other by, oh boy . . . the other kind. The undesirables, Dad called them. Dope migrants coming off the Greyhounds through the Port Authority, who in the last few years had colonized the streets outside here, a few-blocks' circuit of methadone clinics and needle exchanges and fast-food joints where they hung out all day, every day, zombie-walking through the bright lights. Rudy as the house brawn was meant to man the barricades, he guessed, fling them by their scruffs if they dared so much as peek inside, though they seemed less like a problem to him lately than a warning—the ghosts of Christmas future. He could almost see it, a few years down the line, if worse came to worst, him standing on the corner in a dead man's coat, holding a sign for the liquidation sale at Petland Discounts. . . .

"So I told him . . . I *told* him . . . if you can't handle the dermatitis, then you don't deserve— . . . Yeah . . . yeah . . . no . . . no. No, he hasn't responded yet . . . A couple days . . . six days . . . Yeah. I think he's like, I think he honestly, like, can't believe I had the *nerve* to be like . . . yeah. No . . . no . . . no . . . I *know*."

Oh, Tracey, Tracey, Tracey. Tracey never talked to anybody, like she was too good for the place, just talked super loudly on her phone about her problems, which were many by the sounds of it. Her whole girlboss bag didn't suit her one bit. You could picture her otherwise, in a simpler walk of life, getting on just fine. Working with animals, or in a lighthouse someplace, no one to pass judgment on her, make her so defensive. But they'd had to send her here, like for maximum cruelty, stork-dropped her on the city as a twentysomething ad rep for a meditation app. Baroque New York with its great expectations, its meretricious freedoms, its glamazons and players. Her with her iPad case that said *All the Feels* (what *was* that shit? Was that a band?), her snake oils of self-love. Bamboozled by dudes, shanghaied by her gurus. . . . No one with two eyeballs and two ears anywhere near their head would buy that she was winning for one second.

Then again, she had a salary, and health insurance, probably, and a cell phone without tape on it. That he could see. Hell, maybe Tracey *was* winning.

Dad came waddling in like Scrooge McDuck just then, jingle bells chiming as the door brought in the cold. Like some Great Depression barman in his newsboy cap—did he think that thing looked good on him? Jaunty?

"Boss!" said Gary.

"Jimmy," Hector said. "What's happenin'."

"Merry Christmas, everyone. Elaine."

Dad shook the hands and slapped the shoulders, in his element. The bar had been in the family almost eighty years, passed down to Dad by his dad, by his dad, a retired steamfitter who'd come through Castle Garden. Rudy was meant to take it over someday, though he couldn't really see it—same show every night, drunks bellowing, the burghers yakking. Sweating

6

over the hiking price of maraschino cherries while the landlord nibbled at your heels. What the hell else was he gonna do, though, act for a living? He'd got caught his sophomore year at Purchase selling methamphetamines to the local youth, there'd been a fine, a whole commotion, and he'd been quietly relieved of his scholarship, his record scrubbed by a clerk friend of his uncle's, a favor hardly worth involving his judgmental ass, when Rudy was still too paranoid to so much as dip his toe in a legitimate line of work. Part of him thought Dad was secretly happy for his crack-up, that the whole better-future-for-our-children bit was just for show, for his speeches at the Sons of Erin dinners, the Salvation Army clambakes, that Dad *really* wanted him where he could see him. Hung up on the walls, preserved in wax. He'd barely had a day off in six years.

"Son. How are we here? You need change?" Badly. "Kegs okay?"

"We're good here, Pop. Just some quarters for the pool table."

"All right."

Just knowing Dad was in the house made things a lot less festive-feeling. Now was the moment to fill up, while the old man's back was turned. He mixed some Jameson's into his Dunkin' cup, a little Dexedrine to keep from getting sloppy. Easy.

She'd been on his case about that too, toward the end. But that was just the rat race in her ear. That was just some pilgrim's progress, city-on-a-hill, gift-to-be-simple BS. Only in the USA was pleasure a pathology—Rudy loved his country or whatever, but still. There was too much pressure to be good. It would backfire if you weren't careful. Only in the USA did clean-cut, family-values senators get caught with boys in motor inns with their pants around their knees, stoned stupid, wearing chokers. All that pressure to be decent. It was baked into the founding myth. . . . Johnny Appleseed astride the land with his milk pail and his clear head, takes some sherry once a decade, has to *lie down.* Says never again, why imbibe, when the Lord is kind, and the harvest is plentiful? But he had fields and churches, horses, and we've got—what—some asphalt, HBO, and they expect us not to *drink*? We drink. *We've earned* that shit.

Oh, but he was hardly in the coal mines was he . . . the taking a load off had *become* the load, and it was heavy on him lately. Heavy. From stud to dud these last few months, whiskey-limp a couple times during the act. If he'd known that was the last time with her, the other night, he'd have had his wits about him.

TEN O'CLOCK AT NIGHT: They came pouring in from the arena. All the blood sport and Kid Rock made people extra thirsty. Hostile too. This one box-seat type in a mohair scarf was flashing his Centurion card, taking twelve minutes to order, all *What's your red like*, when take one look around here, what do you *think* it's like? It's like Welch's grape juice with subtle notes of vermin shit and death, then getting all uppity like *Rudy* was being uppity to rush him when they were backed up thirty customers deep and just trying to keep things moving; and then the guy not tipping him a cent. God knows Rudy needed it—he'd just lost three hundred dollars on a parlay. In spare minutes now he tried to check the action on his phone and the overhead TV. In Brooklyn they were shooting poison daggers at his heart. He hadn't had a night this bad in years. Now Dad was in his face, with a puss on.

"She can't be here," he said, and pointed down the bar. There was a lady sitting slumped in her barstool in the corner, drugged out of her mind, probably. "I sure as hell hope you weren't serving her."

She had asked for a 7UP. Was probably mixing it with cough syrup under the bartop. Rudy hadn't noticed.

"She's just, like, sitting down. She's not bothering anybody."

He was backed up to the wall, and besides nobody gave a shit. It was Saturday night in the pleasure capital. They would trample over corpses to secure their Michelobs.

"Take care of it, Rudy. She can go outside, where she belongs.

She broke the rules. Nothing consumed on the premises but what you pay for here."

What Dad meant was he didn't want the cops around while they were knowingly serving underage TikTok hotties from Long Island. Those rule-breakers he was all *about*. But now was not the time to make a stink. Not when after tips were pooled and rent was squared, Rudy would have approximately thirty-five dollars to be living off the next two weeks.

"Fuck. Fine. Whatever," Rudy said.

She was skin and bones, the woman. She gave a little mewl as he picked her up and struggled with her to the door.

"Comin' thru," he said. "Excuse me, people. Move it, please. Yoohoo. *Excuse me.*"

There could've been a hundred bodies pressing into him, way too close. Dentists' sons from Westchester, the bachelorettes of Murray Hill. The moneyed rabble slumming it in midtown. . . . Rudy couldn't stand these kids. Shoveling data for the corporate brass, their rosé picnics in Sheep's Meadow—*they* were the sheep—however many tons of waste to keep 'em in shampoo. One young man in a Giants beanie was grinning at the drama, apparently amused. A face on him like the historical depraved. You could see him in some square of old, in a tricorn hat, jeering while the witches burned. "Fucking *move*, please," Rudy said, about to bitch-slap him. "Move aside."

They stumbled out into the cold, the woman coming to.

"Don't touch me! Faggoty-ass *bitch*," she said, and hocked a loogie on the pavement. "You're gonna *die!*"

"Nice, real nice," said Rudy. "You don't even know where you're at, miss."

"I know where *it's* at, faggot!"

Now he got a proper look at her—she was younger than he realized. She was just a kid. She might've been miss majorette, twirling a baton as late as last year in the Pleasantville High Christmas pageant, for the time-lapse number these drugs did on people.

9

"You'll be all right," he said. His heart was palpitating crazily. That extra half a Dexedrine had been one too many.

The woman almost fell, then righted herself against a garbage can.

"Get your sea legs there," said Rudy. "If you're not feeling well, there's a detox place on 42nd. They have beds. They can't arrest you."

There'd been incidents before. Rudy'd shooed the one away. Saw the item in the blotter the next morning: how he or someone of the same description was found cold in a men's room in Penn Station. It's not that it was Rudy's fault of course—some folks couldn't be helped. Still, there were nights he saw that pitted face, gaunt and imploring in the wee small hours.

The girl turned down the block. Skulking away beneath the streetlight with her scarf piled round her head she looked like some old vagabond, some hobbled prophet from the Gospels. But for the sweatpants that said *PINK* on the ass. "Stay awake!" he called. His heart was skitzing in his cage. He had to clutch his chest and lean against the grating.

"Nazi *bitch!*" she said. "You're gonna *die!*"

She must have a lot of fun with that. Barking spooky, technically true shit at people, like the village oracle, trying to make the normals flinch.

Did she mean, like, tonight, though?

• • •

"THIS CHRISTMAS? Oh, got me a little chalet upstate. Airbnb. Sleigh ride with the wife and kids." He was cleaning glasses. It was 3 a.m. "I'll be here, sweetheart." They always stayed open Christmas Day, Dad springing for Chinese takeout for the lonely hearts. "Come and see me."

"You know I will," Elaine said. "You always take good care of old Elaine."

Like the Island of Misfit Toys in here now, the young ones off to clubland or back home to make curfew. Only the regulars were left, masters of the late-night filibuster. Things were on the level for now, though they threatened to turn maudlin any minute.

"Is that *blood*?" Elaine asked.

Rudy wiped his nose, by force of habit. He hadn't touched that shit in days.

"Up *there*." She pointed to the hard hat above the register. "Is that a streak of blood? I've never noticed that before."

"That's blood all right," said Gary. Him you couldn't get rid of, not since his wife had left him earlier this year. If they were open, he was here. "That's—Jimmy will tell ya. Tell it. 1970. How they walked all the way from Centre Street and donated it to Liffey's bar. *Tell* it." There was some story behind the helmet. Rudy didn't know.

Dad said, "It sounds like *you* wanna tell it, Gary."

"All right, okay. If you insist. Another Powers, please."

Gary lived for this shit. He probably did it in the mirror nights.

"It was almost fifty years ago. Some college kids, they went to City Hall to protest the war. This was right after Kent State. And they were waving Vietcong flags, these ungrateful snots, and these workmen on their lunch breaks from building the Twin Towers, they came and, well, they did a counterprotest. They showed the kids who was boss."

"That sounds sorta sinister," Elaine said.

"Well, there was a dustup. Nobody *died*. But they were showing them which way the wind blows."

Rudy was sick and tired of people talking history and politics in here. They never talked, they barked. They went off, egos rubberized by drink, like pull toys with their stock takes, their flimflam declarations of what they thought they knew.

"—and Mayor Lindsay knew where his bread was buttered, right. It was the hippie liberal vote. He's up there having a pow-wow at Columbia, wearing beads, passing the pipe, saying we love the students and the poor misunderstood criminals and we hate Nixon and we hate the war. Some of these workmen

11

meanwhile are veterans. Risking their lives for their country, for their city. Men who literally built this town, the streets, buildings, and bridges we all take for granted. So they're pissed off, right—"

"So?" said Hector. *Oh, here we go now. Here we go.* "So that means they get free rein to beat somebody's brains in while a cop looks on and does nothing? I hate this story. That flag was lowered at City Hall for the kids at Kent State as a show of respect, a show of basic respect for life, of basic solemn . . . *solemness*, and some Archie Bunker asshole raises it back up, because America? That's just heartless."

"They were down there waving Vietcong *flags.*"

"They were *kids.* Don't you have kids? Teenagers? Kids are *dramatic.* Didn't I hear about your daughter posting some crazy shit online about—"

"*HEY!*" Gary stood up in his chair, red as his Santa hat. "You don't talk about my daughter ever. *Ever! Understand?!*" Rudy had to stifle a laugh. It was jarring to see sometimes, how seriously people took themselves. "*Understand?!!*"

Rudy didn't know what they were talking about. Or care really. At all. Smoke break time. . . .

Eighth Avenue could not be shittier or more depressing if it tried to be. He lit his cigarette in the light of the T-Mobile store. His buzz had hardened on him in uncharitable ways. It was bitter cold outside, but it didn't feel like Christmas.

He'd give anything to be celebrating somewhere else this year. Wales maybe. Montreal. Someplace with cobblestones and old-time streetlights. Softer footfall. Snow. He'd been excited at the thought of Colorado. Going west, finding work slinging toddies in a lodge somewhere, meeting people. Scoring a small but meaty speaking part in some plugged-in sunbird's producer friend's movie, and when the Burbank honchos saw it they'd go, "Who *was* that guy? That young man, yes, who played the brother . . . there's just . . . something *about* him . . . something wonderfully *alive* about him." And then? The world. Speedboats on the Riviera.

No matter what, New York was through for him. The dance hall days were over. There were no more serendipities. There was nobody to *meet*. Not like he'd been told from the stories in the bar, not like how he'd pictured them, from old movies with his grandmother. . . . No guys named Fats, pinky-ringed, in need of an apprentice. No lonesome dowagers leaning out their windows summer afternoons, looking for a fine young man to move a bureau for them, and not rush off right after. No party girls with hearts of gold and awful Okie childhoods to live down, like whatsername, Golightly, from that movie Allie liked. Every path was formalized, heavily credentialed, everyone so damn type A and *square*. And the ones that weren't? The type Bs? They wouldn't even let those folks *sit down*.

Back inside Gary and Hector were getting ready to murder each other.

"I'm just sayin', I'm just *sayin'*—" Gary said. "It was just . . . it's a sad state of *affairs* is all I'm saying. Twenty-five years earlier to the day, to the *day*, the Germans had surrendered. To the *day*. All kinds gathered in Times Square. People cheerin', kissin', and huggin'. Watching the ticker tape. And then . . . a quarter century, and what . . . pffft. People spitting on GIs. And *nowadays*—"

"Well, Gary, Gary," Hector said, sitting up in his chair now, "maybe coming home to a firetrap in Spanish Harlem after risking your life killing Nazis in the name of, what—democracy?—wasn't quite as hunky-dory as some shit about V-E Day in *Life* magazine would have you think it was."

"Oh, oh, of course, I forgot. There were no good old days. Fuck it all, fuck Christmas, let's just bomb the Sistine Chapel while we're at it, 'cause da Vinci had a racist thought when he was nine."

"Huh?"

"You people are *obsessed.*"

"Ho! You people? You better walk that back right now."

"Gentlemen," Elaine said. "Boys . . ."

It was starting to snow. A man moved down the street outside. Rudy would see him on his way home in the early mornings, the dude just starting out his day, collecting empty cans and bottles in shopping bags from Western Beef. Not a tweaker from what Rudy could tell, just someone who had lost his way. Spending his earnings on a *Daily News*, lining up to have a shave, bathe like the French in the bathroom of the Wendy's before the crowds arrived. Rudy had to hand it to him—he had his rituals. His own little pantomime of grown-up life, of the world of profit and obligation, that meant his time meant something to him. That even if he lacked a vocation, or dependents, or a place to be, that the day itself meant . . . something. That wakefulness was halfway worth it to him. This homeless man had more self-command and enterprise in his ass-cheeks than Rudy had in his entire body.

Elaine said, "Boys, boys, I come here to . . . to *relax*." Rudy should have stopped her two rounds back. "I don't wanna see somebody's *blood* . . . where I'm all about my nice times, my *relax* . . . some *friends*, some—"

"Elaine, yes," Hector said, "I'd like that taken down. It's never sat quite right with me, but, for some reason, tonight, that thing just . . . that thing just turns my stomach tonight."

Dad was quiet for a minute. He seemed to weigh his words before he spoke.

"With all due respect, Hector, I remember the day a good man left it here. My father, Rudy's grandfather, hung it up there. It hasn't been moved in almost fifty years, and it won't move until they take the place from under us."

Gary slammed his fist down. "Damn right," he said. "That helmet built the *towers.*"

Rudy stood up on the bar and reached above the register.

It wasn't hard to move the thing. It only looked stuck. Rudy put it on the bar and said, "It's a helmet."

"Yeah. *Yeah*, it's a helmet. Are you drunk? *I know* it's a helmet." Dad looked like his eyes were gonna pop out of his head.

"And what's a helmet gonna do for us?" said Rudy. "It's gonna save our lives? Not hanging on the wall it's not. It's gonna bring her back?"

"Hey!" said Gary. "My personal business is not your people's *business!*"

"It's not the Sistine ceiling."

"What goes on these walls is *my* say-so," Dad said. "I own the place."

"Dad . . . Dad . . . you're renting. We all are."

"What is that, some existentialism crap? Honestly, Rudy? Just go home."

Jesus Christ. So fuckin' rude and touchy.

"All right, okay," Rudy said. "Have your helmet. Give it a smooch." This was what happened when you hadn't got your rocks off in some twenty years. One foot in the grave, clinging to the décor while your parts crusted over.

"No, I don't just mean tonight," said Dad. "I've been thinking it might be for the best for you to step aside, and now's as good a time as any."

The way he went right back to his Sudoku's, not even that worked up, made it almost seem like he meant it.

"Sure, sure," Rudy said. He had *made* this place. He was the only living person *in* this place. The customers adored him. Hector and Gary were agog, and Elaine too swacked for human life. "What'll it be then, fuckin' Chieftains CDs on the overhead? That'll keep the shots flowing on a Saturday night."

"You think you're the only *young* person around?" said Dad. "You're not even young. You're twenty-six years old. I'd replace you in a second, and better. *And* cheaper. You think I don't know you've been stealing liquor from me for years? It's not enough

15

I've got to spot you money you pissed away on what, the Draft Kings, you're napping off your benders on the couch, with your pants off."

Maybe one time. Wait, were there . . . *cameras* in here?

"All the while you have the nerve to second-guess me," said Dad. "To turn your nose up, like you're better than us all." Was that not . . . was that . . . in dispute? "Letting druggies go a number two in my bathroom, let them shoot up in my bathroom against my express wishes, not to mention the *law*, 'cause you're such a special, friendly guy? Such a good Samaritan? You don't know the meaning of the term, Rudy."

"Oh, and you *do*? You think you're some beloved old publican, holding the neighborhood together? Upholding the fine standards of Eighth Avenue. This place ain't Cheers. It's not even McSorley's. This place is just the waiting room for Amtrak. Nobody gives a fuck."

"You ungrateful son of a bitch. This place paid for your *life*. Much good you've done with it."

"Oh wow. *Burn.* Willy Loman for the win. Such a good upstanding man. Such a good Christian, throwing some poor girl out onto the street—"

"Those strangers aren't my responsibility."

"And what was *she*, huh? A stranger?" Fuck it—he may as well go all the way now. "Shows a little weakness, stick her out at Betty Ford to rot."

Dad started taking deep breaths. Crazy deep. Like he was about to hyperventilate.

"You have *NO* idea—" he said. "I *always!*—" His voice was gonna crack in two. He gathered his breath and said, "You're just like her, you know that? Two peas in a pod. Always fooled herself that she was good. Always a pain in the ass about everything, all deeper and realer and holier-than-thou. Screw another man at an ashram and call it free expression. Disappear on us for months. She was just an addict, and an improv artist, and her only concern ever, *ever*, was getting what she wanted out of the next fifteen minutes. That was what *she* cared about. Not *people.* Not *new experiences* . . . and sure as hell not *you.*"

It was the most Rudy'd heard mentioned of his mom in years. Dad always talked about her like she was dead. Last Rudy heard she wasn't. She was living in a women's sober house, near Buffalo.

"Well, I'd rather be living for the next fifteen minutes," Rudy said, getting on his coat, "than for some shit about a helmet that happened fifty years ago. Good night, Merry Christmas, bless us, everyone." He gathered his tips from the jar. "And don't think for a second you'll be pooling this. Consider it my severance."

Outside it was stupid cold. He hadn't realized he was starving until now. There was nothing open he could see, and no one on the streets. Even the hopheads had been scared into their hiding places. He would have to walk awhile.

The wind came howling into him. It rattled in his bones, sending street signs swinging. He wished he'd brought some gloves with him. Gloves and a scarf, a hat—those were the type of totally reasonable, simple things he never thought to own, or if he did was always losing places. He needed them stapled to his person, like a dummy. Strung through his coat, like a little kid with mittens.

He remembered that like yesterday—in the foyer, at their place in Flushing. Eight years old, bundling up, having a world-class conniption. Always talking back. . . Saying *I don't need 'em,* saying *Dad, it's not that cold out.* But then, when you got out there, it always was. It was.

ANOTHER CABBIE SUICIDE; STRING OF DEATHS CONTINUES

DECEMBER 21, 2018

A body found floating in the East River has been identified as Zhongqing "Kenny" Zhou, of the Bronx, a taxi driver. This marks the sixth suicide in five months for New York's cab drivers, in economic peril over ride-sharing services and plummeting medallion values. According to friends, the 63-year-old had been struggling to pay off an $800,000 mortgage on his medallion, the plastic emblem that allows cabs to pick up passengers on city streets.

The tragedy comes after a month of eyebrow-raising headlines for the taxi industry. On November 20, Avram Balan, another driver, killed himself with a shotgun in front of City Hall.

In the days leading up to his death, Balan, originally from Kosovo, had posted long diatribes on his Facebook page blaming New York's politicians—the governor, mayor, and TLC officials—for imposing unfair taxes and regulations on yellow cabs even as they allowed Uber's presence in the city to grow unchecked. He also placed blame on unscrupulous moneylenders, whom he claimed pushed enormous loans on low-income drivers to buy medallions, creating a bubble that, some experts and insiders say, was bound to burst regardless of Uber's disruption of the industry.

"It was bonanza," said Dr. Cameron Hulce, a professor of economics at Columbia. "The lending practices were absolutely, undoubtedly predatory."

Balan also alleged that he was being pursued by a debt collector, whom he believed the credit union that had secured his loan, Blacktop Lending Corp., had hired. Twice he had his car seized, and once was confronted on the street at night by a man brandishing a gun, he wrote. A

18

spokesperson for Blacktop dismissed these allegations as "pulp fiction."

The medallion system dates back to the Great Depression, when the city government intervened to prevent unlicensed cabs from flooding its streets. At the time, people desperate for work were hiring out their own vehicles to make ends meet.

"The irony, is that's exactly what Uber's doing now," wrote Mr. Balan, in his final Facebook post. "But the city's doing nothing to stop it now. When they're the ones who started this mess."

In the early 2000s, the Taxi and Limousine Commission ran an aggressive commercial campaign touting taxi medallions as a recession-proof commodity, a "passport to the American Dream" that was "safer than the stock market." Before Uber, Lyft, and other start-ups upended the industry, banks and credit unions made hundreds of millions of dollars encouraging drivers to take on no-down payment or interest-only loans. Meanwhile, many drivers leveraged their medallions to invest in their and their families' futures, in a pattern of risky borrowing and refinancing that would come to mimic the home-equity bubble. Mr. Zhou bought a stake in a Popeyes restaurant in the Bronx. Sunil Singh, of Woodside, Queens, sent his daughter to medical school.

Now a generation of cab drivers, facing retirement age, have been left penniless, saddled with a devalued asset and often forced to use their entire income on repayments for their loans.

"Maybe if you're [in your] thirties, forties, you can think about paying it back and surviving," said Mr. Singh, a friend and colleague of Mr. Zhou. "Guys like me, like Kenny, we are getting old. Maybe we borrowed against our medallion to buy a house, or start a business. Now we have nothing. And now we don't have time either."

Many claim the loans were first brokered under fraudulent or nontransparent terms, often to drivers with poor English-speaking skills who were not fully aware of what they were signing on to. Mr. Singh first bid on a medallion in 2006 with the help of Maverick Financial Corp., a publicly traded finance company headed by Jacob Cohen, one of the most prominent lenders in the industry. As the repayment deadline for his loan approached, he received a call from Mr. Cohen's office offering to extend the terms and lend him an additional $200,000. Mr. Singh said no credit check was performed at either meeting, and that Mr. Cohen discouraged him from consulting with a lawyer.

Mr. Cohen could not be reached for comment.

Mr. Singh's and Mr. Zhou's stories mirror the plight of many like them: financial hardship compounded by personal misfortune. Mr. Zhou's wife had recently been diagnosed with breast cancer, and they had been forced to pull their twenty-year-old son out of college so he could care for her while Mr. Zhou worked fourteen-hour days. When his son revealed that he and his wife were expecting their first child, due in May, a father's joy was tempered with dread. Said Mr. Singh, "He was so excited about becoming a grandfather. But more than that, he was scared. He was depressed."

Police responded to a man's decomposed body floating in the East River near the Brooklyn Bridge on Friday morning. Mr. Zhou had not been seen since Tuesday evening.

"He was a good person. He was always nice, always worked hard. He bought me coffees at Kennedy airport, and we would talk and have a cigarette," Mr. Singh said. "I can't believe he's really dead. His American dream . . . it became a nightmare. Now I look around at all the guys and I think . . . who of us is next?"

2

UNCLE MEYER had her cornered the whole party. Daddy had said stay away, that Meyer was a nut, and a phony intellectual, living off the family dime while spewing his anti-corporate bull, the type of busted second son who was catnip for cult leaders. He seemed all right to Marley, though—friendly—and he had no one else to talk to really, and Daddy anyway was nowhere to be found . . . trapped in his cigar closet again (that happened last year).

"Don't you listen to them," Meyer said. He was standing near the Christmas tree, with spitty crumbs on his lapels. He taught a class in anthropology at City College, though he'd just been asked to take some kind of leave. "Not your mom and dad, and not your little friends. So what you're not miss popular at school"—said who? Who'd told him *that*?—"You've got something, Mary. A mind of your own. A *rare* condition . . . though I hear they're working on a cure."

Mom made her *I need you* face across the room—probably an issue with the salmon puffs. She was in a snit the last while, Mom. Chopping pillows like she meant them harm, and telling Marley to close her legs, even when they were barely open. She and Daddy had been *railing* at each other in their room a couple nights ago, back from the opera. . . .

" . . . Love?! You don't want *love*, Nora. You don't care about *love*. All you care about's appearances. You don't want my hand on your ass. You just want your stupid friends to *see* my hand on your ass so they'll know you've won, so you get to be the champion in the rich bitch Olympics! Well I'm not playing anymore!"

"I'm the one concerned with appearances? *Me?* I saw you the other night, at Polo Bar, ready to crawl out of your *skin* when Jacob Junior stuttered ordering his hamburger. 'The young man doesn't have all night, son.' Since when are *you* looking out for waiters and their time? And you're sure this is the *Dover sole?* You're *sure sure?* Mr. 'Could you check the fucking *crate* it came in?' He's your *child!* And you're *ashamed* of him. Of your own child! What kind of man—" but then they turned the fan way up.

"Screw 'em anyway," said Meyer. "With their, what is this—" He tried to sit down on an end table and almost knocked a lamp over. "What's this. Oh! A *lamp.* May God bless and keep the precious lamps. *We're* going to be living like primitives soon, and there'll be blood in the streets, and what'll they do then, hmm? With their beautiful, beautiful lamps?"

Marley didn't really know what to say to that, so she said, "Um, I think my mom needs me. In the kitchen." Which was true.

"Ah, yes, of course. Of course she does. Go with Mother. But remember." He wagged a hairy finger at her. "When the levee breaks, they'll be first to drown, from all the *shit* they're carrying. Don't you wait for 'em. You swim ahead . . . You swim ahead, little Mary."

Maybe it was right what Daddy'd said. Maybe Meyer *was* nuts.

HOME USED TO BE really grand and shabby like a haunted mansion out of *Scooby-Doo,* with scrolly woodwork from the Gilded Age and a grandfather clock and a pitchy old upright piano Grandma used to play a lot, and lots of peed-on (by cats mostly) velvet cushions, then last year Mom needed a "big refresh" and hired a decorator, a *major* operation, then in the kitchen all day every day for months on end with binders full of God

22

knows what—Daddy called it the Situation Room—and now the place was like one big swanked-out hotel lobby in Miami Beach with vases shaped like lips and fake-o pop art, and couches that barely squished at all when you sat down on them. Marley thought it looked too white, the walls especially, but when she said that Mom said that's not white, that's Chestertown Buff.

The party was going great so far, though Cousin Benny was taking his sweet time arriving. There were waiters in tuxedos with trays of champagne flutes with sugary red rims and pomegranate seeds like sunken treasure in the bottom. Those looked fun. Maybe they could see about nipping one or two of *those* later.

Marley didn't know what Meyer was on about anyway, telling her she had such a *unique mind*, when he couldn't even get her name right, and her teachers certainly didn't seem to think so. Granted she could do the whole crossword puzzle in her mom's *People* magazine start to finish without any help from the time she was six—which was pretty impressive apparently, 'cause not that many kids her age knew who Wynonna Judd was—but she wasn't smart about the things that *mattered*, and she wasn't talented at all.

Last year Mom had taken her like some high-class Mama June to hoof it on the youth arts and culture circuit around Lincoln Center, first to the Metropolitan Opera Children's Chorus, where she'd completely flubbed her scales with the scariest Hungarian pedagogue you've ever seen, in nightmares even, in a long creepy skirt and hobnail boots and a high collar of ebony lace, probably to keep her head attached, and then across the plaza to get laughed out of the American Ballet Theater, where they told her she was "far" too old to start training (!) and that even as early as ten her ligaments and bones had already been "unpromisingly set," and then finally to an audition for an understudy for Girl Orphan #3 in a Wednesday matinee production of *Newsies*, when it was mostly just senior citizens by the busload in the audience anyway, and even *that* had fallen through. That was the city for you. You thought you had landed on a nice little *niche experience* for yourself ("In niches there are riches," so went the motto of Daddy's taxi medallion lending corporation) and there were ten thousand other people who'd had the same idea. There must've been three hundred kids there that day, girls with buns so tight, so industrial-strength shellacked to their skulls they could barely speak—not that they were about to, not to her—stretching and plié-ing and doing vocal warm-ups in the halls, all mi-mi-mi-*mi*-mi-mi-mi, and all Betty-Botter-bought-a-bit-of-better-butter, and this one girl arguing on the phone with her emancipation lawyer, thin as a matchstick, poised as a magistrate, her face like an angel's, but sour. . . . Of course, she had gotten the part.

Mom was in the kitchen now, talking to the caterer. She used to be a model, back in the day. There were photos by Daddy's bedside of her smoking near a pool in chiaroscuro by Herb Ritts (so she claimed) that were pretty racy.

"Everything good, Mom?" Marley said. "Where's Daddy?"

"Oh, hi sweetie. Everything's great, yeah. One sec."

She seemed distracted, touching her hair a lot and fiddling with the straps on her dress (low-cut, tartan). She was dressing pretty crazy lately, like Kris Jenner. A party was one thing, but there'd been *quite* severe pants and epaulets just to go to lunch and spike heels on a Tuesday, like the easier and blander and vanilla-creamier Mom's days got the harder and more big-time she was trying to look, her wardrobe hoarding all the thunder. They had read that part in school in *The Great Gatsby* with Daisy crying about the shirts and Marley didn't get it at all at first, but sometimes standing in Mom's walk-in closet with the clothes so grave and husklike on their hangers and the closet quiet as a tomb she could kind of understand it—how luxury was sad sometimes, and clothes were all the action, if you really liked them *that* much, you were probably too *clothes-minded* to be getting.

"Is Daddy around?"

"Your father? Oh. No actually. He went out. Quick meeting."

"Like, one of his church basement meetings?"

"Excuse me, Andre . . ." She pulled Marley aside, out of earshot of the caterer. "No, a business meeting."

"During our *party*?"

"You know your father." She picked a shrimp up off a tray and chomped its head. "He lives to serve."

Daddy was in business with something called medallions. Most people thought medallions were a sex thing from the '70s you wore around your neck to show your preferences, but they also had to do with yellow taxicabs—proof that you owned and could operate them. Daddy's bank issued loans to fleet owners and drivers to buy medallions and he had made a ton of money doing it, but now there was some kind of crisis with drivers defaulting on their loans, and everybody using Uber wasn't helping, and he was pretty up against it, Daddy, with a lot of phone calls, and a *lot* of meetings, with all kinds of "high-rolling, low-life associates," as she'd heard her mom describe them. They didn't tell Marley too much. Or, they told her too much, but not the facts.

"When are Benny and them coming?" Benny was her favorite cousin.

"They should be here soon. No use getting too hung up on Ben, though, baby." What did *that* mean? Did she think Marley had . . . feelings? "You know who might be coming later, though, is Noli. It'd be so fun to see her, wouldn't it? Anyway, you go . . . have fun."

Noli was Noelle, one of the really cool popular girls at school whose mom was really good friends with Mom. Mom called her Noli just now to try to make her sound *familiar* and *accessible* . . . nice try. She and Marley had been thick as thieves when they were little, sure, when it was grounds for life-defining friendship just to run around the park together neighing, but now that they were thirteen more was expected, and whatever it was Marley couldn't bring it.

Those girls . . . what was it about those girls? Not just Noelle, but her whole crew at school. They were made of different stuff, those girls. Pinafores hiked up yea high, and joined right at the hip. You could never ever picture any of them being alone ever, so blood-deep was their socialization. They moved in packs, but not just that. They *lived* in 'em, and even when they weren't physically together, even in their sleep, even in the bathroom, like with tummy troubles, even alone at home during a historic blizzard with cell phone service down for miles and nothing to distract them from the dirty doggone no-avoiding-it-anymore business of the self, those girls were still *together* somehow, still *of* one another and their scene in this force field of shimmery insidery belonging, perfumed in peerhood . . . whereas Marley could feel totally alone pretty much anywhere, at any time, with any number of companions (except for Benny maybe), at school, on a bus, on the dance floor at a bat mitzvah doing her "roll it, now dunk it" move . . . she could just . . . be all zipped up inside her thoughts, and solemn as a stone.

It was because she'd never gone to sleepaway camp. She knew it. She'd not been broken in right. Well, she *had* gone once, last summer—she'd been hearing a lot about this *camp*, and she'd looked them up online and found one, which was easy enough to do, up the parkway a couple hours to a place with lakes and cabins and Algonquin names, redolent of pine, where her parents had been really (like really really) excited to drop her off, but then the first three days she had sobbed so hysterically, so convulsively, so much like someone being violently tortured that the camp director called them up and said, "Frankly, this is just . . . this is getting a little bit painful" (painful for *who?*) "and frankly . . . she's just . . . she's gonna have to get a grip, or we'll have to ask her to leave" (she said it just like that, in *such* a wenchy way) and sent Marley and her bear and bag on the train (no Uber for her) back to Grand Central Station.

Mom and Daddy had been pretty annoyed about losing the deposit, and almost had to cancel their trip to Mykonos, but instead left her with Grandma for three weeks, which was fine—*fine,* she *loved* Grandma—but how lame was *that?* To just wail for home like a goddamn baby when on the other side of that tiny bit of homesickness was *camp,* the thing that would finally pixie-dust her world, just . . . bippidi-boop!—a felt-up tween in cutoffs with a tan, and not a scared scrawny pasty nobody stuck in the city all August long, buying onion rolls with Grandma and her brother J. J., and watching *Funny Girl* for the five hundredth time, and reading magazines in bed, like some polio case? How lame was *that?*

"Sweetheart, sweetheart." Speaking of Grandma, she was sitting by the fire. They'd just left her there alone with her chicken pieces. She could choke. "Sweetheart, come and visit. How's my beautiful baby?"

She pulled Marley toward her, onto her lap. She smelled great, like rosewater and nicotine-replacement lozenges, in the same shade of Helena Rubinstein lipstick she'd stockpiled before its discontinuation decades—epochs—back. "How are you?"

Strident was the word for Grandma. Or used to be. Always out and about, in her plumage, going to the theater and the grocery store and to lectures called things like "Joyce Before *Ulysses*" and "1848: Springtime of the Peoples," and to dinner with her hairdresser Vicente and her professor friend and sometimes-boyfriend Harold. And she actually read the *New Yorker* and *Atlantic,* rather than just sort of leaving them around like Mom did, like she hoped a little cultural literacy would just . . . *waft* into her. . . But now something had gripped Grandma, or let her loose, more like. Some people when they lost the plot you hardly noticed, but with a super-sophisticated lady like Grandma it was pretty freaky.

"And school? How's school?"

"It's winter break now, Grandma." Thank God.

"Oh, yes. I see."

She had better start soaking it up. School. Oh God, school.

Just the thought of school moved like a millstone over her soul. It was just around the corner, but miles and miles from home. Just the thought of it made her chest constrict. Why?

It's not like it was classically brutal or anything. It was all girls for one thing, and quite famously progressive, and you'd be sooner shunned (at least in theory) for being insufficiently liberal-minded than for having, say, a unibrow and smelly armpits, or a strumpet for a mother. But there was something sinister about that place. . . .

Girls like Noelle would make a big show of their *passion for equality*, taking selfies in pink hats and posting cute pics with their moms on international women's day (Annabel Wyckoff posted one of her and her mom both looking really, really pretty on the beach in St. Barts in bikinis and beady sarongs with the caption, *Thank u for being such a strong + brave beautiful mamma to me and showing me how its done*. How being super pretty and buying stuff all the time's done? Nice work if you can get it!) and saying how women and girls instead of "tearing each other down" should "lift each other up" *no matter what* (which itself seemed kind of hollow and infantilizing really, like some red-herring idea trotted out on Twitter among dueling starlets) and then *terrorizing* this one girl from Hewitt, or Ho-itt as they called it, one of Annabel's foremost sexual rivals, spreading rumors on a made-up Instagram account that she'd been hooking up (as in going all the way) with her ex-stepdad on the regular for years. This Hewitt girl had tried to kill herself after, with pills, and now she went to a special school for at-risk youth in Connecticut, where she peed into a Dixie cup each morning and walked the hilly grounds on a *leash* attached to a personal nurse. That's what Marley had heard anyway.

But no, no, school wasn't classically brutal, not for her. And she should thank her lucky stars nobody there had made it their business to try to *tear her down* (like they'd even bother). But she didn't feel too *lifted up* either. No, no . . . not altogether *lifted up*. Grandma said, "And school? How's school?"

"It's winter break now, Grandma."

"What's that?"

"Same as yesterday, pretty much, Grandma!"

They had had lunch at Saks, the two of them. Nice time. Though Grandma kept calling her Anna. Anna for Grandma's older sister who had died when she was little, run down by a milk wagon crossing Clinton Street, before the family moved to Great Neck.

"And your father? Is he . . . behaving himself?"

"Well, I think so. He's really busy, he's—"

"How's that?"

"He's busy!" Marley said.

"He always was a naughty, manic little boy."

That was another thing—Grandma'd started talking about Daddy like he was small, calling him a *naughty number*, and asking if he'd had his tuna sandwich yet that day, and one night last week at dinner describing in *some detail* how she used to "powder his peanut" (?) after bath time. ("Drop it, Ma," he'd said. "Just knock it off," he'd said, like *he was her mother.*)

Grandma said, "That's always been the family. Half of them wanting to scrutinize the soul, and half wanting nothing to do with one. Someone once said to me, 'You Cohens, you Cohens . . .' How did it go, what'd he say, he said . . . oh! Oh! He said—" She was *really* shouting. People were staring. "He said, 'You Cohens, you'll end up half in Yale, and half in jail.' I loved that! Though of course, you know, we haven't gotten *quite* that far on either count. *Yet!*"

Jesus Christ. Who'd said anything about *jail?*

"Fetch us a cookie, why don't you. Just a small one. That's a good girl."

BENNY WAS HERE, in the flesh. Daddy and Meyer had a sister, Brenda, the oldest of the family, and she had three kids who lived across the park, on Riverside. Benny was just an hour—

not even—older than Marley. There were pictures of them with their highchairs abutting, in grave negotiations over mushy peas, and they'd been getting on like a house on fire ever since . . . kindred spirits, two travelers on the same road. *Soulmates* wouldn't be too grandiose a term.

Last year for Grandma's eightieth they'd all gone down to Florida to the Fontainebleau for a week to celebrate. Meanwhile there was some kind of high-level mudslinging going on with the grown-ups having to do with estate planning that the kids weren't allowed to know about, but she and Benny didn't even care to know the score, they were too busy having the *time of their lives*. Deputized as parents, raiding the minibars, three Toblerones apiece and even a couple rounds of vodka Red Bulls after hours, and racing on the waterslides and hitting the swim-up dessert bar as often as they wanted, and having pillow fights with him holding his leg on top of hers for a whole minute on the bed one time, and in the lobby gift shop pretending to be tourists from Germany looking for diarrhea medicine, which got the visored troll lady who worked there's heckles up pretty bad, and sitting on the balcony at day's end eating ice cream sundaes the size of their heads while the littler cousins watched RuPaul in the suite, her and Benny feeling totally Zen and sun-kissed and tuckered out from all their hijinks while the moon rose over the Atlantic, feeling not like parents—that'd be lame—more like Wendy and Peter Pan, young and old in all the right, most perfect ways. It was *so much fun*, that week. It was probably the best time she'd ever had. She hoped that Benny felt the same, and that he thought about it all the time like she did.

He walked around her room. He seemed so big in it. *So male.*

"It's looking pretty goddamn pink in here," he said. "Though I think you missed a spot. A square inch, right there by the radiator."

"Ha ha." He was too funny for words. He was hysterical.

30

"Whoever made unicorns a thing again really struck a chord, huh? Anyway, what's up? How's tricks." He sat down on her beanbag. It was true what Mom had said, when they came in just now—he *had* shot up, just since Thanksgiving. "What's up with Grandma?" he said.

"I dunno. She is acting a little weird. She called me Anna yesterday."

"She just called me Meyer, which I'm choosing not to take personally."

"Oh, he's not so bad really."

"Mom's been super upset about it all. Dad was talking about putting her, you know, someplace easier. Out near us." Out where? On Riverside? "Like a living facility."

Marley didn't even want to *think* anything negative even related to Benny, but sometimes Daddy called Benny's dad that human haircut from Ohio who was always butting his fake-patrician nose into Cohen family business. Brandon had always been perfectly nice to Marley, but she sometimes saw what Daddy meant, and anyway what kind of a name was Brandon for somebody's father?

Marley said, "Grandma? She could never. She wouldn't stand for that. I have a medical news alert on my phone and it actually sounds like they're making a lot of progress on the dementia front. I think it should be fine soon. And crossword puzzles help." Though maybe not the ones in *People*. "And, like, by the time we're old it won't even be a problem."

"Good, 'cause I think we'll need our wits about us when it's Fury Road out there."

"Yeah."

She didn't understand all this casual talk of the apocalypse. Sure the specter of catastrophe loomed large, probably larger than she or he could really wrap their heads around, but lately people seemed to slip their visions of flame and flood and cataclysm edgewise into conversation almost just to sound provocative.

31

Almost like they *wanted* to be violently purged of the status quo. It seemed like an old impulse of the super-privileged, this.

"Anyway she's like the smartest, most spitfire-y woman ever, Grandma," Marley said. "She can handle herself."

"I dunno. I think people get to an age where personality's not really a thing anymore."

"That's depressing."

"Yeah . . . what are you gonna do."

"I don't know, maybe she should see a doctor?"

"No, I meant rhetorically, like, what are you gonna do."

"Oh."

They were quiet for a while. It was never awkward when they were quiet. Except right now it kind of was.

"Did you get anything good for Hanukkah?" she said. They were both half Jewish, half Catholic, among the zillion and one things they had in common. "I got some pretty cool stuff." She guessed he probably didn't need to know about her sheet mask advent calendar for combination skin—that was kind of embarrassing—but maybe he'd be impressed by her new *Art of Mondo* coffee-table book. He loved the movies too.

"Slim pickings this year, for moi." He took a drag on his Juul and blew some cool Os, like the magic caterpillar. "But Mom says there's no use overloading now, 'cause we'll get more stuff when we move into the new place."

"Oh, you guys are finally moving in your building?"

"They didn't tell you? No. We're *moving* moving. To Pelham."

"Pardon?"

"How did they not tell you?"

She felt herself sort of float above her body.

"*When?*" she said. "What's Pelham?"

"After New Year's. Dad's been wanting to leave forever, and then he saw someone dropping a deuce on the steps of a church, and well"—she felt her blood draining out of her—"I didn't see what the big deal was, but that did it for him apparently. He was saying something about a subway slasher too, which I think might be a lie. Anyway Mom was all, *What about their cousins, what about the diversity, what about the Met.* But then she saw the bathrooms, and she fell in line pretty quick."

"Well, but what about it? All that stuff?" And *her?* What about her?

"I said we've been to the Met once in like six years, for one thing. And there's stuff up there too."

"Like what?"

"Well, *nature,* Marley. Ever heard of it? Plus there's a Benihana that's like a five-minute drive."

"There's a Benihana here."

"It's not the same. The one here's super small and shitty."

That was true.

"Wait, so you *wanna* move? What about school? I suppose Trevor Day's just going to let you up and leave in the middle of the school year, like some Culkin sibling."

"Uh, *yeah.* It's not the gulag. They let people leave. Anyway, I think it might be cool. Different, ya know. Don't get *upset* or anything, Marl," he said. "It's not the boonies. It's less than an hour away. Dad's not even switching offices."

Less than an hour? It was galaxies away. And how could he be so easygoing, so well adjusted . . . such a total yes-man chameleon about it? They were city kids to the bone, the two of them. Terminal cases, Grandma said.

"I mean, I'll miss the city of course. And I'll definitely . . . well . . . I'll miss you. Like a ton. But we'll still chill and everything."

"Benny . . ." she said. "I'll miss you *terribly.*"

Was that too much? The "terribly"?

But well, what would she do without him right across the park? It wasn't just a matter of his company, you see. The character of everything, the weight of every observation, the heat and traction of living itself, it was all him. It was all bound up in him.

He went to stand by the window.

Across the street was an old hotel, a storied place apparently, a relic of swing-time New York with a famous cocktail bar. Charlie Parker had died in one of the rooms—Marley didn't really "get" jazz but Daddy was obsessed with him—his body so ravaged by heroin the coroner had put him down for twice his age. The hotel had just been bought by a conglomerate from Hong Kong and would be turned into condos in a couple months. She'd miss having it there outside her bedroom, right across 81st Street. It was like a living dollhouse, or the cityscape from *Rear Window* (though if Mom and Daddy knew some of the things she'd seen, like grown-ups having sex one time, they would probably board the windows up stat). On the upper level was an SRO-type room where a maintenance man lay on a cot now in a dirty undershirt, his head blocked by the lampshade so you couldn't see his face, reaching down every so often for a bottle and bringing it up over his belly while the TV blared the Knicks game in the corner. And of course there was the ghost. At least Marley was pretty sure she was a ghost. All old hotels had one. Though Marley wondered if she'd survive the renovations into condos. Probably not. Some changes even ghosts couldn't survive.

"Seen any more hookers lately?" Benny said. "I love that place. Not, you know, for the hookers." He took another drag on his Juul. "Not *just*." He was a man now, basically. "I just mean, I'll bet they don't have this kind of thing out in Pelham is all."

"Well, they won't have it here either pretty soon," said Marley.

His hand was almost touching hers.

When the door opened they both jumped. It was just J. J., her little brother. She could've sworn Benny gave her a millisecond's look like, *There goes that.* There goes *what*, though?

"Aunt Brenda wants you guys to come out and be s-s-s-sociable," said J. J. "Did you get your rock?"

"My what?" said Benny.

"Your rock. Make sure you get one before you leave. Well, Marley lives here, she's my s-s-s-sister, so I can give hers to her anytime."

"Okay, sure, sure, J. J. That'd be great." He was so nice to J. J. all the time. Like she needed another reason to adore him.

J. J. had some "quirks," as Mom called them in mixed company with a fake shrug and fake light-heartedness whenever it came up. His "quirks" weren't one thing or the other. He wasn't like one of those kids who was really good at math but really bad with people, or like one of those "inspiring" kids who was really bad at math but really good with people. He was pretty bad at math, and just okay with people. You had to know him.

Mom had struggled for a long time, years in fact, to get pregnant with him, and then he'd been born thirteen weeks early 'cause he wasn't growing right in her belly, deprived of some essential fluids in there, and there was one night at Lenox Hill when things were "touch-and-go" and Daddy's voice was breaky and the air back in the apartment was thick and turgid like the night Pop-Pop had died, but then things improved, and he pulled through. He was mostly fine now. Mostly. He had alopecia, which meant he had no hair anywhere, which was unrelated to the birth apparently, and some issues with his speech and coordination and vision, and he had to wear a pair of rubbery glasses like swimming goggles so they wouldn't come off his head when he was running, which he often was, to nowhere in particular, and one time on the playground she'd heard this abominable child in Gucci-Vans collab sneakers say "What's his *deal?* Is he, like, a squirrel or something?" 'cause of his facial twitch, but he was mostly fine. Fine enough for Buckley, though Mom and Daddy had basically renovated it eight times over trying to keep him there among the bonny princelings and future senators through his not-so-stellar academic performance, and his humming all the time in class.

Anyway nothing was his fault, he was her brother, and she loved him, but goddamn *rocks?* Was he for real?

"Anyway, the rocks are under my b-bed for when you n-need them."

"Great, J.J." said Marley. "Anyway, Benny, we should probably make plans to hang out a lot in the next few weeks. You know, really get some stuff on the books. Otherwise the time, it's just going to slip through our fingers, and—"

"Sure, of course," said Benny. "We're going to my other grandparents' tomorrow, for Christmas, but then we'll be back in a few days, for a few days."

These other grandparents of his . . . she didn't like the sound of these *other grandparents*. She always pictured them like that man and woman in that famous painting with the pitchfork. Thin-lipped, parsimonious. Farm people. She hadn't actually met them ever, but they just didn't sound like her kind of people. Or like Benny's kind of people. Though apparently they *were* his kind of people.

"Guess we should head out there," Benny said. "I guess the party misses us."

THE GROWN-UPS WERE extremely drunk by now. The place was rammed. Noelle gave Marley a phony wave from across the room, like "Hiiiiiii." So she had deigned to show up after all. She was dressed like some cool girl from France, like she was just stopping by on her way to someplace better, in jeans and a sparkly top, with a leather jacket from IRO that probably cost five hundred dollars and Golden Goose sneakers (sneakers, to a Christmas party!), not like an overgrown toddler from the 1940s like Marley. Not like Anne Frank on picture day, in a dress with a Peter Pan collar and goddamn puffed sleeves and a sash.

"Holy smokes," said Benny. His eyes were all *ahoooga* in his head. "Holy shit."

Marley couldn't get a read on if Benny had done things with girls yet, but, well, he *had* gone to camp. He actually had a lot of friends, Benny. He was a pretty cool, chill guy, who sometimes

36

went to parties. Marley never went to parties. She went to the movies, though, sometimes, with Daniela Friedman.

(Though the thing about Daniela Friedman was . . . well, she had moved to Scarsdale in second grade and Marley hadn't actually seen or heard from her since, but she didn't want Mom and Daddy thinking she was going out alone and being unsafe or, worse, that she had no friends, and Daniela Friedman had one of those plausible but totally forgettable Jewish-with-a-twist names that ticked exactly the right box in the mind of a frazzled, slightly indifferent parent. She didn't . . . *talk* to Daniela or anything. Not that she was aware of. She wasn't *crazy*.)

"Who the hell's *that*?" said Benny.

"Oh, her? That's Noelle. From my school."

"Holy shit. You go to school with *her*?"

She *was* really, really pretty. No two ways about it. Her hair was this not brown, not blond, sort of naturally bronze color, and it grew out of her head in a really nice swoopy way, no grease or cowlicks anywhere, and it fell on her face in perfect curtains over not really a widow's peak—that sounded too creepy to describe anything about her—more like the tippy-top of a heart. And her features were this perfect balance of delicate and plush, with dewy, poreless skin, and even the school uniform, which was a *uniform* after all, just hung on her frame better and more crisply than on Marley's or anybody else's.

But she wasn't Benny's type at all. She was a little bit thick. Not dumb—she got really good grades, actually, better than Marley's—but her mind moved on a highly conventional frequency. You just couldn't be that pretty and also have original thoughts. It just wasn't possible. Maybe somebody would say that that was sexist, 'cause no one was telling super good-looking *boys* that they lacked curiosity as a matter of course—though a lot of them did, as it so happened—nor that any depth of insight was particularly off-limits to them, but it was different for girls. You just couldn't be that *seen* and still see things for yourself properly—the force of all their eyeballs on you just got inside your brain and debased your thoughts no matter what, like how some Native American tribes in the nineteenth century thought their conquerors' camera flashes stole tiny bits of their souls away (they were onto something). And even when some model wrote an essay in *Vogue* about her endometriosis journey and people said it was well written and deep what they meant was it was deep *for a terminally beautiful person*, not actually deep, and if you met an actually deep woman who was also really pretty you could bet your bottom dollar she'd not been looking too good in the eighth grade—even Taylor Swift had been piggy-faced and not-that-cute for a while, in middle school, and that's how her songwriting had so much pain.

"Not to be mean," said Marley, "but I should warn you. Her mind is pretty, pretty basic."

"Who needs a mind with a body like *that*?" he said. "I think I'm gonna go talk to her." And off he went. Had he licked his lips just now? Oh God.

Tonight just wasn't right at all.

These parties used to be the social highlight of her year. She and Benny and J.J. rushing around like the kids in the beginning of *The Nutcracker*, except not a total snoozefest, and Daddy's whereabouts accounted for, and J.J. still young enough that the chasm slowly announcing itself between his actual and developmental ages was easier to ignore, and the tree of course—the grand tree at the far end of the living room, majestically aglow, beribboned in gold, and decorated up and down with handmade ornaments, splendid knickknacks, wooden drummer boys and a frosty glassblown ballerina and a prancing caribou, its nose dusted with glitter snow, a beautiful, real Douglas fir, and not some tacky fake feathery crap with only blue-and-white baubles Mom got on Wayfair and thought looked good but actually looked like something from the lobby in a Chase, and Grandma still upon the terra firma of her seventies, and not just sitting by herself staring at the fire, spouting spooky half-remembered wisdoms like some exile from her own life. They were all on thinner ice now, weren't they, come down from a place of richer colors, greater elegance, more automatic love. They were all worse at themselves now. The enamel had worn thin.

DADDY CAME BACK right as everyone was leaving. His briefcase and his umbrella, his fine Italian shoes—these were the Daddy things. A great relief to see them in the foyer. It must have been snowing out. They were all wet.

"Daddy," Marley said. She caught him sneaking down the hall, trying to make a run for the bedroom.

"Marley . . . honeypop, I—"

"Is everything okay?"

She went to hug him, and he tensed a little. But then he loosened, and he hugged her back. And then he really, really her hugged back, really tightly. What was going on with him?

They hugged for what felt like a long time. Despite being five foot seven he was really very big, Daddy. Hairy and full of life. The forearms with their tensile strength, olive-toned in summer, iconic in their way. Always with a beautiful watch and signet ring. She loved him so. Technically she loved Mom too, but her and Daddy's love was different. Just melty love, no recoil to it.

After a minute he let go of her and said, "Everything's perfect, baby." It didn't seem too perfect. He didn't look good at all. He looked tired and rumpled, brutalized by work. Adrift in the charmlessness of his affairs. He was nearing the age when businessmen dropped dead on treadmills.

"Why won't you tell me anything?" she said. They kept lying about whatever was happening with his work, or with their marriage. Outbursts and salty, ugly talk, and then all this back-pedaling, saying everything was fine. As if Marley didn't know by now it wasn't all lollipops and roses out there. It wasn't all lollipops and roses in *here*.

"I know there've been problems," she said. "I know there are, because I hear you. And if you guys are trying to shelter me, well, frankly, you're doing a half-ass job." She couldn't believe herself, that she'd said *ass* just now. "It's just like, you're always saying everything's fine, and then running around, in like a panic—"

"You know what?" Daddy cut her off.

He knelt down and hooked his hands around her waist, like he used to do when she was small.

"Not everything's great. Daddy's tired. Daddy's at his wits' end some days. There are fires, and I've been doing my best to try and put them out. But I'm not panicked. Panicking is something critters in the woods do. I'm a man. And you're a smart, wonderful kid, you know that? I've got guys in my Rolodex who aren't half as intuitive as you. If they taught that stuff at Wharton, the world would be a better place." Grown-ups always talked about "the world" like *they* weren't the ones running it. "Now let me get myself cleaned up. You won't blow my cover, will you, with the peanut gallery in there?"

"No. No, of course not, Daddy."

"That's a good girl. I just wanna know one thing . . . do you have any idea how loved you are?"

"Well, yes . . . I think so." She knew it was a lot. But she didn't know what it was worth.

"Well . . . okay. That's good enough for me."

Later he and Mom were talking in the living room. Marley spied on them from the hallway. They seemed to not be fighting, which was a surprise, frankly, with Daddy having been gone all night and missing the whole party. Mom was looking a little . . . a little bit loose. Her makeup smeared, leaning over in her chair and eating a pastrami sandwich.

"It sounds like a good fit for them," she said, chewing. She *must* have been soused. She never ate. And definitely not pastrami sandwiches.

"That goy was always just a moonlighter," said Daddy. "He's not cut out for New York. He belongs back in Evanston, or wherever the hell he's from." Were they talking about Benny's dad?

"I'll bet he's got his lawn laid already. He's not cut out for New York."

"'That goy'? Oh Jake . . . don't flatter yourself."

"What's that mean?"

"You take the subway once a season on a lark, tip a barbershop quartet forty bucks a singer, your little farthing for the year to humankind, and then you go home to your palace on Park Avenue, saying 'New York, gotta love it!' Feeling like a man of the people. I'm not saying I'm any different. I just mean . . . if they could afford to live here the way *you* live here, on your own terms, they would probably stay too." When did Mom get to be such a ballbuster? Since getting her GED? Marley kind of liked it. Sometimes. "*I think Pelham sounds beautiful.*"

"It's the making it seem like it's some victory that gets my goat," said Daddy. "*Such a charming downtown* and *oh, the choo-choo train museum. Like we're the ones drinking the Kool-Aid. Wait until he sees the property taxes.*"

She pictured Benny out there, next year, in the country . . . drinking forties on a football field at night, like Jason London in *Dazed and Confused* (which she'd just seen for the first time and completely lost her head over), or steaming up his Chevy on a lover's lane, some cheerleader by his side, while meathook-wielding hitchhikers roamed the hillsides. Him drawing her closer to him in the backseat, against the darkness, kissing her tenderly . . . different indeed. The country was so *primal*. With fewer lights, you could really see the stars.

"I'd worry more about Marley," Mom said. "Benny's practically her only friend." Well now, *that* was just—"except for this Daniela Friedman person. Honestly, I think she's infatuated with him. It's unnatural."

Well! Okay. Okay. Well! Okay.

Was it, though? Was it so *unnatural*? In the old country, in Silesia or wherever, she and Benny would be married to each other with three kids by now, and statistically only *one* of those

41

kids would be, you know, not right. When Mom was one for two. And what was *her* excuse? Oh, but that was mean. . . .

In the hotel folks were still up, some of them just starting out their nights apparently. On the twelfth-floor corner a bald, divorced-looking man was shaking a cocktail shaker and dancing along to "Blurred Lines"—you could hear the pilfered bass notes floating across 81st Street—a real happening guy. The super was looking out the window with his bottle. He scratched himself, then drew the blinds.

Marley lay upon her coverlet, time dragging, racing forward. Time itself seemed different nowadays. More threadbare in its progress, the objects shifting, losing magnetism. But maybe that was just growing up, the brain maturing in its casement. Like, she used to think her and Benny having the same birthday was the most insane mind-boggling celestially ordained thing ever, the hand of God plainly at work, but maybe it wasn't that big of a deal. Maybe the brain made myths of things like that, and people, to coddle you against the spareness of your passage. Maybe there was nothing too, too special about anyone.

But no, that wasn't quite right either.

In any case, Benny was right: it *was* pretty goddamn pink in here. She ought to talk to Mom about, you know, changing it up some.

3

UP AND AT 'EM! No excuses. He needed to get out today, stay out. Enough of this sitting around and licking wounds. There was lead in his apartment, and his phone was doing him grave harm.

Rudy didn't mean to sound alarmist about this—he'd seen one too many puff-piece headlines about screens and the internet changing people's brains, transforming the whole social fabric, and he'd never cared too much for the philosophizing. Big whoop, he'd thought. Folks had probably felt the same unease about their TV sets back in the day. Maybe some beatnik wrote a pretty deep poem about it. But these last few days, cooped up in his apartment, scrolling, scrolling, waiting for a sign, he'd felt it too—that thing would be the death of him. The point of no return.

Now you almost missed the Man on the TV, trying to sell you things—at least he was a man, and had a face. At least the things were *things*. Now he opened up his phone and what he saw were lives, lives, lives, lives, lives, whole epochs compressed into the tilework on his Instagram. There'd be a picture of Kate Moss and Johnny Depp in the '90s, looking sexual in a way that made you wonder if the fucking you'd been doing in your life had even counted, then a picture from *The New York Times* of somebody in Yemen yesterday cradling her son's dead body, wailing, and you felt terrible for the woman, and grateful for your life and safety, but only for about three seconds, 'cause then it was more pictures, of more crap, some girl from his high school and her baby at Santaland (had she airbrushed her kid? Its eyes looked weird) and his friend Christian with his girlfriend looking like a couple of Staten Island tryhards at Carbone's for their anniversary the other night, the caption all *your my rock, your my queen, I put you on a pedistle*, when Rudy had it on pretty good authority the guy'd had a restraining order taken out against him by a dancer at the Hustler Club named Paige, then a picture from eighty years ago of some kids in London playing hopscotch in the wreckage of the Blitz, and Teddy Roosevelt as a young swashbuckler in Mexico, all of it, the times, the styles, the wars, the glam, the T&A, the suffering, friends and strangers, near and far, scourges, babies, the legends and the no-names, the '60s and the 1890s and last Wednesday night too, all of it hitting his brain in a symphony of total noneventness, like the more pictures he saw, the less he believed that anything besides his thumb had ever *really* happened.

It was no wonder then that the truthers and conspiracy kooks were having a field day out there—they had their work cut out for them. There must be people all over whose brains had turned to jelly, their circuitry fouled up, numbed by the pictures, confused by life's variety, sick of their own selves and in dear-god-awful need of some *beliefs*. Some angle on the swarming world, however wrong and crazy. Rudy wasn't gonna fall into the trap, though. Not today.

What he needed now was people, action, life, the city. To get his head out of his ass. To see things for *himself*. That's what he'd decided anyway. But all this pounding the pavement wasn't going all that well so far. The real world was no picnic either, see. Everybody looked like shit, tired. They dressed like shit. Nobody had any style. And the ones out here who did, who could afford to, they were all the worst kinds of people.

He had said "Good day, miss" to a lady just now coming out of the subway, on 28th Street. It wasn't a come-on, not at all—he knew better than *that*—it was just to be friendly. Just 'cause it was a nice day, brisk and Christmassy, and he hadn't been out

44

this early in like seven years, and she looked like a cool person and it seemed like a cool thing to say—whatever, it was stupid—and anyway she'd scoffed at him. She had straight-up *groaned*, like she'd been *shot*. Way over-the-top, like ugh, *ugggghhhh*, how *dare* he, how dare he be so patronizing and old-fashioned and intrusive as to even *look at her*, and she'd stormed off down the street.

He felt like such a dummy now. Absolutely breathless with how dumb he felt. Puzzled by the whole exchange, if you could even call it that. "Good day, miss"? What kind of a line was that? Like some lunkhead out of *Midnight Cowboy*, doffing his cap, bewildered at the modern ladies.

Well, screw her and her grinchy ass. Let her moan about it to her friends at The Wing later, how some inked-up outer-borough Joe schmo who wouldn't be fit, or would only be fit, to fix her freezer had dared look in her direction. Let her fix her own fucking freezer. Screw her. No, no, that wasn't right. There was no need to be cruel about it. He didn't know her story any more than she knew his. Screw *himself*, screw *himself*, that after twenty-six years of living, many blows and blessings, long talks, deep thoughts, still he lacked the inner resources to take in stride the total nothing that had been that interaction. He was losing his edge—too much time among the old folks at the bar. He was losing his looks too, maybe. Otherwise, that might've all gone differently.

You could see the changes in just the last five years, his face getting puffy and poached-looking, with the pre-jowls. That saline, past-prime Mickey Rourke look to the skin over his cheeks. Too many drinks and smokes. Some days women would stare at him on the street, men too, and he'd think, eat your heart out, people, convinced they were all just *dying* to fuck him, then he'd catch himself in a storefront window and realize what he'd seen in all their eyes was maybe not so much lust as . . . concern.

It was a city lost. Lost to him, and the mad market of the streets made it clear.

He'd been all over town this morning. He'd looked at an apartment out in Bushwick, a godforsaken hovel. He had no choice but to move, though. They were raising the rent in his building. About a year ago they'd offered him five thousand dollars to break his lease. Sitting pretty in his love nest, a rent-stabilized walk-up on 3rd Street, with a steady pipeline from his baby's parents covering half, he had told those slumlords where to shove it. But then they'd gotten more aggressive. Turning off the heat in winter, nerve-grinding construction day and night, no peace, no quiet, and this ex-cop henchman of the owners' stealing people's mail, threatening undocumented immigrants he'd blab on them to ICE. Prowling the hallways in a beard and glasses he probably got at the spy store, posing as "Inspector"—inspector who, Gadget? He'd planted a dead rat on one Korean family's doormat when they wouldn't take a buyout. And the live rats, well, those came standard.

Rudy was sure what they were doing was totally illegal, but they had ins, these people. They had probably greased the palms of however many civic bureaucrats to look the other way. And what was he gonna do, go Mr. Smith on the Department of Buildings? Fine print was not his thing at all. He had no money for a lawyer. He would take the buyout in a second now, if they wouldn't bust his kneecaps just for asking. . . . Thinking he would never need it—those were the days. In love and invincible. Thinking on the zero percent chance that things went south between him and his lady fair he could always move back in with Dad to get his footing. Ha. Those were the days.

Onward. He was starving. His stomach was making crazy dial-up noises. He had a little time to kill before seeing another apartment in Kips Bay.

He went into a diner on 38th Street. Usually he felt jumpy and self-conscious sitting alone, but in dumps like these all bets were off.

"It's just me," he told the waitress. Was it ever.

"Sit anywhere you want, doll," she said.

He sat down in a booth near the back. He appreciated being called "doll," actually. Very much. He knew some girls who got pissed off when people called them "doll" and "sweetheart," like it was condescending to them, but for a certain kind of man at a certain point in life, "doll" was music to your ears. "Doll" meant you weren't a *total* creep.

She kept poking at the edges of his mind. His ex. Popping up. He'd have to hash it out at some point, get the facts straight in his head before they curdled any more on him. She'd just moved to the city when they met, twenty-one years old. He must've seemed to her like a steady pair of hands at first, a city boy, a few years older. Tougher than the rest. Not like these straw fedora film majors and milquetoasts from her college dorm. And him, well, he had put up no resistance. It was like some dream of teenage love he'd not gotten right the first time, the first renditions wasted in mediocre company, the mall rats and trashtalkers of his misspent high school years in Maspeth, the Dinahs and Rachelles, landlubbers all, with their spray tans and their strappy heels, so bound and tethered to their womanhood, peaking at eighteen.

This girl was something else. An open book, smart and kind and interested. Small breasts, and untroubled by them, her hair untouched by dyes or goops, the same strong God-made auburn hair she'd had as a horse-crazed kid in the Midwest with buckteeth and a sweet smile in a picture on her dresser.

But time went on, and she showed her innocence. She was not long for the city. Fucking *shaking* crying when a homeless woman called her a cunt once on the street. She was a college girl, through and through, full of principles but wispy at her core. And so bright-eyed all the time, so easy to impress, so *moved*, not even in a phony way, 'cause she really meant the things she said. All, *My semester abroad in Florence was so, so enriching, probably one of the most enriching, eye-opening experiences of my life* and making him watch this unbelievably boring independent film from Ghana 'cause her friend who interned for the Criterion Collection told her it was good, and she was so completely owned by other people's opinions, and so new to anything cool or different, and so primed by a lifetime of guilt for being white and well protected and from Lincoln, Nebraska, that she couldn't even get it through her head that not liking this movie from Ghana was even allowed, then spending an hour of his Friday night when he could've been out getting loaded or making bank trying to convince him that him not liking this movie was actually 'cause he was *culturally programmed* not to, when he just hadn't liked it, and why was she so mad at him about it, what the hell was she trying to prove? And after a while he kind of missed the girls from his old stomping grounds in Queens, who had their hang-ups but at least had some pride of place about them. Some attitude. Who at least would call things as they saw them. Who weren't secretly terrified of Black and brown people while always giving little lectures on the richness of their cultures. He had started off thinking *he* was the provincial one, but then he realized she was.

So the bloom came off the rose, in her eyes too. His bad-boy-with-a-heart-of-gold routine not holding up so well, taking on a darkness in her eyes. Almost a doom. He'd gotten totally, completely, almost hall-of-fame-level smashed at one of her friends' birthday parties toward the end, another barely-a-party party in Brooklyn Heights where you had to take your shoes off at the door, and no one got fucked up at all or fought or said anything remotely aggressive or off-key, just talked about work and their summer travel plans, all the girls with weird short bangs and tiny tasteful tattoos sipping red wine, and he made a scene, which was just as well, to give them all something to remember him by. She'd been pissed off after that but they'd hung on for a bit, her coming home one night spewing some shit her therapist had told her about how he was really a narcissist and you couldn't love a narcissist and he was just a stand-in for her numbskull socially regressive stick-in-the-mud alcoholic father and she'd been trying to please men like him her whole life and she never would and she should stop trying blah blah blah.

He was nothing like her dad, anyway. *That guy?* Her parents had come to the city once, to have lunch with her and Rudy before their matinee of *Beautiful: The Carole King Musical.* A geography teacher, who wore pants with the zips that turned them into shorts if it got too hot. Rudy didn't know what the hell her therapist was talking about.

She *had* loved him, though—that was a fact. (Wasn't it?) And he'd definitely loved *her.* That he knew. And he *had* gotten through to her, awhile. Almost two years. Not nothing. (Though it sure as hell felt like nothing *now.*) And that he'd been able to get through to somebody like her, somebody so different from him, to make her laugh and cry, and come, had once seemed like a minor miracle, like a message from the gods that he still had it, that the light of life was still in him, and he could still surprise himself. But that all seemed very dusky now, and very much in doubt. And had she really come? Really? She was a little over-the-top about it, sometimes, and nothing if not suggestible. . . .

His sandwich was like eating shoes. The lettuce tasted horrible, like all the foot traffic of Chinatown. Someone had left their *Daily News* in the next booth. He scanned the classifieds, though they didn't really list jobs or apartments there anymore. Not the kinds you wanted. They were testing a new dialysis drug up at Columbia and needed volunteers. He wasn't quite there yet, but it was good to know there was a lower rung to fall to. The paper and the internet would only do so much for him, though. He had to put out feelers with real people.

He had a cousin on his mom's side in Stamford, Connecticut, he could call. She lived near the railroad tracks on the Metro-North New Haven line and managed a Sephora in a strip mall, but she was quite a cool person, and seemed to get a kick out of him. Plus how bad could Stamford be? Maybe she could get him a job. Though he didn't know if they hired dudes at Sephora.

49

There was always Uncle Mike of course. But something told Rudy to tread lightly with Uncle Mike. Rudy respected him, which complicated things. Besides he'd already crossed him once, burned that bridge with Mike's construction friends and not thought twice about it at the time. He had sat in on a job site the summer before senior year, building a luxury high-rise on the West Side, fetching Coolattas for the crew, then nearly braining some guy lifting a crane bucket. He'd hated every minute of it. The heights, the *wind*—it was windy up there like you couldn't believe. He'd be so much better off now, though, if he'd stuck it out with that. Not just money-wise. Blood-wise. In body, mind, and soul. Doing hard, proud labor all these years, up early every day with the city, working with his hands. The road not traveled. Now it felt too late to go legitimate. Still, he shot Uncle Mike a text. Better to get to him before Dad poured poison in his ear about what a failure piece of shit his nephew was.

There was an old woman in the next booth over, her bags piled next to her, all dolled up with a fur coat and matching headband, taking a long, long time getting her eggs into her mouth. Her hand was shaking every which way. Parkinson's, maybe. What the hell was *that* like? Being old and sick? Did death blacken her every thought and move, or was she happy just to keep the motor running? Happy with her scrambled eggs, every hard-won bite of them. Happy just to see a baby smiling at her in the street. She'd probably been his age or older when they'd first landed on the moon, this woman. And something told Rudy that she hadn't spent the last five decades feeling sorry for herself, crying for her lost loves, missed opportunities. Wailing for her days of wine and roses and Sinatra. No, something told him that this lady had gotten the fuck on with things.

No more making friends with old people, though.

Uncle Mike texted back to say to come by his office for lunch tomorrow. Very terse. No greetings, no exclamation points, but that was just his style. It would be great to see him. There was no salvation but in others. Things were looking up.

Now if only he could do something about his social life. He wasn't gonna wind up alone in some gentlemen's club on Christmas Day. He needed wingmen. Plans. The more he got out there the less nervous he would be. He should call up Brendan Heggers.

Brendan had been a few years older than him at school. They'd been on the varsity baseball team together. Always down for a good time, Brendan, a worse cutup than even Rudy, at least in high school.

Rudy instantly regretted pressing Call. The phone rang for a long time. Calling an old friend out of the blue was desperate. Crazy. He could always hang up right this second, text Brendan to say sorry for the butt-dial—

"Hello?"

Too late.

"Oh, hey! Waddup? Happy holidays!"

"Rudy, Rudy. It's been a minute. Are you all right?" Had he heard otherwise? "Everything okay?" He sounded weirded out that Rudy'd called.

"Of course. It's great. I'm great," said Rudy. "Just, you know, in the city, out and about. Workin' hard, playin' hard. Was wondering if you wanted to grab a drink one of these days. Just, you know, feeling festive. My treat." Huh? He definitely wasn't good for it.

"A drink? Oh . . ." There were kids crying in the background, and a really loud TV. "I'm at my mother-in-law's, in Jersey, actually, with the kids. We're here for the week."

"Kids? I knew you and Elise got engaged—are there kids already? Kids plural?"

"She's pregnant with our third, yeah."

"Jesus Christ. Holy shit, man! Congratulations." What was he, a Mormon? This guy was twenty-eight, twenty-nine years old. What the fuck was he doing with three kids? "Hey, how's your sister?"

"Oh, she's really good, yeah."

"What's she up to these days?"

"She actually joined the Peace Corps after college. St. John's."

"Of course she did. She was always going places," Rudy said.

"Not like the other girls, am I right."

"Yeah."

"So where's she at?"

"Ecuador, actually."

"Holy shit, that's far."

"Uh-huh. Yeah. It's crazy."

"So she's not, like, around tonight?"

"What, they don't get Christmas break in the Peace Corps?"

"Ha ha, no man."

"Oh, too bad . . ."

You could practically hear Brendan's attention wandering. See the walleyes through the phone. He'd always been a bit of a dullard honestly. Rudy didn't know why he'd even called him. They hadn't even been that close.

"Anyway, gotta go. My youngest just pooped. You know how it is." He said it like he'd just been summoned to the front lines. People were such goddamn martyrs about their kids. "Great to hear from you, though. We gotta catch up soon. Next time."

"Great! Great to hear from you too. I mean, glad I called. Good luck with the cleanup! Ha ha."

He had already hung up.

So much for that. The Peace Corps? Jesus Christ. Rudy'd had it so, so bad for her in high school. Mallory Heggers. They were always ships passing, though, never made it happen. Was a time a crush like that was the very spice of life . . . just the thought of it sustained you, made the school day interesting. And even after graduation, the idea of that person out there in the world kept you on your toes a little, kept you young. It was like a little sitcom plotline but real, all that will-they-or-won't-they business.

He sounded like a total sleaze, but well, he wanted to know. It was like pulling teeth, with these two-word answers.

Well . . . they won't. They didn't and they don't. Or if they do, it don't work out.

Back on the train he felt another wave of dread and panic. Not knowing where to hang his hat. Not knowing what the hell life would look like a month, even a week, from now. Of course many had faced much worse uncertainty, which didn't make it any better. It just made you feel like an asshole for not worshipping your privileges.

Walking around was so *exhausting.* Maybe he had some kind of an autoimmune disorder he didn't know about.

He used to walk all over, all the time. He used to love it. Stepping out, teenage mojo, teenage money, the world giving him that energy back like it gave a shit that he was in it. Back then the whole city seemed like copy, like a book of life that he was reading. Now it just, it was what it was. A tiresome theater, not nearly worth the cost of his admission.

Stalled on Grand Street he studied an ad on the subway platform with a veiny woman pumping iron that said Life Begins Where Your Comfort Zone Ends. . . . It had fucking better.

His comfort zone in any case was naught—he couldn't have stayed there if he'd wanted to. That property was now condemned.

Uncle Mike worked out of an office above a car wash in Astoria. They'd always been close. You had to think twice before coming to him with a bleeding heart, though. He had no tolerance for blubbering. In his world introspection was a passing fad, or some contagion from a Kurt Cobain song, which was about as hip a reference as he cared to know.

As a younger man Rudy had resented all this hard-boiled realism, always with his talk about "the real world," its chumps and suckers, some of it straight out of a second-rate noir. But maybe the proof was in the pudding. Uncle Mike had done well for himself, no doubt about it. He was no master builder, but he'd

53

done well, high up in his union and the trades council, a spread with Doric columns on Long Island, a nice, beautiful family, two little girls. There was a picture of him hugging Governor Cuomo at a ribbon-cutting for the Tappan Zee Bridge, part of whose labor he'd negotiated. And Dad had been riding his coattails all the while, like some invalid big brother, just as full of Catholic bile and muscle-bound proverbs, to be sure, but without the flair and confidence and people smarts to put them to good use.

"I heard you had a little falling out," Mike said. His sandwich was full of foldy meats. It looked disgusting. "What are you having, eggs? Is this breakfast hour to you?"

"I've been up since nine," said Rudy. "I just like eggs."

"Oh, *nine*. Wow. Well in that case . . ."

"What'd he tell you? How that self-righteous ass axed his own son? So much for family first."

"He's upset. It'll blow over. Hopefully by tomorrow night, but if not, well, you know I can't disinvite him. You'll have to work it out among the two of you or find other arrangements. Karolina won't have tension at her table. This is solemn business, as you know. I think she killed the pig herself this year."

Mike had only settled down at almost fifty, with a woman fifteen years his junior whose father he had worked with, an Albanian. Very old-world, the way they'd gotten together. Mike was always saying *she's a pistol* and *she wears the pants*, which meant of course she didn't. Otherwise he wouldn't joke about it. "Maybe it's for the best, honestly, you going your separate ways, professionally."

"Really?" Rudy had been expecting a rebuke. "I thought you'd be pissed at me."

"No. No. Look, I mean no disrespect to the place, or to Jimmy. But the last time I was there, somebody called to say they'd left their dentures on the bartop. You—you're a young man. All that watching the wheels is for retired persons."

"That's what *I'm* saying."

"And now, well, you're getting to an age where you're gonna start feeling left behind soon. If a man doesn't make his own moves by thirty, he gets jumpy. He can start to lose his way."

"What do *you* know about it?" Rudy said.

He'd always seemed so self-directed, Mike, like a rocket fired into the world. No time for looking back, or inward, no groveling for anyone's approval. Rudy admired that.

"What do you mean?" Mike said.

"What do you know about feeling left behind?"

"Rudy, stop thinking you're the only one with feelings, okay? It's not doing you any good. Lots of people have feelings. Lots of people feel like shit. If you stop thinking it's something *special*, maybe you can start getting over it . . . So? What are you gonna do? You're not still trying to be an actor, are you?"

"No, no. Not really."

"What happened to that sheriff thing you were considering?"

He had tried to enroll with the sheriff's office, a little-known enforcement arm for the Department of Finance. It sounded appealing, actually—the pride of public service, but less stigma than being a cop, and less sad-sack to announce at parties than being a social worker. Keeping the peace, making sure deadbeat dads weren't behind on their child support payments, checking up on mentally ill people in their homes. But when he got the brochure he found out most of what he'd actually be doing the first few years was towing cars, and the crew at the bar gave him a load of shit about it too, Gary and Hector saying "Howdy partner" and whistling the theme from *The Good, the Bad, and the Ugly* every time he walked into the room. Still, it was his own fault for buckling so easily at a little bit of jibing. Typical Rudy, always looking for an out.

"I definitely feel that left behind thing," Rudy said. "My whole class at Ignatius, everybody's up to something. Matt Galapo's worked for the same company for six years, risen through the ranks. He's bringing home 90K now."

"Him? What company . . . Fat and Sons?"

"H&R Block. And you remember John Urias? I remember that kid always sticking his hands down his pants and sniffing them. I swear he had the same booger in his nose for three whole years. Now he's prosecuting bigwigs for corporate malfeasance. Bringing home the bacon *and* doing right by the people. Why not me? Actually, don't answer that . . . Anyway, I've got my ten-year coming up May after next. Can you believe that shit? I'm already shitting bricks just thinking about it, trying to save face."

"Well, fuck that," said Mike. "You'll figure something out by then. And if you really did right by yourself, come 2020, you'd have better things to do than talk memory lane in the school gym with a bunch of lawyers and accountants."

"I dunno . . ." said Rudy.

For all his ragging on the straight-and-narrow, Rudy wasn't sure he could have been a lawyer or accountant if he'd wanted to—he'd been too far out to lunch to make the moves. Now his great shame looking back wasn't that he hadn't joined up with the grind and made real money, the shame was that in lieu of it he hadn't made real memories even. That he could remember anyway. Even in his wilding out, all the characters he'd met, the 3 a.m. epiphanies, the heart-to-hearts with random Dutchmen and Australian girls, he was none the wiser about human nature than the eight-to-six office ants he used to turn his nose up at. It had all just passed right through him.

"Sometimes I think those people had things figured out way before me," he said. "Anyway, if you could put your feelers out, that'd be great. Any and all offers welcome."

"Well, there might be something, actually," said Mike.

"Oh?"

"I know the owners of a building on Park Avenue. Did some plumbing work for them a few years ago."

"Oh yeah?" Real estate. Wheeling and dealing. Rudy could get down with that. Absolutely.

"They're looking for a doorman."

56

"Cleaning up shit after little Pomeranians in shoes? Sounds like a lateral move."

"Are you gonna be snobby about this? 'Cause you're in no position to be snobby about this, Rudy."

"I know, I know, it's just, isn't that a union job, with, like, benefits? Don't they open up their rolls like once a year?"

"Like like like. What are you, some valley girl?"

"I just mean, who am I to take the place of somebody with mouths to feed, a mortgage. Somebody who really needs that job."

"I don't understand. You're too good for it, but you're not good enough for it. I swear, your whole generation. It's like you think by *pretending* to be conflicted about things that you're somehow squaring the ledger for the disadvantaged. It's a job. You need one. Take it, or don't . . . It's only temporary anyway. Just filling in while one of their guys has taken ill."

Rudy seriously needed the money. He could always say yes now and hope something else would pan out over the next few days.

"Okay. You're right. I appreciate the offer, Uncle. I'd be happy to try it out."

"No, no, there's no trying it out. If I make this call, there's no try. You show up. Immediately if they ask. It's not if you feel like it, if the sun is shining and the mood strikes. You show up."

Mike was such a hard-ass. A real alpha, always hogging all the credibility. Rudy liked to think of himself as a pretty straight talker usually. A leader, even. At least among the blind. But half the time he was with Uncle Mike he found himself feeling like some mealymouthed six-year-old shifting in his seat. Why'd he let Mike do that? Make him feel that way? No more. It was time to sit up. Show up.

"What about, you know—won't I need some kind of a background check?"

"Don't mention that. Okay? That's in the past. You were not convicted of any crime. So don't go mentioning it just to clear your conscience."

57

"Yeah, okay. You got it," Rudy said. "You name the place. I'll be there."

"I'll let you know. Now, you can both stew in your shit for a little while longer, but you and Jim'll have to hash it out at some point. He's your father. He's not getting any younger. Give it a few days. Anyway, what'll you do for Christmas? I was sorry to hear things didn't work out with whatshername—"

"Yeah, yeah."

"Though frankly I wasn't all that surprised. Nice girl, pretty, but she seemed a little bit . . . you know."

"A little what?" He wanted to hear *this*.

"Granola, I guess. Bit of a do-gooder for you. Didn't seem like the right fit."

"Yeah, well, she didn't think so either," Rudy said.

Did people think that that was helpful, saying how they'd called it from the start? Like, *phew, you dodged a bullet there.* When what they were really saying was you had bad judgment, and there was no dodging *that* bullet. And anyway why was a do-gooder not right for Rudy? Rudy could do good. Couldn't Rudy do good?

After lunch he walked back to the overhead train. Half-trapped, and half-relieved. He went past houses with aluminum siding, red-nosed reindeer and nativity scenes in people's yards. People went all out this time of year, out here.

He'd been minded just to skip town, get out once and for all one of these days, but maybe it was just as well to do a bit more time and make a plan. But not get stuck. No way. Not wake up at thirty as a doorman. Make a plan. Not let the years keep getting away from him.

It was always at the thought of leaving New York, really doing it, that the thing would seize him. He couldn't say what it was exactly. They said people sometimes had that feeling about life when they'd decided they were going to kill themselves, for real this time. How they walked around for days beforehand feeling almost high, and carefree, full of sweet regard for the world and all its things, suddenly so optional. He got the feeling for the city once last summer, in the evening, exiting the Lincoln Tunnel, rumbling in after a weekend on the shore. Ace Frehley on the FM, by sheer coincidence . . . emerging into the hot throat of the far West Side, the tangle of Depression-era roadworks, the blatting trucks and billboards all accosting him with heritage, the whole city's transmissions coming through to him, so tough and clear. This feeling that for all its grime and power and profanity New York was not the boss of him at all, how badly it required complicity, more so than any place on Earth. People said big cities were indifferent to the human scale, but mountains were, and rivers. Great cities begged for love.

The feeling wouldn't last long, and it wasn't worth much anyway. It would be no help to him back in the thick of things, in housing court, or stuck in traffic, enraged at all the crowds and filth. But in those passing seconds Rudy could appreciate whatever thing about New York the poets and the charlatans had played to death and still not killed, or even named, and he'd think, okay, all right . . . Stamford can wait.

IT WAS SUPERMARKET SWEEP up on the seventeenth floor—a socialite had died and her kids had come to pick over her loot, Rudy running up and down all morning with the movers. The apartment was some grotty aunt's idea of perfect opulence, like Greta Garbo's death lair: Persian rugs and red walls, African masks, hat mannequins galore, a little staircase for the dog, leading up into the canopy bed. . . . You'd half-expect to see the old bat lying there in effigy.

The woman's daughter was some kind of mash-up of Gwyneth Paltrow and a crow, skulking through the kitchen on her cell phone, all, "but Mother promised *me* the sterling silver gravy boats. Yes, *and* the cuffs from Van Cleef . . . *and* those early sketches . . . Well, but they'll go in Sloane and Sawyer's playroom . . . Well, but you don't *have* any children, Judith . . . Oh, sure, *sure* you might still," snapping her fingers at Rudy and the other guys to mind the wainscoting. In the living room they were packing up some paintings, one or two that looked familiar to him actually, of a fruit bowl with a pitcher, and another of a naked woman, very matter-of-fact in her expression, lying on a chaise lounge. . . . Those painters must've been rolling over in their graves right about now. Imagine, broke and obscure, dying of the clap in a garret in Montmartre, despising and despised by all the bourgeoisie, and your life's work ending up with *this* cow, a fertilizer heiress in six-hundred-dollar pants. Rudy liked the paintings fine—he wasn't a *total* rube—but there was something in these folks' whole art-loving routine that to him was

61

more deplorable than if they'd just gone full white trash about it, spent their money all on tiger pit bulls and plasma-screen TVs. . . . These folks were giving Truth and Beauty a bad rap.

He'd arrived bright and early this morning to get the rundown from the super, Ron, before his first shift started. He was a dying breed, Ron: pug-nosed, smelling of breakfast sausage, with a Yonkers accent thick as his arterial walls, and some kind of gout-nubbin growing out of his jawbone.

"I've worked in this building almost thirty years," Ron said. They were in the boiler room. "Back of house mostly." No kidding. This guy made Ernest Borgnine look like Zac Efron. "First things first, you learn everybody's name. Everybody's. Their kids' names, their dogs' names. Nannies' names, and where they're from. You learn to spot the kind of people who've got business coming in the building. You learn to have your, you know, your *scruples* about yous, without giving any folks the third degree. Though I will say, I *will* say, the way some of these young ladies are dressing nowadays, with the sweatpants half the time, with the nurse shoes half the time, like a buncha frumpy Frannies, it can be hard to tell what's what. Who's who. Know what I'm saying?"

"Sure, sure," said Rudy. This slob was one to talk.

"That's why you've gotta pay attention. Say for instance the woman in 12F has had some kind of a procedure done. She comes in looking like I don't know what. Like Freddy versus Jason. She comes in maybe you don't recognize her, 'cause her face is in the dumpster somewheres, and she's got tissue from her backside's been injected into her mouth, her undereyes, what do you do? Think fast!"

"You um, well . . . you—"

"Do you *scream*?" said Ron. "Do you *startle*? Call for help? No. No. No. You don't *scream*. You don't *startle*. You don't so much as *flinch*, even for a second, or there'll be hell to pay. You say, 'Good afternoon! What lovely weather, Mrs. Cunningham!' Real pleasant, like nothing's happened. You recognize her from her shoes, or from her handbag. Or from the pattern on her Hermy's neckerchief. *That's* using your noodle. People aren't paying this kind of money to live here to feel judged about their own personal choices. Not by the likes a *you*. You understand?"

Rudy nodded as Ron led him out into the lobby. He'd been picturing more twentieth-century—'60s-mod, white, clean lines—but it was like some gold-and-iron vault from the Knights of Malta. A tapestry of a hunt, a creaky-looking antique bench with claw-feet. Everything but a moat. This lobby wasn't fucking around.

"Now," said Ron, "say someone calls saying they haven't heard from their Aunt Teresa in a couple days, they're worried, they need you to go check on her. What do you do? Think fast!"

"Well, you go up there and check on her," said Rudy.

"Wrong. Never. You never ever leave your desk when you're on desk duty, unless it's to hail a cab. And maybe Aunt Teresa doesn't like these relatives of hers. Maybe she's avoiding them on purpose. Maybe, *maybe*, they're not who they say they are. You don't invade nobody's privacy ever, and you never ever make assumptions. You wait until your desk is covered, and you go up there, and then, if there's any reason to be concerned, such as for instance a funny kind of a smell coming under the door, *then* you knock. If no one answers, you can use your key to infiltrate the premises."

"Okay. Then what?"

"What do you think? You call the coroner's."

"Really? Jesus . . ." Rudy said. "Does that kind of thing happen a lot?"

"Only sometimes. Anyway, Anatol—that's the vice head of maintenance—he'll talk you through the mail when the time comes. And the elevators. Sometimes the service elevator gets stuck in the shaft in the basement, so always, *always* look before you step, unless you wanna go kerplop. That's it for now. I'm going home."

"Where's home?" said Rudy. You had to try to be friendly with people, even the Rons of the world. Especially them.

"And don't go thinking you'll be raking in the Christmas checks. Don't go thinking you'll be coming in here like

Johnny-come-lately, the day before Christmas, scooping up the Christmas money. You've got to earn that sort of thing. There's an old couple upstairs, sometimes they come down, hand out candy canes. They like it. Maybe if you're lucky, you'll get one of those. A candy cane."

"Great. Okay. That's great."

"And it's Yonkers. My wife's laid up."

"Oh yeah? There's definitely something going around lately," said Rudy.

"It's cancer. In her rectum now."

"Oh . . . my God. I'm so sorry to hear that."

"Yeah, well, life's a bitch and then you die. Anyways, good luck. You'll do fine. I was about your age when I started working here."

Jesus. Was that how this story ended? Spat out on the other side as Ron the super?

He'd been on his feet like crazy since then, slated to work three days straight as some kind of hazing ritual. First the move with the dead socialite, then packing all the cars up for the holidays. JFK to West Palm Beach and Aspen 'til the new year. Like the royal caravans of Babylon, piled high with junk—hobbyhorses and lacrosse sticks and tennis rackets and mono-grammed Louis Vuitton diaper bags and three different kinds of rain boots for different kinds of rain. It'd make your head spin to think of what a goddamn *operation* life was for these people, for their kids. All the choreography, the cash involved, the courtiers. An army's worth of handlers for every well-born child. Chess teachers and nannies and coaches for their lisps, and eighty thousand bucks a year on schooling, and all the poking and prodding and planning even before they were so much as whispers in their parents' loins, with these mothers pushing fifty, and their daddies' Mesozoic sperms—speaking of which, someone had left a package at the front desk to be mailed that said LIVE SPECIMEN—DO NOT WARM!; he'd better not screw *that* one up.

Rudy didn't want to imply it was all a total waste of money or effort or anything like *that*—how cynical could you be. But, well, some of this stuff was clearly splitting hairs. What did those people in 4E think, that a *lisp* was the thing holding *that* kid back? Closing in on puberty to look at him, and Rudy'd heard him in the courtyard earlier, calling a bird a "tweet-tweet." *He* didn't care about this shit. *He* didn't need things monogrammed.

Maybe Rudy was just jealous 'cause his folks had swung too far the other way, not done much of anything to pad his nest. No, no, his mom had deigned to cut down to half a pack a day and just red wine when she was pregnant with him, 'cause some dum-dum neighbor of theirs (Janine Silvestri, he could still see her tacky self across the yard in fuzzy slippers) had her convinced that that's how they did it in France (who the fuck did *she* know in France? A plumber's wife) and how the *stress of quitting* would've been worse for mother and child than the toxic chemicals and poison they had pumping through his itty-bitty fetal organs. Dad saying how he'd tried to intervene, but then he'd find her in the bathtub with it.

Rudy was lucky he wasn't, like, mentally slow or anything as a result. Wait, wait . . . wait a second . . . maybe he *was*. That would explain a lot. Why despite the Jesuits' best efforts he was dressed like Sergeant Pepper, closing car doors for a living, and signing off for ringworm meds for the Aristocats; why for all his schemes in love and money he had a cellophane-wrapped peanut butter sandwich to look forward to for Christmas Eve dinner later, alone in a break room off the front desk with a hot plate and a hot rods calendar, like a stage set from some classic play about the sorrows of the working class. . . . It would explain a lot.

BY EIGHT O'CLOCK Park Avenue was dead, the early birds all tucked in bed, most everybody out of town. Rudy stood outside and lit a cigarette, a big no-no, but who was watching.

65

He couldn't help but feel a little bit excited it was Christmas Eve, which was obviously stupid. What did he think, Santa was coming? He'd known since he was twelve years old that any holiday was just a day. Even more so, actually—holidays were grayer for the pretense of good feeling. But every year he got the same idea into his head, that life had something up its sleeve for him. That sooner or later the darkness of December would be bearing fruit.

It was better to be here tonight than at his apartment, anyway, heartsick, bugging out, freezing his nips off with the heat turned off. *Or with the family. . . .*

They'd be having dinner out at Uncle Mike's right about now, headed to midnight mass later at Blessed Sacrament. Dad all solemn and proper about it, his nickers in a twist the whole meal about getting there on time to get a good seat. Rudy didn't get that at all, Dad's hard-on for churchgoing. It seemed completely arbitrary. This was not a man given to spiritual matters in the least. He would hardly even pray, just sit there shushing the little kids in the next pew for goofing off while he himself took two, three minutes to loudly unwrap a breath mint, God forbid he have to sit through the whole service without snacks. But *the ritual, the ritual.* You had to go for the ritual.

Well, Rudy didn't hate church *that* much. He would almost miss going this year. Almost. Sometimes sitting there he got a whiff of something. Not belief—nostalgia maybe, for some old notions, old times, how bright things seemed to burn back in his choirboy days. He liked the smells, frankincense and newsprint from the missalette, the rotted woodwork, the tang of wine and BO from the homeless men who slept there after hours, that deep, deep, rankling, Catholic smell, serious as life. And the music—"Greensleeves," medieval canticles, he liked some of that too, more so at least than the word-salad sermons from their banshee of a priest, Father Fahey, droning on and on and on, living in his stories from two thousand years ago all 'cause he lacked the courage to go get a fuckin' life and just be gay. It was always the same feeling after, letting out, like a rocketman come back to Earth. Northern Boulevard at 2 a.m., dime bags, late editions underfoot, drinkers on the prowl, and hit-and-runs about to happen, the night's whole dirty DNA uncoiling, and part of Rudy wishing that all that—back there in church—had meant more. Shown him something real, for the road. But church was no match for the world.

"Hello? Excuse me? Hello out there!"

Rudy nearly jumped out of his skin to hear the words. He killed his cigarette. He slicked his hair and put his cap back on, going inside. He could get fired on the spot for smoking on the job. Maybe nobody had seen him.

A man was standing near the front desk, bleeding from the forehead. Just Rudy's luck to have somebody die on him his second shift.

"Are you all right, sir?" Rudy said.

"Sure, sure I'm all right. Could be." The man touched his head. "Oh, oh boy. Would you look at that. I think—it may be I . . . I bunked myself. I *think*. I'm not so certain. I'm on this new medication, you see. For my heart."

He couldn't have been older than his forties—too young to be non compos mentis. He talked like an old man, though.

"You ought to sit down, mister," Rudy said. "Should I call a doctor? Do you need to go to the hospital?"

"Oh, oh no. No no. No hospitals for me. You have a Band-Aid back there somewhere?"

Rudy rummaged for the first aid kit behind the desk. There was a lockbox with a tourniquet, some Band-Aids. "It's just . . . they're Paw Patrol."

"Would you mind doing the honors?" the man said. "I can't see so well."

He came closer to the light above the desk. It felt odd doing something like that for a stranger, up close and personal all of a sudden. He smelled like rich dude, like caviar burps and aftershave. He kept looking out the front door over Rudy's shoulder.

"Thank you, thank you. That's great," he said, patting his head. "Was someone here?"

"You'll have to be more specific, sir."

"Did somebody come up?"

"To which floor?" Did he think he'd been attacked or something? "No, no one's come in for a long time," Rudy said. "Some party guests went up around seven, to the penthouse."

One of the few people left in town over the holidays was having a black-tie dinner on the twelfth floor, some hedge fund guy, Ratner. They'd been sending magnums of champagne up all day, a Christmas tree for every room—all ten of them.

"Oh. Right. Right. The party. I heard about this *party*. I guess my invite got lost in the mail. Can't imagine how . . . I think I'd better sit down now."

"You should. You should."

He sat down on the claw-foot bench.

"That's better. I'm sorry for the inconvenience. Just need to get my bearings here a second. I've not been sleeping well."

His speech had something distinctive about it, a Long Island paunch. To the blind eye he was just like all the other bankers in the building: work shirt perfectly starched, Patek Philippe with three time zones. But there was a wonky factor there too, something hackish, like a lawyer in a personal injury commercial. Little arms, gumby in their way, a puppy-dog droop to his features, and something in his gait like circus music ought to follow him.

"You know I usually love this time of year?" the man said. "Not Christmas, not Christmas, the week after. In the city. It's like August. There's something special about it. But this year—I don't like this year . . . We had a tiff. I had to work. So I said, let's stay in town. And she—she really let me have it. I deserved it, I guess. I deserved it. We've got a little place in Bridgehampton. You know it?"

"No, not really," Rudy said.

"Want some Orbit?"

"I'm good, thanks."

"But better to be here solving the problems than out there, on the phone the whole time, fretting, right?"

"Right."

"You must think I'm loopy, talking like this. Are you new?"

It was about time somebody asked him that.

"Yeah, yeah I just started. I'm just filling in," said Rudy.

"I'm Jacob Cohen. You can call me Jake." He came and handed him his business card, which seemed unnecessary. It was a little bit déclassé, with a clip art-looking picture of a checker cab. It said PRESIDENT AND CEO, MAVERICK FINANCIAL CORP. "We're working on the business card. Getting something more refined."

"I'm Rudy Coyle."

"Pleased to meet you, Rudy."

"You're in taxis, huh? That must be interesting." There was a ton of money in it, from what Rudy'd heard. It was practically a cartel, or used to be.

"That's one way of thinking of it. Lately, Rudy, I don't know. One of my ex-partners, he's had some legal troubles. I don't know if you read about him. And a driver from his fleet, he— pffft. He did himself. Clocked out. Outside City Hall, no less."

He had read something about that actually, a couple weeks ago. It was horrible. The guy had been from Macedonia or someplace, strapped for cash to repay his loans for his cab. Blew his brains out in broad daylight. "You were connected with that?"

"You'd think I pulled the trigger, Rudy, from the way that they're reporting on it. You know 'So-and-so could not be reached for comment' is code for 'This guy sucks.' It's code for 'So-and-so is a guilty, craven, complicit bastard and a despicable human being.' That's what that means. I hate how they do that . . . journalists. Don't you? Give it its own paragraph, to really stink your name up . . . Don't you hate that?"

"Sure, sure," said Rudy.

He seemed to really be feeling better. Self-rationalization

69

was like some kind of life force. They ought to show coma victims pictures of their enemies—they'd be up and talking soon enough.

"My secretary, she forgets to tell me things. Like, *'The New York Times* called. Maybe you should call them back.' And what am I gonna do, fire her? She was my grandfather's secretary. A dear old woman. She's worked there since before I was born . . . And I feel badly for the situation, I do. I really do. I really do." He really did. "But to blow himself away like that, in the middle of rush hour, with a double-barrel shotgun, when there are little kids walking by him on their way to school? That's just . . . I'm sorry, but that's just . . . you've got some Travis Bickle wackadoodle, and they're calling him a hero, 'cause they're paid to extrapolate, and they love to grind an axe for the have-nots against guys like me. Or who they *think* we are, when they don't know. When they're glib, and they don't know. And they secretly applaud the spectacle—the anarchy of it. They're lapping it up. They've got spittle on their lips. When what happened to that man . . . that's not the *system,* that's not *corruption,* that's him being mentally unwell and unable to deal with things in a normal, appropriate, reasonable, normal fashion—"

"Right—"

"Which of course they'd come right back at me and say *but that's also the system.* Everything's the system. The weather's the system, the behavior of bumblebees is rigged against the poor man! No. No. I'm sorry, but no. To live or die, to wake up in the morning, and to try . . . *that's* a choice. And now I'm meant to feel ashamed that I'm alive, and sane"—Rudy wouldn't be too sure—"with a roof over my head? I earned it, Rudy. It was no picnic for *us,* mind you. My grandfather escaped the Nazis, drove a taxi seven days a week, without a lick of English, bought his first medallion here, in 1937—"

"So . . . so your grandfather earned it?" Rudy said.
The man was quiet for a minute. He looked confused, blinking

a lot. Maybe Rudy was going out on a limb leveling with him, or getting cute, but he might never stop talking otherwise.

"Pardon? How do you mean?"

"I didn't mean to overstep, sir. I'm sorry."

"No, no, please. Call me Jake. I want to hear this."

He sat back, suddenly amused. In his mind Rudy was probably no more than a caricature—the smart-talking butler, born to keep the rich man real. In which case he could do no harm.

"Well. No offense, but you sound just like my father," Rudy said. "All, my ancestors had it bad and I ended up okay, therefore screw everybody else for the rest of time. Like if Dad was in that cabbie's position he'd have a fraction of the energy required not just to drive a cab around for fourteen hours a day, but the smarts to learn a whole new language, send himself through night school, learn to code, go work for IBM or whatever, pull himself up, like he's such a self-starter, when the man can barely change the channel without asking someone else for help."

Jake was quiet again for a second, then he said, "I'm sorry, are you mad at your pop or something?"

"What? No. I mean yes, but—"

"Cause my pop and I, we—boy—we really slugged it out. Too much alike."

"I'm just saying, with all due respect to your grandfather and, you know, his entrepreneurial spirit. It's apples and oranges. The water's deeper now."

"Well, that's a whole other conversation. But you're right, Rudy, you're absolutely right . . ." He leaned forward on the bench, eyes flashing with authority, like he sensed a soapbox moment. "You've got people coming here, competing not for opportunities anymore, not for a piece of the pie, but for the prayer of a crumb. And everyone who's not a card-carrying xenophobe is too afraid of going back on all the leftist piety to admit that it's not 1937 anymore. That maybe this country has enough problems. That maybe the last thing the world, the *planet* needs is *more* American consumers. But the liberals are too busy grandstanding—and Trump, well, love him or hate him, even a broken clock's right twice a day."

Some ringing endorsement there. So this was what was meant by the Trump coalition. From Liffey's to Park Avenue, handymen and tycoons in the same fucked-up, hellbent boat. There was no question who was steering, though, and who would wind up in the water. Not this guy. . . . Still a little part of Rudy actually *wanted* to see Dad, see the Garys of the world drowning, just a little bit, just to punish them. For what, though? Not their politics. Not exactly. Rudy didn't even vote.

Anyway, he knew better than to get too deep into any of it here.

"It just seems to me, whatever side you're on," said Rudy, by way of wrapping up this interaction, "it's you titan of industry types who make the rules."

"You think *I* make the rules? Oh . . ." Jake laughed, wagging his finger. He was a little bit annoying. "I should keep you around, Rudy. For my ego's sake. You're my new best friend, I think!" Hopefully not. "Those people upstairs? That circle jerk they're having in the penthouse? Talk to *them* about the rules. Major donors to both parties, and it's not just politicians in their pockets. God himself is. The archbishop of New York is up there now."

So that's who that was. There'd been a guy in a robe. Rudy figured it was some illuminati thing.

"—private-equity guys gobbling up the world, leveraging whole communities within an inch of their lives. And they're the toast of the town. Front row at the Al Smith dinners, whole wings at MoMA and the Met. When, me? Jacob Cohen? I think there's a plaque with my name on it at a catering hall out in Brighton Beach somewhere, near a pink-and-purple light-up fountain that spouts vodka. I don't decide anything, and I've always done everything I could, everything I could, to do right by my drivers. I'm just a middleman, believe me. I couldn't have prevented any of this."

Maybe in his own mind he was just some old-time money-lender trying to keep up. An also-ran for class president, cling-ing to Park Avenue by the skin of his teeth. Even his arrogance seemed studied, like an adaptive quality. Plus, with the Paw Patrol Band-Aid on his head, it was hard to feel hard-hearted toward him.

"All right . . . I believe you," Rudy said.

"Would you—no, no, never mind. It's stupid."

"Would I what?"

"Would you have dinner with me tonight? I'm all alone with-out my family and, well, it's Christmas Eve. I made a whole chicken."

"I'm not allowed to leave my desk."

"Of course, I shouldn't have asked. I don't wanna get you into any trouble. But, well—what if we ate down here? I could bring some plates down. You've gotta eat, right?"

"Well, Ron told me to pack a sandwich, for the break room."

"Oh, come on now. Ron's a killjoy. A sandwich. No one wants a sandwich for the break room on one's here. And those people, Ratner's people, there'll be up there for hours. You like chicken?"

Was he pushy or what? Then again, maybe he shouldn't be left alone, with his new meds and all.

"Well, okay. All right," said Rudy. "Thank you."

"Don't move a muscle."

Jake came down ten minutes later with a rolling bar cart and a Crock-pot, wearing oven mitts. He looked adorable in oven mitts. There was one of those silver domes they used to keep plates warm in cartoons. Rudy didn't know anybody actually owned a thing like that.

"You made all this?" Jake had carved a whole roast chicken up. Mashed potatoes, green beans with slivered almonds on them, cake.

"I like to cook. Helps me deal with stress. My daughter made the cake, though."

73

There was a stepladder from the break room Rudy pulled up and they sat on either side of the front desk.

"How long have you lived here?" Rudy said. He felt like he was on a date.

"Eight years. Getting approved by the board? Oh boy. Talk about a charm offensive. It was a real to-do. Flowers by the pound to Mrs. Astor's grandniece or whoever the hell it was. The rarest liqueurs. Calling in favors from friends of friends of dockworkers. I succeeded, by a whisker. And they thought they were really going out on a limb for me, I guess. Really taking a chance on a scrappy dreamer 'cause my father wasn't ambassador to Sweden. Well, I think they're starting to regret it now. I get looks sometimes, lately. Since my name's been in the news? Looks like, *I told you so. There goes that taximan.* Suspicious looks. When I'm not just in taxis. I've got many different business interests. An empire, if you will. But they look down on taxis. They're perceived as an unsavory industry, and why? When their industries are just as dirty, or more so, it's just they've got thicker plate glass between the executive suite and the sausage getting made."

It couldn't have been easy for these taxi guys, working overtime to stop the bleed, when yellow cabs were for the scrap heap. Customers were getting hip. They knew better than to stand in the rain begging to get whiplash in a bald-tired rattletrap reeking of vindaloo. But you couldn't say that.

"My wife, I think she takes it harder than me . . . Wonderful woman, stunning, more elegance and class in her pinky toe than these loafer-wearing drips have in their whole bodies, but she's got a chip on her shoulder, you know? I mean, we weren't exactly *rich* growing up, but her—it's changed her, money. It's made her tense. Image-conscious. It's made *us*—well . . . she says I talk too much. You married, Rudy?"

"No, no. Just got cut loose from my relationship," he said. "She was too smart for me, I think. She's going back to school."

"Oh yeah? Whereabouts?"

"University of Colorado?"

"Well . . . don't beat yourself up *too* much. It's her loss." He had a way of making you feel better, the way he phrased things.

"What I wanna know," said Rudy, "is why you'd wanna live someplace you've got to strong-arm your way into? Isn't your money green enough on its own?"

"What do you mean? Why do people climb Mount Everest?" Jake said. Rudy had no idea. That kind of thing always seemed extremely stupid to him. But anyway it seemed like a bad comparison. "They do it 'cause it's *there*. Because there's a limestone palazzo like something from Vienna in the middle of Manhattan. This building—I *love* this building. McKim, Mead, and White? This building is history. Any white-collar criminal from Malaysia can launder his money in a condo at Time Warner Center. But living in a classic six in a co-op, on Park Avenue . . . that's the dream, Rudy. That's arriving."

"Whatever you say." If Rudy had the money there was no way he'd spend it living up here, among the tombstones. "Meanwhile I'd be happy with a ceiling. They've been drilling holes in the floor above me."

"Oh yeah? Where's that?"

"East Third Street. My landlords, they're real dirtbags."

"Who are they? I might know them."

"Edgar and Bianca Kronman?"

"Oh, oh, I know Edgar," Jake said.

"Seriously?"

"He grew up in the next town over, on Long Island. *We* were pool boys together at the club. Very tough customer. Very competitive. And his wife, I hear she's even meaner."

"She's a fuckin' nightmare," Rudy said.

"I've heard about this. They've done this all over. Lord and lady of their own corrupt little fiefdom. They bought a bunch of apartment buildings in Chinatown and the East Village for

75

peanuts in the nineties, made millions forcing them onto the free market. Did they offer you a buyout ever?"

"They did, a year ago. Not in writing, though. And now I don't know if that's even on the table anymore or what. I'd take anything."

"Never say that. You've got to name your price, and stick to it. These people are predators. You've got to play hard with them. And you've got to beat them to the punch, *before* they try and evict you. You'll have no leverage after that . . . Now, but would they have any reason to characterize you as an unsavory tenant? Smear you, that kind of thing? Any drugs, drinking? Delinquencies? Cause Edgar's not above putting PIs on his tenants. They could paint you as a stumblebum. Things could get ugly, fast." Rudy was feeling sorry that he'd brought it up. "But frankly I doubt it'll come to that. He'd be unwise to try and evict you and get tied up in the courts when time is money. He knows that better than anyone. Besides, between you and me, I know some things about Edgar *he* wouldn't want out there."

Rudy didn't get this person. He was half mother hen, and half piranha. "Isn't that, like, extortion?" Rudy said.

"This man takes home five million a year. Don't cry for him. He'll be fine . . . Personally I don't have the stomach for it really. Battling and all of that." Rudy doubted that, somehow. "But these lawyers, they love it. I'll make a phone call after the holidays. We'll get it sorted out."

"Well, thanks . . . I mean. What can I say? Thank you, so, so much, Jake."

This was shaping up to be some evening. Free four-star meal, free legal advice. This blew midnight mass out of the water.

"Please. You want some cake?" Before he could answer Jake was serving him a slice the size of his head. "I hope you like pistachios."

"I love 'em."

"I like to help people, you know. I like to think of myself as a facilitator. You're fun to talk to, Rudy. I feel better already, just talking like this. As I said I've not been sleeping . . . But you're a very nice, cool guy, I can tell. You're an actor or something?"

Rudy never admitted that to anybody anymore. Too many eye rolls over the years. May as well say you had no ambitions whatsoever.

"I think I missed the boat on that," he said.

"Oh, nonsense. You've not missed the boat on anything. You're not yet thirty, right?"

"I'm twenty-six."

"Twenty-six. My god. Wow. Good for you. Great age. You haven't missed the boat on anything. And the thirties are the best, you know. You're in for a treat there. You're old enough to know something, and young enough to *do* something. My life didn't really start 'til I was almost thirty. Business started booming. I quit drinking—*that* might've helped, to say the least . . ."

"Oh yeah?"

"I had to stop, Rudy. I had to. I was a nowhere man. Blitzed. Beat up. Always running my good times into the ground. I was never going to unleash my full potential, going on like that. I was a schlubby junior assistant in a cheap maroon suit, sick and short-tempered, working for my father, overcompensating for the nepotism by being a know-it-all prick to everybody. Shackled to my own BS. Not realizing *I* held the key. So I cut that out. Once and for all, at twenty-nine. And ever since then? Oh . . . life hasn't been easy, but it *has* been good . . . very good . . . notwithstanding a few hiccups *lately* . . . You a drinker, Rudy?"

He didn't know how frank to be. You gave people an inch, these proselytizers for the righteous path, they'd never get off your case about it again.

"I mean, I *drink*," said Rudy. "Of course I drink. I worked in a bar. I practically grew up in one. That's *my* family business. And I was always a tank, you know? No problem. But now sometimes, these days, I guess . . . *yeah* . . . sometimes you wake up feeling like . . . like—"

"Like Nosferatu. Not sure whose blood you've sucked."

77

"Jesus, yes," said Rudy. A little too eagerly, maybe.

"I've been there, brother. I've been there. And it only gets worse. Mark my words."

He really got off on dishing out the life advice. This from someone who'd been sheet-pale, paranoid, and bleeding from the head not half an hour ago. Rudy didn't mind it, though, for some reason.

"So you just, what, gave it up?" said Rudy. "Isn't that boring? You go to the finest restaurants in Manhattan, have water with your prime rib?"

"Coca-Cola, sometimes. It's not so bad."

That sounded like the saddest thing Rudy'd ever heard. He'd better learn to moderate, and fast, before they took it away. . . .

Maybe just beer for a while. . . .

"Besides," Jake went on, "it's a false association between the glamorous, go-getter lifestyle and excess. Every third person in Hollywood is sober now. Trump. *He's* sober. Love him or hate him, no one could accuse him of not enjoying life."

"No, no, I guess they couldn't . . . Though I think some folks might be better off with their full potential . . . leashed."

"Maybe so," said Jake. "I just highly doubt you're one of them."

It was true that Rudy'd never tried, really tried, on the acting front, and all the partying hadn't helped steel his resolve exactly. He'd never had a rush in his whole life like playing James Tyrone in *Long Day's Journey into Night* his senior year of high school. Just walking into rehearsals he'd felt like a little kid. His theater teacher, Ms. Lowndes—he missed Ms. Lowndes. She'd been totally gaga for him and his performance, locked in a battle royale with his baseball coach over his time . . . nice to be so in demand. Anyway, she was dead now. But she'd said to promise her he'd really try, and not let anybody convince him not to, not the jocks, not the priests, not his dad or his uncle. She said he could be the next John Garfield if he wanted. Too bad nobody knew about the first one.

"Anyway, it's getting late," said Jake. "I'll be out of your hair in a second. I think I'll join my family out east tomorrow, bright and early. Try to make up for some lost time with them."

"You should," said Rudy. "You all good with your, you know, your head?"

"I'm fine. I'm feeling fine. Are you fine?"

"I'm great." He *was* feeling better actually. He'd forgotten how good it could be, just to meet a new person, shoot the breeze with your fellow man. All this gloom and doom, living in his head, who needed it. "And you know, Jake, so long as we're giving unsolicited advice here, I think you could afford to ease up on the throttle too a little."

"How so?"

"I see you, you're living in this building, stressing so hard you're passing *out*, alone without your family Christmas Eve, working yourself sick trying to keep up with the Joneses, when as you've said yourself, the Joneses aren't the Joneses. The Joneses are the Sacklers. And who wants to keep up with *them*?"

"*They* had a place here. No more. Moved to West Palm Beach. They practically drove them out with pitchforks."

"You're driving yourself crazy, and for what?" said Rudy. "And I'm not trying to act like I'm some noble pauper, like I'm above greed. I know greed. Little kids know greed. But at a certain point it's like, what are you guys after?"

"I see what you're saying, I do. You rub elbows with a certain crowd, you get tunnel vision. You forget what's important in your life. And I do think about, you know . . . my guys. What it must be like for them. Driving all night. Coming back to their little dump apartments. And what goes through a person's head, how bad it has to get, before he does a thing like that. I think about that driver's little grandbaby, growing up without his pop-pop. And whatever my issues with these journalists, or these social justice people, who'd have you drawn and quartered for prizing your own hide over a mental Kosovoan's you don't even know—I swear, these people, they've demonized self-interest to the point of absurdity—but whatever my issues with them, I agree with them that it shouldn't have to be so goddamn hard for people to get by. I'm not a *total* monster."

"Of course you're not."

"But, well, you *try* to be altruistic. But then your kid needs twenty-six-thousand-dollar braces, and, well, that's your kid. What are you gonna say, 'No'?"

"I mean, yeah. You say no. You get the discount braces."

"I don't think we'd qualify."

"I just mean as an example," Rudy said. "Maybe there are other ways to live. Other buildings. Other cities, even." Jake almost choked on his pistachio cake. "Oh, no, no, I . . . I don't think that that would work."

• • •

IN THE WEE HOURS, killing time, Rudy looked him up. There was a corporate profile, a note to our investors. Some interviews in business magazines. What kept coming up was his ex-partner's name. Valentin Zalebnik, a Russian. He'd got his start as a fleet owner with money lent to him by Jacob's father, his mentor. Branched out to Chicago, Boston, Philadelphia, buying taxi medallions at way more than their asking prices and sending their values through the roof. He was worth five hundred million at one point. Everybody called him the Taxi King.

There were items in the *Post* and *Daily News* relishing his fall from grace. In the last year he'd been indicted for bank fraud and wire fraud. His secretary'd sued him for harassment. There was a picture of him and Nicki Minaj, who in flusher times he'd hired to play his son's bar mitzvah. Nicki in some kind of latex onesie, gorgeous, smiling politely through her benefactor's halitosis, the bar mitzvah boy looking panicked, like he'd just pitched a tent in his good pants, and Valentin in the middle, gold-chained, oily-headed, with the smuggest who's-your-daddy look on his mug you could imagine, a chilling vacancy behind the eyes . . . he looked like the scum of the earth. It was no wonder Jake had cut ties with him.

The sun was almost up by the time Rudy got back downtown. His whole neighborhood was still asleep. It felt like a proper little village at this hour, innocent behind the shuttered storefronts. An old Ukrainian hobbled back from early mass to the bakery he owned and lived above.

Rudy felt like Scrooge the morning after, light of heart, the bells of London pealing for his absolution. Sometimes a sheer affection for the world and life ripped through him out of nowhere. To think, he wasn't even thirty. For all his grumbling, his bitching and moaning, so weighed down by this bag of bones, he *wasn't even thirty.* It was shameful to be so ungrateful, so tired, squalid, drunk, and angry, when life was sweet and tender, and his gifts were many. He hadn't missed the boat on anything.

There seemed to be some activity going on right outside his building. It was early for people to be moving, and on Christmas Day, no less. Wait, wait, shit, wait, shit—

"Hey, hey, hey, what the fuck are you *doing,* man?"

Kronman's cop was coming out of the building, carrying two garbage bags.

"Hey, hey, I asked you a question!" Rudy said.

"What does it look like?" the man said. "You'd been warned. You're behind two months."

"It's Christmas Day!"

"Your lease starts on the twenty-fifth. We don't make exceptions for holidays."

Anthony something was his name. Six foot six, shaved head, stomping around like the Polish Vin Diesel. He wasn't all that. His head looked like a thumb.

"I sent my check in right on time," said Rudy. "They haven't cashed it yet."

"The leasing office says they never received it."

"That's a fucking lie. I tracked the envelope this time, 'cause I know you've pulled that kind of thing before. I have the confirmation of receipt somewhere here. I took a picture of it." He took his phone out of his pocket. It was dead. He started runmaging through the bags, looking for the hard copy. "You can't just treat my stuff like this, you know. Those are my important personal documents!"

"They'll be suing you for damage to the property, and breach of your lease agreement."

"Damage to the *property*?" said Rudy. "You're the ones opened a fucking hole in my ceiling."

"You had someone else living here illegally. Not to mention you almost set the place on fire."

"Oh, come on. I think that's being a little bit dramatic." He had fallen asleep with a cigarette awhile back. Just for two seconds. Woke him right up. Switched to vaping while indoors now, no problem.

"You're endangering the other residents. The Kronmans are practically saints for not kicking you out sooner. Ling says he can't fit his recycling into any of the bins, you've got so many bottles piling up."

Fucking Ling. Rudy'd thought Ling was his boy. . . . Well, you couldn't blame the old man. They probably shook him down for damning information on threat of extradition or something. He was very honorable, Ling. Very literal-minded. He didn't understand Americans, that bluffing was an art form here.

"You've got more recycling just you alone than the whole rest of the building combined. It's pathetic."

"I've . . . I've had parties."

"That's another violation then."

He wanted to press his fingers into his fuckin' Cro-Magnon-looking eye sockets. But the man was six-six, two-eighty, with some very hawkish friends. There was no use even trying to fight.

"You'll be hearing from his lawyer," the cop said, and got into his car. A Lexus. Rudy went up to the window.

"Nice car," said Rudy. "Those people must be keeping you on some pretty plush retainer to do their dirty work. You think we don't know what you're doing? Hey, hey, roll the window down when I'm talking to you, fucker." The man obliged, like he was humoring an insane person. "You think we don't know what a scam you're running here? You think we don't talk? Cathy, from 4B, she said you threatened her in the shower. I think that qualifies as sexual harassment. You ever heard of a class action lawsuit?"

"Power to the people, right. All you freeloaders will be out of here by spring."

He drove off down the block. Rudy thought he was gonna scream. Maybe he should just run into traffic, get it over with. No. No. Maybe later.

He had to go charge his phone at one of those information stations, those LinkNYC things. He was pretty sure they had one on the next block. Those seemed like a nice idea in theory, useful, with haikus flashing on the screen and facts about Black History Month, though the only person he'd ever seen actually using one had been yelling at the 411 operator to give him back his shoes. They seemed to attract a desperate element. Anyway, here Rudy was. Desperate.

When his phone came back on ten minutes later he called the number of the leasing office. Nobody picked up. Of course. They never picked up, and it was 7 a.m. on Christmas Day. He should call his friend Tara. Or his cousin in Stamford. No. Fuck family. Always a patronizing tone, always strings attached, lording the whole history of your life over your head. Plus he needed this job, and he couldn't commute that far to work. Plus it sounded super depressing where she lived.

He fished the business card out of his wallet from last night. He hesitated for a second, then called anyway.

"Hello?" Rudy felt a little calmer just hearing Jacob's voice.

"Yeah, good morning. I'm really sorry to bother you," said Rudy. "I know you're with your family and all, but . . . it's urgent."

"I'm driving. Honestly? I don't love driving and talking on the phone."

"I get that. I'm sorry."

"It's not your fault. I just don't love it. I'm going to pull over. 'Cause I don't like your tone of voice right now. Just wait one moment." You could hear traffic whizzing by. "He . . . oh. Jesus. Jesus. *Someone's* in no rush. The guy in front of me, he's driving like Mister Magoo. Sorry. There's a Wendy's I'm trying to pull into. You hold tight. Okay. Now . . . I'm all ears. What's the problem?"

"He kicked me out," said Rudy. "I come home and he's putting all my shit out on the street."

"Who, Edgar?"

"That motherfucking Polack cop friend of his. Sorry . . . sorry if you're Polish."

"Well, *they* didn't seem to think so."

"Can he do that?"

"And on Christmas morning. Sounds like a real Edgar Kronman move."

"Fuck them buying me out, he says they're gonna sue me. I know people who are two hundred grand in the hole from this kind of thing."

"I'll tell you what. My lawyer—he's in Anguilla for the week. But we're old friends. I can try him on his personal number. Don't panic. We might not win the lottery here, but we can do our best to help put this behind you. In the meantime, do you have any place to stay?"

"Soho Grand's all booked." He couldn't afford a hotel. Even the YMCA was a hundred bucks a night, when who were they catering to, the *well-heeled* indigent?

"Any family?" Jake said.

"We're on the outs, right now. Me and my dad. I mean, I *could*, but I just . . . I can't." He had asked too many people for too many favors over the years. It was getting embarrassing. Just calling like this was so *embarrassing*.

"Shit. Goddammit. I fucked up," said Rudy.

"Okay, calm yourself. No need for that kind of language."

"I know I've fucked up. I've fucked my life up. I should've

stayed in school. I shouldn't have drank and smoked so much. And I know it's all my fault I wasted time. I know it. I'm not *aggrieved*. I know that having zero self-restraint isn't an actual disability. And I know there are people out there playing better games with worse hands every day. But well, it's done. And I just need to be able to move forward now, and try to . . . to . . . to better myself, without having a massive brand-new hole to climb out of."

He hung his head. He used to almost thrill himself with these kinds of maneuvers. Calling in favors, seat-of-his-pants, his ass saved in the nick of time. Like he deserved for it to be. Like it was something noble or felicitous in him, some alley cat's agility with life. Now he was just so, so tired.

"I'll tell you what," Jake said, "I've got a little one-bedroom I'm fixing up in Turtle Bay, near the UN. You could stay there for a while. I'll charge you for utilities until you get back on your feet. It's more than I'm getting now. There's not much furniture, though. I think the previous tenant left a couch."

"If it has four walls, it'll be great."

"And you might get people walking through sometimes, contractors, inspectors, that kind of thing. Get used to getting your pants on in a hurry."

"Oh, I can do that." His ex—the one before this last one—she'd been married.

"All right then. Okay. There's a keypad. You use a code to get into the mailbox. The key's in there. I'll text you the information."

"I fuckin' owe you, Jake."

"It's not a problem. I'm sure I'll be calling on you soon enough."

"Whatever you need, man. Whatever you need, I'm yours," said Rudy.

"Okay, then. Be kind to yourself. And Merry Christmas."

There were fifteen garbage bags full of his shit out on the street. There was no way he could carry even half of it uptown. There was a wooden footstool Allie's grandfather had made with his bare hands. He'd been a wonderful man, her grandpa. A Norwegian, who'd fought in the Battle of the Bulge and grew soybeans for a living, singing folk songs to his grandchildren. Fuck it. Leave it. What the fuck was Rudy gonna do with it now.

He waited almost an hour for the M15 to come. He kept nodding off at the bus stop, like an elderly person.

He couldn't get it out of his head, the way that cop had looked at him. It was the way the Suitsupply crowd looked at the guy on 33rd Street with the colostomy bag. Polite contempt. Utterly grossed out to be sharing the same airspace, and pretty sure that whatever wound him up there on the street, with his truncated guts, he had probably deserved it. . . . But the colostomy bag guy was one thing. He was probably used to those looks by now. But Rudy—Rudy had been fresh and clean and strong as a stallion 'til not so very long ago. He needed to get back there, to that place of strength. He needed nobody to ever look at him like that again.

When he got to the apartment he was almost too zonked to register how nice it was. Little? It was an airplane hangar.

There was a huge La-Z-Boy sleeper sofa, a fridge you could practically take a nap in. Floor-to-ceiling windows, pristine white walls, totally new appliances. An open-plan kitchen with a breakfast bar, nice finishes on everything. And the view.

You got vertigo just standing near the window. You could see the whole span of the East River. The Pepsi-Cola sign. The Tudor City sign, the UN building. The trams going out to Roosevelt Island. The Trump World Tower like a big black gleaming middle finger to mankind—even *that* he liked the look of now. You could see all of Queens, all the way to JFK, to the edges of the New World. People talked all kinds of trash about these new luxury high-rises. He had too, plenty of times. From where he was standing now, though, it beat the hell out of a railroad tenement on 3rd Street.

(He would miss that little dump of course. . . . The two of them in summer, drinking warm beer on the fire escape. The

86

fridge was always broken. Watching kids play jump rope on the streets below, like in some Weegee photograph. But that all was ancient history now.)

He ought to get some food in him. You could always get Chinese on Christmas Day. He took his pants off and lay down on the couch for a long, long time, staring at the ceiling. It was fucking comfortable. You used to have to think twice about dropping your pants down on the fourth floor. But up here . . . up here only the birds could see you.

HE STAYS IN HIS LANE—AND IT'S A FAST ONE

New York Business World: Life & Style

MAY 2009

"They're like these little golden geese, hiding in plain sight," says Jacob Cohen of taxicab medallions, the commodity that's been his family's bread and butter for more than half a century.

Maverick Financial issues loans for the tin emblems on the hoods of yellow cars that entitle them to pick up street hails. You might not even know they exist, but they're an asset he says is better than gold, bonds, or stocks. (As of the most recent citywide auction, they were going for $1,000,000 each. In addition to financing the loans for medallions, the Cohen family owns fifty of them outright. You do the math.) Mr. Cohen insists his company's about more than taxis, though. As CEO, a mantle he assumed from his now-retired father, Melvin, he's handled over $3 billion in consumer and commercial loans, part of a diverse public company whose subsidiaries range from real estate to art financing to a minor league baseball team, based in Long Island, the Stony Brook Stompers. Speaking of the national pastime, I can't help but ask about the jersey.

Framed on the walls of Mr. Cohen's jaw-dropping Madison Avenue office, where I caught up with him, is the famed jersey Mike Piazza wore on September 21, 2001, during the first professional sports game played in New York City after the September 11 attacks, when the Mets Hall of Famer scored an emotional eighth-inning home run that stirred spirits and lifted the team to victory.

"I was at that game," Cohen, a lifelong Mets fan, remembers. "I wept like a baby. And I wasn't the only one. There were guys who looked like Mr. T bawling their eyes out."

He wanted a piece of it. So he bid $400,000 on it at a private auction. As one does. I politely inform him that some

Mets fans are angry the jersey was ever sold and want it back at Citi Field. But he swears he's not hoarding the goods for himself.

"Once the [9/11 Memorial Museum] opens, I'll be loaning it out for public view. Sure I'll miss looking at it, but I don't wanna be J. P. Morgan here, sitting alone with my Greek urn. This is a part of the social history of this city, that belongs to all New Yorkers. All Americans . . . even the Yankees fans," he adds with a wink.

Suave and garrulous, with a boyish twinkle in his eye, Mr. Cohen has charm to spare. And his credentials aren't too bad either. He was featured in Crain's New York's 40 under 40, the definitive list of movers and shakers in the business, media, and real estate worlds, as a thirty-two-year-old, and has served on the board of the Javits Center, the New York Chamber of Commerce, and We Care, Inc., a nonprofit that helps provide apartments for homeless families. He even wrote a memoir, *Painting the Town Yellow*, that was a *New York Times* bestseller. "Unfortunately for me," he says, "my mother's the one who bought them all."

He grew up in a modest suburb on Long Island, but always had an appetite for the big city. After graduating from Hofstra with a business management degree, he completed his MBA summa cum laude at Columbia University—"I was a late bloomer," he admits—and worked for a few years on Wall Street before going to work for Maverick.

Yellow ran in his blood. Mr. Cohen's late grandfather, Jozef, was a taxi driver and fleet owner who emigrated from Silesia, Poland, in 1937, though, tragically, the rest of his immediate family were eventually interned in the Sosnowiec Ghetto, and later deported to Auschwitz.

"This was a man with a shattered heart," Mr. Cohen says of his grandfather, "but you'd never know it. He showed up every day with a smile and worked, worked, worked. Six days a week. Fifteen hours a day."

He went on to acquire some 200 medallions, running one of the largest fleets in Queens.

"I would always come to visit my dad and grandpa at the garage on Skillman Avenue, in Long Island City," Mr. Cohen says. "We would go to the auto bodies in Willets Point for repairs. The garage—this place was right out of the sitcom *Taxi*. I got to know these people, drivers and mechanics, hardworking people trying to provide for their families, trying to better themselves in America, with amazing work ethics. People from all walks of life. My brother and sister and I would sit there playing chess with them, or do our homework."

When the economic crisis of the 1970s hit, there were fewer and fewer drivers willing to work. The streets were plagued with crime, and driver muggings were rampant. "I'll never forget one of their drivers coming in bleeding from the head," he says of an incident in 1978. "I was five years old. He'd had his wallet stolen, with all his shift pay going back a week. Fortunately the mugger was a bozo. He tried to cash a stolen check. The police tracked him down in no time."

The family business pivoted to selling loans to drivers, and Jozef quickly found he could make more money as a lender than a fleet operator. In the drivers who bought medallions on his credit, the senior Cohen found eager, conscientious customers who rarely failed to make good on repayments, and the fixed number of licenses meant the medallions were a reliable asset going forward. Jozef lived to see the company go public in 1999, a proud day for the family. In the thirty years since its official founding—his grandson is happy to report—they can count the number of defaults on one hand.

Maverick Bank, the company's wholly owned loan corporation, received FDIC approval last year. And the youngest

Mr. Cohen didn't stop there. He saw an opportunity in funding the ads on the tops of cabs, founding Maverick's own advertising subsidiary, and diversified the company's portfolio to include more commercial and consumer lending. He assembled a board of directors of midtown Manhattan power brokers, culled from his personal relationships at the New York Athletic Club, the Fifth Avenue Synagogue, and the Church of St. Ignatius Loyola.

At a time when some feel that New York's monied classes ought to bury their heads in the sand, Mr. Cohen doesn't shy away from relishing the luxe life. He can always be seen, impeccably dressed, hobnobbing with dealmakers at the 21 Club and Enzo's, his favorite weeknight haunt. He's even managed to dine at Rao's, the famously exclusive red-sauce joint in East Harlem, a few times, though he won't say at whose table. ("They'd kill me. Literally. I'd be dead.") He sees nothing inconsistent between his lush lifestyle and that garage in Long Island City where the Cohen legacy was born.

"I see myself championing the little guy. I'm still the David type versus Goliath. All of this luxury is nice, and a very nice perk, but that's not where the heart of the company's vision is. I'm a lower-middle-class kid from Long Island. The first person in my family to go to college. And I reject the false idea that to do well in business you've got to lose your soul, or forget where you came from. I think that's a false narrative in our society, sown to divide and embitter people, when we can all work together to enrich ourselves. And each other."

Accomplished *and* humble. Apologies to the ladies, though—Mr. Cohen's off the market. He wed Norma Jean O'Malley, of Mahwah, New Jersey, a fashion model turned designer of children's footwear, in a 200-person ceremony at the Pierre hotel in 2006. Their four-year-old daughter,

Marley, can often be seen running around the office, now on Madison—not Skillman—Avenue, the company's littlest, and cutest, cheerleader.

Looking toward the future, he says, "I want a whole brood. I want lots of kids, tons of them. I want them crawling all over my head. I told my wife, get ready."

Things are indeed looking up for the Cohen family. But despite his love of all things taxis, Jacob Cohen insists his true passion is in helping people realize the American Dream. When asked if he would consider a bid at public office someday, he just smiled. For once, he wasn't talking.

5

ENZO'S HAD A MURAL of a country villa with a fountain and a naked angel playing the harp. She loved this place. They were out celebrating tonight, because a disgruntled ex-employee of Daddy's, a "coo-coo-la-la" as he called him, had brought a lawsuit against his company and the judge had just dismissed it, which was apparently fantastic news. (Though it didn't *sound* fantastic. Not like you just won an Oscar or found out your crush secretly loves you back, more like one of your ten ulcers has calmed down a bit. For now. But anyway Daddy was happy. So everyone was happy.)

"This was what we call a dysfunctional personality type." Daddy passed the bread basket to Mom. "Truly an odd duck. No friends at the company. No life. Sat there at his desk with a packed lunch every day, with Babybel cheese. This is a grown man we're talking about."

"So you fired him?" Marley said.

"Well, we didn't fire him because he was odd. We fired him because he was lousy at his job, and bad with people. This was five years ago, mind you. Some coincidence for him to come crawling out of his cupboard now, looking for a big fat settlement, when the company—the industry's in turmoil, and he thinks we're too cowardly to stomach the bad press."

"What did he say in his lawsuit, though?"

"Well, all sorts of things. Lies. He accused us of engaging in certain . . . unsound business practices, unjust enrichment, things that would violate something called the SEC. But the judge saw through him and ended up agreeing with Daddy. So justice prevailed. So it's good. It's very, very good."

J. J. played Minecraft on his iPad and swung his legs a lot under the table. He'd agreed to wear his baseball cap tonight, which Mom and Daddy seemed relieved about. They usually had a no-baseball-caps-in-the-dining-room policy here—it was a pretty fancy place—but Daddy had a lot of sway with the maître d' and so they made an exception. In general at nice restaurants Mom and Daddy wavered between wincing in shame at J. J's big bald head and doing a kind of "Let 'em stare!" righteous parent thing.

J. J. *did* seem out of place sometimes. (Except for once, on the way to skiing in Vermont, they'd stopped somewhere called the Ruth B. Hillman Memorial Rest Area, with gumball machines and newsstands and arcade games and every kind of junky treat you could possibly dream up this side of Rye Playland, and all kinds of people, from every state, of every shape and stripe and blemish, and this one Jabba the Hutt-looking lady on a motorized chair with a ventilator attached to it, tenderly smoking a cigarette in the parking lot, and no one in the whole place even batted an *eyelash* at J. J. No one even looked up from their TCBY treats for a *second* to suss him out, except to smile. Marley thought she'd felt a lightness in him there, for however long it was, just an average kid with his box of nuggets and no eyebrows and a T-shirt that said I MAY BE LEFT-HANDED, BUT I'M ALWAYS RIGHT: they'd bought after he'd barfed all over his Lacoste polo in the car. Marley wished that she could take him back sometime, maybe for his birthday, to the Ruth B. Hillman Memorial Rest Area. Out of chilly, sleekest Gotham, and into the arms of America . . .)

They brought her plate of meatballs out, sizzling in a little skillet.

"This is just getting silly," Daddy said. "All this hero worship. I read an article somewhere the other day, about some graphic designer in Brooklyn printing votive candles with his face on them. She's putting his face onto baby onesies and selling them on the internet." Marley'd lost the thread of what Daddy was talking about. He moved pretty fast. "And people actually buy them. People put their babies in them. Robert Mueller baby onesies. I wouldn't want that ghoul's mug on my baby, would you?" Mom said.

"He seems like a decent man," Mom said. "But people should leave their children out of it."

The guy came by with the Parmesan and grater and said *tell me when to stop*. Which was always kind of awkward 'cause if it was up to Marley he would never stop. So at some point he just had to walk away.

"Maybe I'm just an old fart," said Daddy, "but some of these, what are they called, these *memes*, I don't know about these. It's all cutesy crap. They debase the conversation. They turn public figures into little cartoons. Everyone's a hero or a villain. It's a farce. And this'll all be a big nothing . . . wait and see."

"Are you sure about that?" Mom said. She was on her second wine and it was only appetizers. "He looks to me like he's running scared. He's definitely hiding *something*."

Mom had voted for Donald Trump too, but she seemed to place a lot of emphasis on feeling conflicted about it.

"You know how high the burden of proof is for conspiracy beyond a reasonable doubt?" said Daddy. "You're telling me that that silver spoon—Charlie Kushner's boy?—is an international saboteur, with back channels to the Kremlin? No way. I've met him. He's a featherweight. Maybe there were meetings, a bit of strong-arming here, influence-peddling there. But blaming politicians for being handsy with power is like blaming cows for having spots. The connections between dark money and US politics are so deep, so entrenched, it's not the needle in the haystack. It *is* the haystack. And the democrats are in on it too."

"You seem to know an awful lot *about* it, Jake."

"You're not hearing me, Nora. Just saying it like that, in that smirky way. What I'm saying is the opposite of what you're implying. I'm not saying there's a conspiracy so dastardly, so well-hidden the investigators will never find it. I'm saying the ways that foreign kleptocrats influence politics here are so . . . *diffuse*, if there's a story, *that's* the story. But it's hardly Trump-specific. And a lot of it is technically legal. And you'd have to blow the island of Manhattan to smithereens to so much as put a dent in it."

Daddy *did* seem to know an awful lot about these things. He'd even once referred to Trump as a "frenemy," which sounded scary. Though maybe less scary than if he was a friend. Marley wasn't sure.

"I don't think that's right," Mom said. "Saying 'Everyone's corrupt.' 'It's not the player, it's the game,' and dismissing every criticism as stupid and naive. I don't think that's right. He's the leader of the free world for Christ's sakes. He should be held to a higher standard than what's *technically* legal."

"Really? Why? And I'm not against criticism. What I'm against is innuendo. I loathe—*loathe*—innuendo. I think journalists are shooting themselves in the foot by making such a big deal out of hearsay. They're Geraldo Rivera if there's nothing in that box."

"What's that?" said Marley.

"Geraldo Rivera. It was before your time. He was a TV journalist. He made a big deal about how he found Al Capone's secret vault. Al Capone was a famous gangster from Chicago."

"Oh, I mean, I know who Al Capone was, obviously—"

"And he opened up the vaults on live television, much-hyped, thirty million people watching, the television event of the year, thinking they were gonna find, I don't know, the Dead Sea Scrolls, the meaning of life in there, and he found bupkes. There was a half-empty bottle of gin in there, I think."

Mom said, "Maybe that *is* the meaning of life."

"How do you mean?" said Daddy.

"I don't know. Never mind."

She sipped her wine, with a sour look. Marley didn't really know what Mom meant either, but if anyone else made a comment like that Daddy might find it amusingly off-kilter, or at least laugh politely at it, but when Mom said it it was just weird and irrelevant and didn't land. That happened a lot with them. They didn't really *like* each other.

"See kids, liberals make fun of right-wing conspiracy theorists, but they're just as crazy. Even crazier, some of them. Just as thirsty for a crucifixion. Not to mention the hypocrisy of some of them. You can't show a Chinese person eating rice without being accused of grievous stereotyping, but you can basically imply that every Eastern European Jew in the taxi business is a greedy, tax-avoidant thug and get away with it. I don't think that's very fair, do you?"

"Jacob," Mom said, and gave him a look like *don't be gauche.*

"What? They're old enough to hear it. And they should know about their family business. God knows they won't learn the truth about the situation in the papers. Maybe they'll be at the helm someday."

Marley really, really wouldn't want to do that. She didn't know what she wanted to do when she grew up, but it definitely wasn't that. She actually couldn't think of a single thing she wanted to do less than work in taxi loans. Except for maybe be a doctor. That also sounded horrible.

"They should be proud of their family business. You know our company helped plug a billion-dollar hole in the city's budget. Helped generations of drivers to retire with their dignity intact and money in the bank. But now we're being painted as some kind of speculators, all because the city flipped the script and let Uber storm the castle. The city betrayed our industry, because they have no faith. And now, with their duplicitous behavior, a lot of well-meaning people have been left in debt."

"What I don't understand is," J. J. said, "if you're in d-d-debt, and the guy you owe *m-money* to's in d-d-debt, and the guy *they* owe m-money to's in . . . in it, can't all the guys just get together and be, like, let's all just f-forget about it and move f-f-forward?"

Daddy brightened like he always did when J.J. said something halfway normal almost straight through.

"That's a very beautiful idea, son, and some politicians would say the same thing. But unfortunately that's not how it works. There's a baby in that bathwater. You cancel the debt, you destroy the market going forward. Look out for the little guy, by all means, but the big guy, he's a person too, right—"

Marley didn't understand what he was talking about at all. She didn't know the first thing about economics. What was an "infusion of liquidity"? And why did banks need loans if banks also issued loans? And how could you own three houses and ten cars but need to pawn your wife's Birkin bag to keep yourself in codeine? (She'd read a story in the news about one guy, in Miami, who'd done that.) It seemed like debt for some people was a straightforward kind of thing, like paying off your car or your tuition, walking around with a leg-iron for half your life, but for rich people debt was something else completely—it was Play-Doh, and there were whole professions that were all about moving it around before it hardened on you.

"—but what this crisis needs is someone who can see beyond next week. Daddy's been in talks with some investors. High-net-worth individuals who specialize in distressed assets. They're very wise to be interested. They want in on a piece of an iconic industry, and they know a medallion's still a wonderful thing to own, that yellow cabs will always be a part of this city, and will reward those who believe in them. It's the bottom of the market now. The city council just approved a cap on Uber. I swear, we're gonna turn this ship." Marley ran her spoon along the cheesy meatball remnants. "Remember, we got through 9/11. It can't get any worse than *that*."

Even Mom seemed not bored when Daddy did his real-talk speeches about steering the taxi industry back from the brink. He had run for something called the City Council once and Marley could never remember them being so in love as on the campaign trail. She'd been seven or eight then, too young to be grossed out by it even. Mom holding a clipboard, swanning around in her Easter-colored de la Renta dress suits with a

COHEN FOR DISTRICT 5! pin on her lapel. She seemed to really like the idea of public service. Or at least being married to it.

Anyway, he had lost the City Council race, but by something like only fifteen hundred votes. He had felt really wronged after that. He talked about maybe running again someday, maybe even for mayor. Which sounded like a pie-in-the-sky prospect until you thought about who the president was.

"Anyway, I'd like to raise a toast." Daddy raised his Coke. He didn't drink wine 'cause he had "blown his wad" as a younger man. "To the new year," he said.

"Daddy, it's practically February," Marley said.

"I know, but having this creep out of my hair, well, it feels like turning over a new leaf."

Marley raised her Shirley Temple. They all clinked glasses, Mom and J.J. too.

"Cheers."

He seemed like he was in a pretty great mood tonight, better than he'd been in a while, with work and Grandma getting worse and everything, like maybe now was a good time to bring up what she needed to bring up.

"So, um, I thought that we could talk about the summer thing?" said Marley.

"What summer thing?" said Daddy.

"The Cuba thing? The deadline to apply's next week, so . . ."

She really, really wanted to do this study abroad course in Cuba this summer, a literature and film course. Her favorite teacher was leading it, and it was kids from all over the country going, boys *and* girls, for a whole month, and the thought of being with a bunch of kids from other schools who were interested in things like that sounded amazing, plus she was really interested in Cuba. Grandma in a vanishingly rare moment of togetherness had said it sounded fabulous, like the opportunity of a lifetime. Grandma's uncle had actually lived there in the '40s, in Havana, and she had a photo of him in a zoot-looking suit squinting in an orange grove. It looked *beautiful*.

"Is this the first I'm hearing about this?" Daddy said.

"I told you about it. We talked about it for like twenty minutes. You said we'd see?"

"I've already set you up in the internship with Rubin." Daddy was friends with this producer guy who was really important in Hollywood and Broadway. Though apparently he was a terrifying person to be around. Like he'd given his personal assistant PTSD, and the lady had quit show business entirely and now she worked in yoga for dogs.

"You know I can't renege on him. He's an investor. I had to pull a lot of strings to get this."

He said it like he'd really sacrificed himself, when pulling strings was basically his number one passion in life.

"I just thought, you know, you'd want me to do this kind of thing," said Marley, "it'll look really good on college apps, and—"

"Rubin practically owns the drama school at Yale. Your chances'll be worse off having crossed him. Trust me." Like she had a shot in hell at getting into Yale anyway. But Daddy just dug into his veal like the discussion was over.

"I just thought it would be cool to do something different, you know? Colleges especially really wanna see that these days. Not just, like, being in the rat race, but getting out of your comfort zone, and out of, like, this little New York bubble of go-go-go and privilege and—"

"Right, a bunch of private school kids, on a literature course . . . way to abnegate your privilege . . ."

"So you do remember me bringing it up—"

"And I assume all this rubbing elbows with the revolution is free of charge?"

"Well, no, not exactly . . ."

It was five thousand dollars. Not including flights even. Which was obviously an insane amount of money she had no way of getting her hands on for a long time, if ever. Though she knew for a fact that Mom's Armani Casa pouf for her vanity cost more than that.

"It's out of the question. It's a waste of your time. *And* my money. The Rubin thing, it'll be real, honest-to-goodness work. And it's not just suits and wheeling-dealing. It's the mail room, it's on set with the key grips, it's with people from all kinds of backgrounds, people who have to work for a living. You'll see how things get made. You might even learn some people skills." What was *that* supposed to mean? "Besides, Cuba's too far away. Your brother needs you around."

"He needs *you* around. You're his *parents*. And *you're* going to *Greece* for a month."

Daddy's eyes popped, and he did this sort of angry-chompy thing for a second, then he said, "I work hard for a living and I don't need a child's permission to take a vacation."

"I'm not a child."

"You are. You're my child. And you can try to go to Cuba, or not go to Cuba, but you're Marley Cohen. Okay? That's your name. It's the name your mother and I gave to you. Here we were thinking it was a pretty great thing to be, until you tell us otherwise. But you—your name, your so-called *privilege*—that's your ticket. Ride with it, or die . . . *Or* wait for the next life. Who knows, maybe you'll get lucky, wake up as a child in Laos. Then you won't have to feel so guilty."

"Jacob—" Nice of Mom to chime in.

"All this self-flagellation they're teaching these kids, that's not being humble, that's not helping people, that's just raising tortured, self-important little narcissists. I'm sick of it. I worked in an auto shop the summer I was fourteen. This is a chance to work on Broadway. Any kid who wasn't totally naive and spoiled for opportunity would kill for it. But no. She'd rather be off in the sugarcane fields."

Marley drank her whole Shirley Temple down in one big treacly grenadine gulp to try to keep herself from crying. It wasn't about not getting what she wanted, it was just—Daddy got so *mean* sometimes.

IN THE LOBBY there was a new kind of young nice-looking door guy Daddy fist-bumped with and called "My man!" as they came in. Daddy took a lot of pride in knowing all the door guys' names and favorite sports teams, like it meant he wasn't totally detached from life as most people on Earth lived it. She just hoped this guy didn't get to thinking Daddy was his friend or anything. He'd be in for a pretty big disappointment there.

Maybe she could make the money for Cuba herself somehow, like by selling study drugs. J. J. was rolling in all kinds of prescription medicines. But she knew she didn't have the nerve to pull off a thing like that. It was true what Daddy said, she had no people skills. Nor any anything-else skills either, really.

She'd heard it mentioned about city kids being hip and tough and scrappy but that didn't describe her at all. She was practically provincial. In her pinafore and Swiss Miss braids, with a goddamn muff in winter, like some doomed tsarina, moving from one limestone cloister to the next . . . so much for the mean streets.

Though one time before Christmas she'd been out with Mom shopping on Fifth Avenue and some guy with blond dreadlocks and bloody toenails had come up to them and called them "fucking pigs," probably because of Mom's mink coat—*that* at least had been something different. . . . Mom had been all fake-proud and indignant after, all *This coat's an heirloom for Christ's sakes,* and *What could be less wasteful when you really think about it,* and *Last I checked this was a free country,* but you could tell she was completely shook, absolutely cowed, he'd really burst her bubble, that man, she barely said one word the whole rest of the day, and she hadn't worn that coat once since, which was a good thing, frankly, because heirloom or not it made her look like a complete jerk, but did that man know something Marley didn't? *Were* they . . . were her parents . . . pigs?

Grandma's light was off when they got back upstairs. Go figure. You could hear her apnea from under the door, though, which was reassuring. It meant she was alive.

She'd moved in with them a couple weeks ago, to the spare room down the hall from Marley and J. J.'s rooms. Daddy'd gone *berserk* when Aunt Brenda had suggested the old folks' home near Pelham, and how she'd really gone downhill fast, and it was time to make arrangements, and let her live with *you*, Jake, if you're so damn noble, and Daddy'd said you know what, Brenda? You know what? Maybe I am, and so now that's what was happening, though Mom said Daddy was just nailing himself to the cross.

Marley thought it might be fun, like a nonstop sleepover, but so far Grandma stayed in her room a lot, not even coming out for dinner most nights. Retiring early in the evenings, then hobbling through the hallways late, like a specter in her nightie, leaving old-butt smell behind her in the bathroom. Which of course she couldn't help . . . even her Shalimar was no match for *that*.

Marley'd had to go into her bedroom a couple times to check on her and get her pills she needed for her four o'clock soup. That room seemed haunted since she took it over. Mangier, somehow. There were pictures on her mantel some of which were like the stuff of nightmares, of her ancestors in black and white, in the time before smiles. Dour and dusky in their shawls, occult in their expressions—even those little kids were dead by now—and one of Grandma's mom and dad in some-place called Lublin, on their wedding day, looking miserable. It was crazy to think Grandma—happy stylish modern Grandma with the pink pearlescent manicures—had come from *them* . . . poor and pious, scuttling out of steerage, exiled from the land of skulls and scurvy-stricken goats. But when you thought of it that way it was no wonder Grandma'd lost the plot—her life had been so *long*, you see, and stretched so thin over the eras. She'd been born in Brooklyn in a cellar, and swaddled in potato sacks, and she'd grown up and rode around in jet planes and worn tracksuits in the '80s and taken Marley to see *Trolls: 3-D* with Justin Timberlake at Lincoln Center once . . . it was a lot. Anyone would start to get mixed up.

It made Marley's brain hurt to think of all the changes that would happen in the world by the time *she* was Grandma's age. That made her feel peculiar, like she was standing over the abyss, about to hurtle straight through space-time, with no sound and nobody watching.

She had better *do* something, one of these days.

SHE'D BEEN DMing with this guy, Dimitri, by some miracle. So that was something. They'd known each other since forever, but they'd been talking a lot since they'd run into each other at the movies over winter break. (At the popcorn counter she had said her friend Daniela was holding their seats inside, which he totally bought, though she'd had to make a mad dash for the exit the second the credits started, without saying goodbye even, so he wouldn't know that she was there alone. *That* had been a close one. . . .)

His dad was in the taxi business too, an old friend of Daddy's, though it seemed like they were maybe on the outs. He'd come over once a year or so ago, Dimitri's dad, with some much younger girlfriend of his whose butt he kept touching right in front of everyone. She was drop-dead gorgeous, this girlfriend, just gouge-your-eyes-out Minka Kelly gorgeous, and she'd come to Marley's room to pass the time while Valentin—that was Dimitri's dad—and Daddy were talking shop, and Marley thought she'd find her bedroom really lame and little girlish but it was actually the opposite, this twenty-something-year-old woman with the microblading and the five-inch heels and the rhinestone thong poking out over her jeans had sat down on her floor and played with Marley's dolls and stuffed animals for like forty-five minutes, getting *really* into it, giggling hysterically and making up different voices for all the animals, and the more she did it the more it became clear to Marley something horrible had happened to this woman, some kind of arrested-development thing where she'd been sprung from an orphanage in Minsk and sold into the girlfriend experience and she'd never seen or held a toy before, and now the sight of all these dolls and stuffed animals in Marley's room was completely overwhelming to her. Whatever was going on there, it was pretty messed up.

Anyway, Dimitri's family life seemed totally chaotic. He'd just gotten kicked out of his boarding school 'cause his dad couldn't pay the tuition, and now he was meant to be enrolling in some less expensive place near where his mom lived, in Staten Island, but they hadn't sent the money in there either yet. So he was just sort of bumming around the city in the meantime, running wild, like Holden Caulfield or somebody, while he figured out his schooling. Living with *friends*, even, he said, sometimes.

She was looking through his pictures now, for about the hundredth time this week. It made her blood race looking at him, just knowing he was alive, and male, and a junior, and that he might not be completely uninterested in her.

Facially he wasn't what you'd call a pretty boy. He had a dusting of black hair on his upper lip so faint and discontinuous it looked a little bit like crumbs, and his chin jutted and curled in a slightly satanic way, and he smoked real cigarettes by the looks of them, not the harmless crème brûlée kind Benny smoked, but he had something in his eyes that was a little bit . . . she felt embarrassed to *say* it, or even *think* it, but . . . a little bit sexual.

Of course she didn't know the first thing about what to *do*, if it ever came to that. If they ever met up in person. She'd heard things mentioned here and there. Sophie Sexton said a guy would never get you off (off what?) if you couldn't get yourself off whatever it was first, which sounded like pretty good advice. But Ms. Bloy said sex should wait 'til college, which also sounded like good advice, and kind of a relief frankly, because Marley really wasn't ready yet. But Ms. Bloy might not be the best person to ask about that sort of thing, smart as she was . . . with her port-wine neck stain and her rubber shoes with the separated toe compartments, always going on and on about the male gaze. Like it'd ever been anywhere *near* her. Sophie, on the other hand, she really knew a lot. Even her *name* had sex in it.

Dimitri was typing. Writing to *her*: Marley Cohen. *U comin out later?* The words blossomed like flowers in her retinas. What did he mean, later? It was almost nine. *Were chillin herr. My friend dylans place. 89th n 2nd. Come by if u can.*

What was he talking about? It was out of the question. Just . . . it was out of the question. Wasn't it? She'd never been to a party. She'd been to some lunchtime birthday things at Serendipity, and bar and bat mitzvahs of course, but only because your parents made you invite everybody in your grade, every last person, even Tina Schmiege, but she'd never been to one at *night*. Plus she was in her PJs with her face already washed, and some gouge marks where she'd picked her chin pores that wouldn't be unswollen until morning, plus her stomach hurt a little bit from dinner. Plus when she'd said she wanted to really *do* something sometime, she hadn't meant, like, right away. She'd meant more like, some other time. Like down the road.

Also she didn't have any money, and Mom and Daddy monitored her credit card pretty closely.

. . . Grandma might have cash.

• • •

HALF AN HOUR LATER she was in a cab, in a crop top underneath her puffer, in disbelief that she was really going. She felt really nervous, and a little bit guilty, but Grandma wouldn't miss those twenties in the least. No more than she missed anything in life.

The driver was named Dilawar and he had beads on the dashboard and the call-to-prayer on the radio and his dinner in a thermos in the passenger's seat. Maybe he knew Daddy. For a second she was gonna ask him, just making conversation, but then she thought that would be stupid of her. Childish really. The world, it wasn't actually that small, and he probably didn't care who Daddy was, this tired man. And besides she got the sense lately it wasn't anything to brag about.

RUDY MET HIM in his car on his day off, a Saturday. Jake was parked around the corner from the building in a white Mercedes.

"Afternoon, Rudy. Or should I say good morning," Jake said.

"I thought you could use a little extra shut-eye."

He'd sent him out last night on what he'd called a favor. Three a.m., skullcap and all, at an abandoned garage on 43rd Avenue in Long Island City.

There'd been no one there at that hour, rats too fat to scamper, waddling like corgis among the chassis, a dispatcher in a lit booth eating a banana. Rudy with a slim jim in his pocket for busting open car doors and a list of license plates whose rate cards and medallions he was meant to pry off of the vehicles. Jake had insisted it was all very standard practice nowadays, this sort of repossession, legally airtight, and he'd show him the court documents if he had any concerns. What was Rudy gonna say to him, "Show me the court documents"? "I have concerns"? Jake had meant it rhetorically, and Rudy was no legal eagle—he wouldn't understand them anyway. He'd spent the last month running piddly errands for him, grateful but annoyed, unpacking his FreshDirects, buying roses for his senile mother. This was something that took nerve, and skill. A chance to take things up a notch.

"I see nineteen," Jake said, looking through the bag.

"One of the cabs, it was right near the dispatcher's office. I didn't want to risk a confrontation, like you told me."

"Did he see you?"

"No." Maybe. "Would that be a problem, if he had?"

"What'd he look like?"

"White, heavy-set. Handlebar moustache. Midfifties, maybe."

Jake looked nonplussed. What was Rudy meant to have done, busted his kneecaps? "It's no problem," he said finally. "You did the smart thing, backing off."

Rudy took a deep breath. "So what happens to them now?" he said.

"Well, we're consolidating assets. There's going to be a sale. It's hush-hush, though, for now. The details are still being hammered out."

Rudy was confused. He didn't know much of anything about the taxi business, but he'd thought this was the whole thing Jake had said they were trying to avoid. Aggressive repossessions and foreclosures, a fire sale of medallions, and drivers left holding the bag for debt they couldn't even theoretically work their way out of now—you'd just seized their licenses to operate.

"I thought the whole idea was about keeping taxis on the road," said Rudy.

"Of course it is. That's always been my goal. That's what I'm trying to make happen, by taking the power back once and for all from petty warlords like Val."

Valentin Zalebnik. Jesus. That had been his fleet, last night. He didn't look like the kind of guy whose turf you wanted to be caught treading on, legally or not—a Soviet-style heavy. The Caligula of Brighton Beach, whose bloodhound eyes must haunt their share of strippers' dreams.

"Anyway don't get me started . . . you did a fine job, Rudy. That's all you need to know. Thank you very much." He opened the glove compartment. He actually kept gloves in there, beautiful leather driving gloves, like something British counts wore. He handed Rudy an envelope.

"Are you serious?" said Rudy. "I'm basically squatting in your apartment."

"Don't worry about that. What you did, it was important. I really do appreciate it."

It was a bundle. Fifties too, from what Rudy could see. It seemed rude to count it right in front of him, though. He folded it in his inner pocket.

"Big plans for your day off, Rude?" Jake said.

"Oh, not much. Dinner with a friend later, in Queens."

"Oh, well, you can *really* treat her now. Enjoy yourselves . . . If you want, I'll give you a ride."

"Oh no, that's okay."

Rudy wouldn't mind going home, toasting to his newfound wealth, and not moving a muscle until dinnertime. He'd been on his feet nonstop lately, dealing with people and their bullshit. He just wanted to be alone.

"It's not 'til seven anyway."

"Oh, well, that'll work out fine then," Jake said. "I've got to stop someplace out there first."

You couldn't get him to take no for an answer, once he got it in his head he wanted company.

"Okay, well . . . thanks. That'd be great."

He drove east, toward the 59th Street Bridge. It was a classic empty January day. The city could be bleak as hell this time of year. Warsaw-bleak. The silver bells were a distant memory, and spring was twenty years away. Life had no illusions, and no flavor but the cold. Rudy'd found himself feeling less depressed, though, lately, than he'd been over the holidays. It was always like that with him. The good times were the bad times, and vice versa.

"Where are we going anyway?" he said.

"I have to get my wife's car serviced, out in Willets Point."

"You don't go to Mercedes-Benz of Manhattan for that? They're gonna jump you out there, in a car like this."

"Oh, no, I own a couple of the lots. I get a great deal from my guys. Just don't tell my wife." He put a finger to his lips.

Rudy still hadn't met her, though he'd seen her strutting through the lobby a few times, a real glamour-puss. Never a hello. Not so much unfriendly as intensely preoccupied. She had a beautiful face.

"Your kids seem nice," said Rudy. "How old are they again?"

"Fourteen next month, and nine. Marley, that's my oldest, she's my heart. I look at her sometimes and I think I'll burst. I worry about her, though. She's at that tender age. It feels like she could go either way. She could be a leader, a real leader . . . or she could go running into the arms of the first chump who looks at her nice, become a makeup artist or something, just to spite us . . . It's these schools, Rudy. I'm paying sixty thousand dollars a year, and for what? We wanted them to have that traditional education, the kind her mother and I never got at our crappy public schools. Learning Latin, the great battles. The canon. That kind of thing. Now it's all Mandarin and history's a lie. I don't mind them hearing different ideas from my own. But this, this is bordering on orthodoxy. They're grooming a bunch of incurious little robots."

"Yeah. Some of the canon's not so hot though either," said Rudy. "Fuckin' *Ethan Frome?* I'll never get those hours back."

Jake laughed. "And, no offense, but . . . no matter what they were teaching her, sixty thousand dollars a year would still be a ripoff. You're being taken for a ride there. They're just preying on parents' insecurities."

"You know, I think you might be right."

"You've got a son too, yeah?"

"Yes. Jacob Junior. That's my son." He was silent for a minute. "He's nine."

He seemed a little bit off, the son. Bald as a cue ball, for some reason.

"Cute kid," Rudy said.

"Thanks. Yes. Thanks for saying that."

"Real spirited."

"Oh, well, yes. He is *that.*"

Jake's lip curled in a sheepish way. For such an expressive, talkative guy, his reticence to talk about his son, to just address his baldness situation or whatever issues and be done with it, seemed out of character. He didn't wear it well. Shame and evasion were best left to others. Catholics, for example.

"Speaking of family, I should tell you," Jake said, "I know your uncle. Or I mean, I've met him before."

"Oh, really?" Jake seemed to know everybody. "How?"

"I didn't put two and two together at first. But then I thought, Coyle, Coyle—and it turns out I met him a few years ago, when he was doing some work for a housing nonprofit I used to be involved in. I'm not involved with them anymore, but, well, he seemed like a nice man. Solid."

"As a rock," said Rudy.

"Honestly I felt awkward when I realized the connection. I didn't know when to bring it up. People get touchy with stuff like that sometimes. At least, I always was. Feeling like their family precedes them in some way. Anyway I didn't want you to feel awkward. Any work you do for me, it's your own merit. Your own thing."

"Yeah, no, totally, it's all good . . ." Why not just say he knew Mike, and move on? He was a pretty sensitive dude, Rudy supposed.

"Small world, though, huh?" said Jake.

Twenty minutes later they came to the edge of Willets Point, or what remained of it, an old-fashioned bazaar of mechanic shops and salvage yards in the shadow of Citi Field. Rudy'd been here only once, lost on the way to a Mets game with his idiot friend Dave who couldn't drive. It was like a Third World country, no-named streets, roosters passing between concertina wire. An iron-strewn necropolis. A landscape so degraded you perceived it as a kind of test, some challenge from on high for how much ugliness mankind could bear.

"Lots of memories here," said Jake, turning onto the next street. "Lots of them. I've been coming here since I was a little boy, with my Pop-Pop, to get mufflers and glasswork for his taxis. All of this used to be a dumping ground. Can you imagine? A gigantic pile of trash and ashes. Fitzgerald wrote about it. So I've heard—I was never much of a student of literature. Then Robert Moses tried to turn it into a parking lot for the World's Fair. *Then* they tried to build on it as part of a bid for the Olympics. That's when I bought some property here, in 2008."

"You bought property in 2008?"

"I was feeling confident. As were a lot of people in the taxi world, I think. We were unscathed. And it piqued my interest, on a personal level. I thought, all this change is coming to the area, with me or without me. Better for the folks here to be dealing with someone who knows them and respects them than some faceless mogul who'll sell them and their businesses down the river without thinking twice about it."

Did he mean he wouldn't do that too, when the time came? Or just that he'd think twice about it?

"All that, and, well, let's not mealymouth. The land was going to be worth a fortune. It was a very attractive opportunity . . . Of course they've tried every trick in the book to put a stop to it over the years. Digging up some statute from 1949 that says you can't build near this sacred gas main. But it *will* be going forward. The shovels are nearly in the ground, for phase one."

"Money talks, I guess," said Rudy.

"Oh, don't be so political. You sound like my teenage daughter. This could be Queens's next great neighborhood. There'll be housing, half of it set aside for low-income families. There'll be schools, a park, a hospital—"

"Housing for low-income families. Isn't that just a sweetener for developers to shove another megamall down people's throats?"

"Far from it. They're trying to build a real community out here, Rudy. Don't think it's not possible. Besides, what's the alternative? Everywhere you look, there's blight. I'll miss the old folkways here just as much as anybody, but when you're four feet deep in a pothole during a rainstorm, with human excrement and toxic sludge pooling at your pantlegs, you won't be feeling quite so sentimental."

Jake pulled over and ordered two chicken empanadas out the window from a woman selling them out of the back of her van for fifty cents apiece. He gave her a twenty and said to keep the rest, the woman bowing her head like a supplicant, almost crying she was thanking him so much. It was embarrassing. It didn't matter Rudy was a son of Queens, born just a couple miles away from here, or that Jake had come here as a kid, a fact he'd mentioned about twenty-five times in the last hour, they had no business being here. They were conquistadors.

After they ate they pulled into a place called Carlo's Tire and Rims. A man stood outside in a puffer vest, wiping his hands on a rag. Jake honked.

"Señor Cohen!" the man said, and came up to their car. His face was lined but handsome, rutted with years of killing work.

"Rodrigo! Mi amigo!"

Jesus Christ, him with the amigo bit. In his fleece-lined Barbour jacket. He got out and slapped the man's back and shook hands with a crew of three others standing by. Rudy could peg the interaction from the first ten seconds: Jake bending over backwards to show how down-to-earth he was, pleased as punch with himself to know one Guatemalan from the next, this Rodrigo fellow and his friends humoring the boss through gritted teeth, like anything but total desperation kept them loyal. The whole hombres routine was just a thin veneer of civility, your typical American pantomime. They talked about the car for a few minutes, Jake bursting into perfect, fluent Spanish as he told Rodrigo what he needed. Rudy must've looked surprised, 'cause Jake said, "What, you've lived in New York City your whole life and you don't speak any Spanish, Rudy?"

There was an area in back where they were invited to sit down. There were two more men drinking coffee and playing cards around a space heater, and '90s-era centerfolds on the walls with women spreadeagled in neon thongs and ads for Manny Pacquiao fights.

Rodrigo's son was there. He looked just like him. Adorable kid, charming, perfectly bilingual. The pride of his baseball team, Rodrigo said. Eleven years old and bound for greatness. He set to work with his dad, fetching rims and handing him his tools, the father explaining his process to the son with great intensity and patience. Rudy caught Jake looking at them. Wistfully, maybe. Maybe jealously. . . . All the money in the world couldn't buy you a confident child, with light in his eyes, and hair on his head.

Someone broke Rudy's reverie, handing him a Heineken, saying something that he didn't catch.

Jake said, "That means it's Saturday. Take a load off."

Rudy hesitated, after Jake's come-to-Jesus speech about the clean and sober path. He knew he would have to make a conscious effort not to shit where he ate.

"Don't abstain on *my* account," Jake said.

"Well okay," said Rudy, "that'd be great," and accepted it. It was just beer anyway.

Half a pack of cigarillos later he was thinking maybe harmony among God's children was possible after all. Rodrigo had him help replace a carburetor on a vintage V8. He could barely understand a word of the instructions, but it didn't matter, they made it work.

Jake was deep in conversation with a guy named Felipe, having a cigar. Rudy'd had him pegged for a classical asthmatic type . . . a momma's boy, soft and peevish, a child of Levittown, who lacked the constitution for life's guttural pleasures. But there he was blowing cigar smoke out of the side of his mouth, beribboning the air, gesticulating in Spanish. Rudy was a little bit impressed. Here he'd been thinking that the war, if there was a war, would be waged between the haves and the have-nots, but maybe the real war was between the doers and complainers.

Between the grown-ups with responsibilities and the children screeching for their rights. Everybody present was a doer, trying to make a living, trying to take a load off. No social studies belly-aching. Just shared respect.

An hour later they were back in the car. Jake had offered to drive him to his friend Tara's house.

"That's what's the matter with our country nowadays," Jake said, "is everyone's suspicious of each other. People see every-one else for what they *represent*, not for who they are. Those guys in the garage—we're from very different backgrounds, clearly, them and I. But I've tried to be a fair landlord to them. I've tried to make it easier for them and their families to make their plans so that when the time comes for me to sell, they're prepared. But to some people all of that, all of that goodwill, cultivated over years, that's all just lipstick on a pig. It's just as bad as if I'd put them on a platter for Related, Inc., three years ago, and served them up. To them, it's just as bad. Why? They're cynical is why. They want to see the worst in everyone. Everyone with a pot to *piss* in, that is. And the more they do it, the more they poke holes, the more people like me aren't going to be so generous."

"I mean, that's kind of up to *you* though, isn't it?" said Rudy. Jake seemed not to hear him. He was making a complicated se-ries of turns onto the parkway. It wasn't like he was ignoring him.

TARA LIVED WITH her baby daughter in Woodside. Their moms had been best friends back in the day. They'd come over together from the same tiny town on the southwest coast of Ire-land, a couple of Catholic country girls footloose in the city, in the '80s, working as nannies, living by the wanted ads in back of the *Irish Echo*. Those sounded like great times they'd had—bopping babies for the wolves of Wall Street by day, then hitting up Tunnel and the Palladium at night, summers on the Jersey

Shore. Mom looked like some vixen from a Warrant video in all those pictures, young and made for trouble, before the wheels came off for her.

Tara'd always been a kindred spirit, growing up. Straining at the yoke, like him. Talented like you couldn't believe, an incredible dancer, she'd even got into LaGuardia for high school, the *Fame* school, the best performing arts school in the country, but her fat-fuck troglodyte of a father—may he rest in peace—didn't want her in Manhattan with "those prancy fags," so she'd stayed in her shitty high school out in Queens, sleepwalked through an associate's degree in paper pushing, got knocked up, ghosted by the dad, and now she was slinging cocktails five nights a week at a gentlemen's club in Brooklyn, Pumps. She had a bit of the old fire in her yet, always sending Rudy invites to sex workers' rallies and things, which of course he never went to, and trying to help the girls she worked with unionize—which he guessed was cool, more power to her—but frankly it seemed like a misuse of her time and energy, or some attempt to politicize her crappy life decisions. A girl like Tara, she should've never been working there in the first place.

Opening the door she gave him a limp hug. She wasn't a big smiler, as a rule, these days.

"Hey," she said.

"Hey."

Rudy went inside. The baby was in the living room in her walker thing. He hadn't realized she'd be around tonight.

"I think they recalled those things," he said.

"Oh yeah? What do *you* know about it?" Tara said. She took his coat.

"I read it in the business section the other day," said Rudy, "how Fisher Price had to recall those walker things."

"Oh, okay, he reads the business section now. Those fatalities were when the parents weren't watching them for six, seven hours at a time, Rudy. They were out, they were running off their crystal meth, and the kids' necks got caught between the straps. You think I'd ever leave her in there unaccompanied?"

"Jesus Christ. I just thought it was worth bringing up, that's all." He'd just walked in, and already she was mad at him for politely recommending she not let her child asphyxiate.

"Okay, I'm sorry. You're right. I'm just in a shitty mood." No kidding. "Do you mind watching Sophia while I take a shower?"

"No, I guess not." So much for steaks and champagne. Apparently he was here on diaper duty.

He grabbed a couple ice cubes and some whiskey from her freezer. He'd got a buzz on at the garage he needed to take up a notch or he'd risk falling asleep.

Her apartment was a dump. Just a couple weeks in an all-white condominium in midtown was enough to breed a certain contempt for how some people kept their living quarters. It smelled like Rice-A-Roni and Noxzema and there were piles of laundry everywhere. How much fucking laundry could the two of them be going through?

"Hey sweetie, how are ya?" Rudy said, and took a seat on the couch near the baby.

Sophia was two. Or maybe one. One of those. A real cutie, with a single dimple like her mother. Rudy didn't have much to say to kids in general, but he was realizing the key, like with so much in life, was not to be self-conscious. Just talk to them like you would talk to anybody.

He sat back and watched the TV with her, nursing his drink. He didn't know they even still had *Sesame Street.* He'd practically been raised by it. Watching it now made him feel ashamed, though, of the choices he'd gone on to make. These actors, who did the puppets, singing songs teaching inner-city latchkey kids about recycling—*these* were people who could sleep at night. There was a segment about a little autistic girl named Molly and her companion dog. It made your heart hurt. It made you want to be a better person. Just gentle and upstanding and clear-headed. No more cutting corners, no more drinking. No more bullshit, all this toxic guile, lapping at his soul. . . .

But he was still a young man, with many wants and needs. It was too early to be good. Or too late, maybe.

"Hey."

Tara came out of the shower in her robe. She looked so young without her war paint on. He forgot sometimes that she was only twenty-four. The party'd ended for her so abruptly.

They'd had sex one time. More than one time, but just one night. At first it was weird, like fucking your sister, and then it wasn't. It had only just happened when she'd found out she was pregnant with this other guy's kid, and she'd balked, and Rudy'd balked. She assured him that it couldn't be his, and sure enough when Sophia came out, she was brown as a cocoa bean. Rudy was relieved, and a little disappointed maybe, but what was he gonna do, start things up with Tara anyway, raise another man's kid? No fucking way. He wasn't *that* nice.

She sat down on the couch, rubbing her hair with a towel.

"How's it being a doorman?" she said.

There was something in the way she said it that annoyed him, very much.

"Honestly? It's kinda great. I've met some really interesting people."

"Mm-hmm."

"You gonna have a drink?" he said.

"No, I've got work later."

"Oh. Really? What the hell. I thought we were hanging out."

"We *are* hanging out."

"If you say so." She *was* in a lousy mood.

"So what happens after it's over? It's just a short-term thing, right?"

"Who knows? One of the guys in the building, he might have a job for me. Maybe in LA, even. He says he knows some producer who could get me set up out there, with auditions."

Her eyes did a buggy, half-roll thing.

"What?" he said. "What's with the face?"

"It's just, like, when are you gonna call it, Rudy?"

"Call what?"

"Just, call it and admit you're one of us already."

"One of who?"

"Just, like, a regular person."

"What do you mean? Clearly I don't know what you mean."

"It's just . . . every time I see you the last few years, it's some new thing. You're going to join the Marines. You're going to LA. You're going to Colorado. When . . . just being a regular person, it's not that tragic. I know maybe it looks bad to you. Maybe you come here from Park Avenue and you think it's so depressing and beneath you. But it's not. Honestly? I'm glad my life looks different than I thought it would, maybe than you thought it *should*, 'cause I have her." She nodded toward the baby.

"Don't take this the wrong way," said Rudy, "but . . . you don't look too glad."

"Maybe I'm not floating on *air* all the time, maybe the day-to-day can be heavy sometimes, but it's worth it. Like, I'm glad I was forced to sacrifice certain things and just knuckle down." Knuckle down? She was a cocktail waitress in a strip club, not a CPA. "It's all worth it, for Sophia."

"I don't know . . . You say that now, 'cause she's still cute. Wait 'til she's fifteen and hates your guts. With one of those Skrillex hairdos. Then you'll be singing a different tune about the sacrifices you had to make. And of course by then they won't be having you at Pumps in hot pants."

She shook her head. "You're such an asshole, Rudy."

"I'm not saying it's *right* they wouldn't hire an older lady. *I don't make the rules.* I'm just saying how it is. People fall in love with their mistakes, saying *ooh, oh, everything happens for a reason.* Like hell it does. That kind of reasoning's for suckers. It's Stockholm syndrome. I'm sick of it."

119

Maybe he was being a little bit nasty. His tongue was looser than he'd realized. But those buggy eyes, those goddamn buggy eyes made his blood boil. Those eyes made everything short of murder feel like fair game.

"Listen," he said, "I'm not saying Sophia was a mistake. I mean, *technically* she was—listen, I love her and everything. She's wonderful and a blessing and everything. And you're a great mom. I just mean, if I told you you could be at Alvin Ailey right now, wait to find the right dude, have a kid at thirty you'd be just as obsessed with, who'd feel just as meant to be, don't tell me you wouldn't consider it."

"Right, 'cause people get to live their lives twice. Cause Alvin Ailey's really something someone like me ought to have banked on for their future. You think you're Mr. Clear-Eyed, Rudy, Mr. Tell-It-Like-It-Is? You're deluded. You think if you'd have chased that girl out there to Denver you'd be pleased you did it? It'd be like the end of that movie. The second the thrill's over he's sitting there staring into space thinking, *Oh fuck, oh God, what've I done?* That's what guys like you do. That's your whole MO. You see your shadow, and you run from it, and you see it again, and you run from it. You're an empty vessel. And the women come and go."

"Oh *God*, don't give me that."

It drove him nuts when women did that. Got all high-minded and philosophical about the Folly of Men, to throw you off the scent of their *own* dysfunction. This all from a girl who'd once driven a car into her ex's living room.

"Don't give you what?" said Tara.

"That fuckin' Carly Simon, Stevie Nicks bullshit. The wise-woman routine. You don't get to write the book on me."

"I don't know what that means. Carly Simon?"

"I mean you're just as vain and psycho as I am. Just 'cause you're stuck with a kid all day makes you steady hands all of a sudden. And all that stuff about men running away, that's about that deadbeat dad of hers. That's not about *me*."

Wait . . . *was* it about him? *Was* she mad he hadn't made a grander gesture? She'd acted like she'd wanted him to just disappear, all those months, she'd been so moody.

"Okay, I think you should go now, Rudy. I've got work soon anyway."

"I thought we were having dinner. I just got here." It was always rough-and-tumble with them. They could get into it, and then snap back, like nothing had even happened.

"And now I'd like you to leave," she said.

"I didn't mean to be an asshole. Okay? I'm sorry. I just thought you of all people would have a little bit more faith in me is all. *You* know what it's like. Explaining to your elders over Guinness pie at some cirrhosis case's wake that you're trying to be an actor. Or a dancer. Or whatever. That you've got . . . notions, about your time on Earth, that don't involve being a bartender or cop, and watching them look at you like you just confessed to being some kind of a molester. All those nobodies, fine being nobodies, needing you to be a nobody too, just to keep up their morale. I thought you of all people could relate to that . . . frustration. I thought you were like me. I *thought*."

The baby started wailing, and Tara picked her up.

"No one's like you, Rudy. Isn't that what you really wanna hear? You're a very, very special person."

She said it with such dead eyes, such a flat, sarcastic, hateful tone, it chilled his blood. And the way she held that baby as he headed for the door, shushing it and burping it, making a big show of her motherhood, in love with her own wholesomeness . . . he saw right through it. Like she was some kind of a saint now. Our Lady of Pumps. Anyone could shit a kid out and take pretty decent care of it. It couldn't have been *that* hard.

Walking out he could feel the wad of cash inside his coat pocket. Just the heft of it was reassuring to him. There'd be a Chase somewhere on his way back to the city.

• • •

ON MONDAY MORNING the lobby was crawling with detectives. There had been thefts from some of the apartments, jewelry mostly. The residents were all asquawk, some of them already firing staff they were suspicious of, maids and nannies walking out red-faced throughout the morning, one of them carrying a bucket with Pine-Sol and a broom, the saddest severance package in the world.

The thefts were meant to have happened over the Christmas holidays, when everybody was in Florida and Jackson Hole. Right when Rudy'd started working there, coincidentally, which wasn't a great advertisement for his vigilance. Whatever . . . *he* hadn't done it. Ron the super played the drill sergeant, chewing everybody out, waxing official with his little speech about how those who failed to report important information would be swiftly punished, how the eyes of 811 Park were on them all.

It *was* probably an inside job, if not a doorman then one of the army of helpers and servants and maintenance workers going in and out on their say-so, and whoever'd done it, frankly, they'd had the right idea. The items hadn't even been reported missing until the last weekend in January, which showed you how much these people valued their fine things. Had a diamond bracelet worth twenty thousand dollars just hanging around, not even worthy of the safe, and didn't notice it was missing 'til it happened to complement your eveningwear. That they'd noticed at all was really a coincidence, and now their precious items were so far down the Silk Road on 47th Street there'd be no tracing them. Whoever did it was untouchable. Not to mention rich. Rudy was a little jealous.

Late in the afternoon, a rainy Tuesday, somebody came in he didn't recognize. A youngish man, white, or mostly, in a distressed leather jacket two sizes too big for him, soaking wet. He pretended to look at the tapestry for a while, shifting on his heels. He seemed nervous.

"May I help you, sir?" said Rudy.

"Me? Yeah, yeah, I'm looking for somebody." He came up to the front desk. "Jacob Cohen. Does he live here?"

Rudy couldn't imagine what kind of business he'd be here on, though it couldn't have been anything good, to look at him. . . . Mark David Chapman vibes. He had that frenzied, sickly aura to him, a deadness to him. Full of violent premonitions. It set the room atilt.

Rudy hadn't had to deal with this kind of thing before. The place was like a fortress, and the people in the building, they weren't celebrities. They were more powerful than that, and more anonymous, and if there were those on the upper floors with skeletons in their closets, or sins to answer for—oil spills in the Amazon, corporate graft—they were not the kinds of things the public knew about. People didn't just wander in with scores to settle.

"May I see some ID, sir?" Rudy said.

The man fished around in his pants pockets. A bunch of loose change fell to the ground as he came up with his wallet. It was a New York State license. From way up near the Canadian border. Parishville. Jeremy McLean was his name.

For a split second it occurred to Rudy that this was some kind of ruse, that he was one of Valentin's goons trying to get back at Jake for trespassing. But, no, no—this man was no hired hand. Too hapless to be representing anybody but his own lost, bug-eyed self. And he didn't have that Brighton Beach style about him. He was pure country. The nu-metal beard, the pupils like pinpricks. Rudy'd seen faces like his in a phalanx around midtown. The walking dead. He might have even kicked him out of Liffey's once, with less tact than he was trying to muster now.

"What business are you here on, Mr. McLean?"

"It's not business. I mean, it is. It's private, though. Don't he live here?"

"I think you must have the wrong address, sir. There's no one by that name that lives here."

"I don't think you're right, man. I saw it. I read it in the paper."

He took a crumpled-up piece of paper out of his coat pocket. The ink was smeared with rain. It was an article from the *New York Post* from this morning, about the thefts. Jacob's name had been included in a list of high-profile residents of the building. Under other circumstances, Jake'd probably be thrilled as hell just to be mentioned in the same breath as Bruce Ratner.

"There's no one by that name who lives here, sir."

"But it says right here—"

"It's possible he moved out before I started working here, and they were basing it on outdated information," Rudy said. "Do yourself a favor, don't believe everything you read."

"Well, I don't mind if I take a seat a little while. My leg hurts. It's raining outside, you know?"

"You can't sit there. This is private property, and only residents or guests of residents are allowed to sit there."

"I'm a US veteran—" the man said.

"And I appreciate your service."

"And who the fuck are you?"

"I'm someone who'll be calling the police if you don't get the fuck out of here immediately."

The elevator dinged. An old woman from the tenth floor walked past, carrying her little dog.

"Good afternoon, Mrs. Arnold," Rudy said. Big phony smile. She just kept walking. The whole building was on edge with the robberies. Even tighter-assed than usual.

"Well, you can tell him I'll be back," the man said. "And I don't believe you for one second that he isn't here. You can tell him I'll be seeing him. And soon."

Rudy felt like a piece of shit watching him leave. Not just for failing to invite a serviceman to sit, just . . . there was no good way to handle that kind of situation, without both parties feeling cheaper for it. The guy seemed like an asshole, and quite possibly deranged, but Rudy could only begin to imagine his exasperation, what a cold and mawkish circus New York City must be to somebody like him. And maybe it was the cumulative weight of many interactions like the one they'd just had—being read the riot act, being told to go away—that turned people like that man from misfits into mall shooters, and Rudy'd had a part in it. He called Jake.

"Jeremy McLean? Doesn't ring a bell . . . No, doesn't ring a bell at all." He let out a deep breath. "It's Whac-a-Mole, Rudy, it's Whac-a-Mole. Eliminate one source of stress, and there's another. It's the death threats, it's—"

"Death threats? You don't think this is related to, you know, this weekend."

"Oh no. No no. *Val?* Not that he hasn't threatened me before. Plenty of times. But even Val wouldn't be stupid enough to lash out now. He's done for. He's been arraigned in just the last few days for about the fifteenth time. Caught hiding his money in the Cook Islands or somewhere."

"But death threats . . . death threats from who?"

"Oh, that's just the cost of doing business, Rudy. It could be anyone. Some four-hundred-pound person living in his mother's basement, who couldn't approach me if he tried. He couldn't fit through the front door. People read things on the internet, they make false connections, they grow obsessed. And for every wealthy, influential person daring to live his or her life there's a sick, lonely individual sticking pins into a doll, thinking his idleness will somehow right the wrongs of capitalism. But that's one thing. Actually approaching where I *live*, well, that's, well . . . that's another . . . that's very disturbing, that's . . ." This person hadn't seemed like what he was describing now at all. He wasn't some misguided zealot. He *knew* Jake.

"Listen. I'm meant to take a trip next weekend, to Atlanta. It's the Super Bowl. There'll be some business associates there, possible investors, and, well, I have to show my face."

Was he asking him to come along, as his personal security detail, to the Super Bowl? Yes. Fuck yes. Rudy would love to.

"What I'd really appreciate is for you to look after the family while I'm gone. My mother, she's a little bit . . . she wanders off at night sometimes, and with the robberies, my wife's completely shook. We've been spared so far, thank God, but that kind of thing makes you question the moral character of whoever's minding the shop downstairs. It's outrageous."

"Yeah. Yeah, it is," said Rudy. "Outrageous."

"You I trust. And it'd be a heck of an easy commute."

"You mean, stay there? Are you sure your family would be comfortable with that? I've barely even met your w—"

"And of course, it goes without saying that I'd pay you."

7

"OF COURSE Mother thought the worst of Melvin. When she *first* met him. She thought he was a slicker. He loved business. On my side of the family were all artists and musicians. Uncle Isaac played the harp once for the czar."

He was sitting in the kitchen with Jake's mother, Anna, and his kids. Jake had said how his mom was losing it and she couldn't live alone anymore, though she seemed all right to Rudy. Very chatty, her hair all done. Granted she repeated things, and needed things repeated, but so did people he knew in their forties, in their fifties. And at least the things she said were worth repeating—stories of her travels, of growing up in old New York. Not like how Dad almost served a pot roast once to Benny Goodman.

"And what are you," she said. "Are you a German?"

Their kitchen was unbelievable, like something out of a magazine. They had some totally over-the-top limited edition Dolce and Gabbana–designed espresso machine, red and gold, with little Renaissance idylls painted on the body. Rudy'd seen it once at a home goods store in a mall and wondered what kind of pervert would spend their money on a thing like that. Now he knew. It actually looked okay.

"Me? Oh, no. I'm Irish," Rudy said. "Rudy's just a nickname. I had pretty bad rosacea as a kid. It was Ruddy, then it was Rudy, then—it's not a good story. But it stuck. It was easier than Oisin."

Anna shook her head. "There was an Irish family in our building, when we lived up in the Bronx. One day the young woman and her baby jumped eight stories from the rooftop. Flew right past my window. I was six. *I* thought it was a pigeon . . . But it turned out how that baby was her son, *and* her brother. Can you imagine? That bloodstain stayed at least until we moved. Maybe longer. It was like those atom shadows from the people at Hiroshima. They had to scrape them off the sidewalk."

"Grandma," said the girl, eating her pancakes. "Please."

"You're good-looking, though. What are you, some kind of gigolo?"

"Gigolo." The son laughed. "That s-s-s-sounds like J-J-Jell-O."

"That's true . . ." said Rudy. "But, no. No, I'm the doorman. I'm a friend of Jake's." They'd been over this a couple times. "There've been robberies in the building, so he—your son—he wanted some extra security while he was away."

"But what if you're the robber," Anna said.

"Well, you're right, I could be. But don't worry. I'm too slow. And I look terrible in diamonds." He got half a giggle from the kids for that line, lame as it was.

There was something dour about the two of them. The boy all hunched over eating his cereal, cowering like a golem. The sister with the pimples and the milkmaid braids, and dark rings under her eyes that looked like the sign of some kind of a vitamin deficiency. For two such flashy, polished parents, always on the make, seeing, being seen, some wires must have gotten crossed somewhere in the gene pool to wind up with such ghoulish children. Or maybe Jake and Nora's plans to fit in with the aristocracy had backfired; they were making all the right moves, raising them, but in the wrong century. They didn't realize being death-pale and reclusive were no longer signs of high-class breeding.

"Anna. It's time for your medicine."

Jake's wife, Nora, came into the kitchen. She was a terrifying person, especially with that syringe.

"Oh, sorry," Rudy said. "I shouldn't be in here. The kids invited me."

"It's fine," she said, like it was anything but. "Don't forget we're leaving at eleven, kids."

"Oh, you guys going out today? Anything fun?" said Rudy.

She injected Anna with her insulin, pretending not to hear him. She was passive-aggressive as hell, this lady. He could understand her feeling put upon by a stranger in her house, but he'd practically become her husband's right-hand man. All persecuted letting him in last night, making a face like he was really pushing it when he'd asked her where to find a bed-sheet. Like there was one square inch of the apartment *she* had earned. . . . Oh, but she'd been a model for ten minutes when she was twenty-one years old. A real career woman.

An hour later the kids were dressed and ready to go, headed to a birthday party somewhere. Rudy wasn't sure what he was meant to do all day—Jake had been extremely vague about it. Just told him where he kept the gun, and to make himself at home.

"Excuse me, please! Come here, please! *Excuse* me!"

He heard a voice from a distant wing, and followed the sound down the hallway. Nora was standing at her bedroom door, in a silk robe and with an eye mask on her head. She'd been up and dressed an hour ago.

"Are you all right?" said Rudy. "What's going on?"

"I'm meant to take them to this—this—this *thing*, at Chelsea Piers, but I can't go now—you'll have to take them."

"Jake said to keep close to home."

"And I'm saying for you to take them."

"Can't Anna take them?"

"No, what? No. Of course not. She's eighty-two."

She seemed completely fine, Anna. And he wasn't her fuckin' nanny.

"Can't they just . . . not go?"

"It's Henry Blount's *son's party*," she said. Like he had any clue who the hell that was. He just stared at her.

"So?" she asked. "Can you *do* it?"

129

He knew he could only stay so long in Jake's good graces if he didn't do exactly what she told him, and watch his tone while doing it. And she did look genuinely not well, whatever was going on with her. Though frankly she seemed like a miserable cunt who deserved it.

"There's a present on the entryway table," she said. "It's Chelsea Piers, the hockey rink. Blount is the name. Make sure they have their mittens, and their pom-pom hats, and they should text me the *second* they get there. *And* before they leave. And absolutely *no* cake or pizza if it has gluten in it. Make sure to ask. It gives them terrible cramps. This is for the cabs." She practically threw a fifty in his face. "I'm expecting change," she said, and slammed the door.

IT WAS A LOT FASTER just to take the train. It took each kid about ten swipes to get the MetroCard through. There was a line of people forming behind them, Rudy apologizing to everybody for the holdup. There was an old Black woman with a covered wagon's worth of groceries from CTown, looking pretty ready to get where she was going.

"What, you've never taken the subway before?" said Rudy, when they finally made it through.

The girl, Marley, looked sheepish. "I mean . . . we take cabs," she said.

Some pair they made on the train, in matching peacoats, holding hands. A homeless veteran came through the car with his tale of woe, collecting alms in his Chicago Bulls cap. They looked completely shocked and awed. The girl had a little coin purse from Kate Spade she emptied out, fifteen quarters' worth, then nudged her brother to do the same. She searched her pockets for anything else and came up with a fiver in Great British pounds and a buy-one-get-one-free card to a frozen yogurt place. He guessed they meant well.

At 42nd Street a seat opened up, and Rudy sat down next to them.

"You think everything's okay with your mother?" he asked.

"Well, she gets these migraines. Really bad ones," Marley said. "Where it's like her brain is being cleaved in two, for hours. And they come on really suddenly."

"Oh, wow, that's terrible . . ."

"But sometimes I think she also uses them as an excuse to just, like, exit life. You never know what's actually going on with her. With either of them really."

"What makes you say that?" said Rudy. The mother was one thing, but Jake seemed like he'd be the most emotionally available parent in the world.

"Just, no reason really, it's just . . . they're super slippery is all. Mom, she can be kinda grumpy."

"Oh . . . really? No . . ."

"I think she might be really unhappy. And sometimes I don't even think she wants to be happy. I think secretly she'd rather sit around sulking about how Daddy stole her voice or whatever than actually do something." She was pretty forthcoming, for such a shy-seeming kid. Once you got her talking. "And Daddy. He's so dismissive. Like if I tell him to recycle a Chobani container or something he's all, Okay, Greta Thunberg, like the whole world's a joke to him. Like anyone's being mindful or careful or conflicted about anything is them just being trendy, or weak, or a weasel. It is so infuriating it makes me want to scream. Or just do something, like, really drastic, just to get him to know I'm not joking around."

"What do you mean, drastic?" You heard about these kids going apeshit on their parents just to make a point, slitting their wrists for show. "Drastic like what?"

"I don't know, maybe getting really drunk sometime."

"Oh, well . . . that'd be fine," he said. "I mean, no it wouldn't, just . . . don't do anything."

"Honestly sometimes I think they're gonna get divorced. Are your mom and dad divorced?"

"Well, they're not together," Rudy said. "But my mom and dad were never married."

"Really? That c-can happen?" J. J. said.

"It can happen . . . it's been known to happen."

It had been a huge point of shame for Dad, in his piety, that he could never get his mom to take the bait. Lying to everyone that they'd eloped to Atlantic City. Rudy only found out he was a bastard on his eighteenth birthday, Dad pulling him aside, practically in tears. Like Rudy gave a shit.

It was just as well. You could not imagine a more mismatched couple in creation than his parents. Except for maybe these kids' parents. The thought of how Jake and Nora had even got together, that was science fiction to the mind. . . . She must've had some money issues, daddy issues back in the day. Charmed by what a loudmouth he was, glad to let him take the reins, the very things she'd come to hate his guts for down the road. He must've thought she looked good, some shiksa goddess arm candy, 'til he realized how her poise was just stone-coldness by a nicer name. Poor Jake. He was a mensch. Full of energy and love. No wonder he was always running around, working like a dog, and spending his rare days off trying to get Rudy and the Carlo's Tire and Rims guys to hang out with him. He needed to get away from her.

"And Daddy's businesses," said Marley, "there's so much secrecy involved. It's like he's making all these sketchy deals, and—"

"Why, did someone say something to you?" said Rudy. "Has someone ever threatened you or anything?"

"Oh no. Nothing like that. Though one time my Uncle Meyer told me how Big Taxi got rich off the backs of impoverished immigrants and that our money's really blood money, and that by living in my father's house I'm complicit in it. I didn't tell Daddy about it 'cause I knew he'd go berserk—he really doesn't like him, Meyer—and I was too young to really know what he was talking was about."

"Well, that's completely insane. You're a kid, first of all. What are you supposed to do, move out? How your dad makes his money, even if it was that bad, which it's not, it has nothing to do with you."

"Yeah, I *guess* not . . ."

She wasn't buying that line for a second. She was probably being fed a lot of stuff at school about the sin of privilege, whatever it took for the powers-that-be at Chapin or wherever to perform their civic virtue while charging sixty thousand bucks a year to keep the plebs out.

"Some people are just nuts," said Rudy. "You can't listen to them. They hide behind their outrage just to fill a void in *themselves*. You think your Uncle Meyer would give two hoots about Karl Marx if he was better-looking?"

"When did you meet Uncle Meyer?"

"Oh, I haven't, yet . . . but I was a bartender. I've met everybody. And I've seen pictures."

"So you guys are really close now, you and Daddy."

"Your dad's a very open guy. Very generous. Don't let anyone but *him* convince you otherwise."

He felt bad for the girl. She was in dire need of attention. Jake was by all accounts a loving father but could barely sit still, and was probably not much of a listener, if Rudy had to guess, and her mother was a frosty, imperious shrew, and this girl was stuck somewhere in the middle. Reading Russian novels to her grandma as she fell asleep, bringing her brother to physical therapy if it conflicted with their mom's colonic. Doing her homework in the waiting room while he got rolled around on a bouncy ball. . . These poor kids. What was the point in being rich if you looked like shit and you never had any fun?

Childhood, adolescence hadn't been no cakewalk for Rudy, with his mother gone, and money always tight, but he'd always had a good time. Always. He'd always been a happy kid. At J. J.'s age he'd been unstoppable, convinced the moon was hung for him alone. No doubt in his mind the road would always rise to meet him. An obnoxious youth, in his Slim Shady phase, already having touched a tit, gangsta-signing in every photograph with absolute conviction. The doubt, the loneliness, the what-am-I-here-for . . . that all came only later.

The parents had rented the whole Sky Rink out at Chelsea Piers, which probably cost as much as some folks' weddings. The grown-ups gathered near the end zone, the dads in their Citibank fleeces and the mothers with their highlights and plastic glasses of prosecco, everybody smug as hell, talking and laughing their heads off. J. J. got shepherded into a group of boys and handed a hockey stick and mask, not a single kid from his class even acknowledging he'd come. The birthday boy, Henry Jr., looked like the future preppie killer-rapist of America.

Marley got them some doughnuts and coffee and they sat down in the stands. At least they didn't have to talk to anybody but each other.

"What about school, though," Rudy said. "How's your social life?"

"Oh, God, it's a disaster," she said. "People are always telling you to be confident, and get out there, and then you do, and it, like, blows up in your face, and you wish you'd just stayed home."

"Yeah, I hear that."

"I went to meet up with this guy I know, that I kinda like, I guess, at this party the other week, and he seemed really weirded out that I'd showed up alone, and he kept disappearing with his friends to go smoke cigarettes on the balcony and I ended up just hanging out with the person whose house it was's dog and eating Popchips by myself. He texted me to say he was *sorry*, but . . ."

"Well, there you go," said Rudy. "That's something. Most guys wouldn't even be capable of *that* much."

She should take whatever action she could get, this girl. She couldn't have been bound for an easy time in that department. All the guys her age, raised on porn, the permatans of Instagram . . . hers was not the kind of look to be setting fuckboy hearts aflame.

"You gotta meet up with him when he's not distracted by his stupid friends, though. Teenage boys and their friends are toxic. Meet up with him one-on-one. Someplace where it's just the two of you. I don't mean in, like, an *alleyway* or something. You know, be smart about it. But try to get to him alone."

She nodded.

"And I'm sorry, but . . . you can't be showing up to parties by yourself. It sucks that solitude is frowned upon, but you've gotta have a wingwoman. Even if it's someone you don't even really respect or like that much that you're just using as a human prop to get you in the door, that's okay. You've gotta have somebody, anybody, and the rest will start to fall in line."

"But not, like, Tina Schmiege," she said.

"Oh, I don't know her but, no . . . maybe not her."

She finished her coffee. She was like a miniature woman, very sophisticated in her way.

"Sometimes I feel like with people," she said, "like even if I like them, like I'm always a little bit removed, no matter what, you know? Like there's some joke I missed the beginning of five years ago and now I can follow along and nod and pretend to laugh at the punch line but I still don't *really* get what they're talking about, or what's so goddamn funny, and I never really will. Did you ever feel that way?"

"At your age? Never—not at all," said Rudy.

"Oh."

"But now? *Now* I fuckin' feel that way. All the time. But you're better off like this, believe me . . . Peaking early is a curse."

"I've got, like, nine missed calls from Mom," said Marley, on their way up in the elevator.

135

Nora was standing in the kitchen when they got back, dressed, arms crossed, apparently recovered from her episode. She seemed to waver between being a falling-apart basket case and totally composed and officious; it was a very unappealing spectrum.

"I need to talk to you," she said, and pulled Rudy aside into the hall. His stomach dropped. The kids had had their fill of cake and pizza at the party, but there's no way she could've known that. Though she probably would soon.

She said, "Anna's gone."

"As in . . . deceased?"

"I mean, she left. She wandered off."

"Weren't you with her?"

"She always has her nap at noon. So I thought nothing of it. Then I went into the room to check on her and she was just . . . not there."

He knew it. He shouldn't have listened to her when she told him to go out. His whole job was to sit vigil. Jake had been extremely clear about that.

"Well, she seems pretty with it, though, right?" he said, trying not to panic. "Maybe she went out for a walk. She's capable of getting back on her own . . . right?"

"Her phone, keys, and wallet are all in her purse, in her room," she said. "And her glasses."

"Her glasses? They're for reading, though."

"I don't think so."

They were for trucks. They were for seeing fucking trucks coming at her.

"She goes into this sort of . . . trance sometimes," Nora said. "She's only made it as far as down the hall before, maybe to the lobby. But I've looked everywhere. I would say we all go out, but I don't want to scare the kids."

Downstairs he checked the security cameras and sure enough she'd wandered out an hour ago. Walked right past the front desk without a coat, knocking into things, with that nothing-for-brains fatty Dominic sitting right there, making love to his chicken parmigiana. No wonder there'd been thefts in the building. The place was being manned by morons.

He went outside. She'd have died of hypothermia already if she'd managed to avoid a dozen other hazards. It'd been an hour already. A whole hour. Anything could've happened in that time, and whatever it was it would be his fault—Nora wouldn't think twice about throwing him under the bus. And as nice as Jake had been to him there'd been flashes of that other side, that pit bull in the business world. You didn't want to cross him by so much as refusing the offer of a lunch, let alone killing his mother.

He called the major hospitals, the senior center on Third. No sign of her. He couldn't call the cops and bring them into it. Not yet. Jake was the type to be on chatting terms with half the precinct.

He had to *think*. How far could she have gotten on her little legs, at her age? Wherever she was going, it had to have made sense to *her*. Though who could know the mind of a bat-blind, memory-addled, eighty-something woman. (Then again, *he* could, if anybody could . . . dead-in-life more times than he could count, a blackout case somnambulating through the streets, the hours, the curbs shapeshifting on him, speaking doggerel to himself. And yet he'd always somehow been okay, some inner pilot guiding him toward home. Some beacon in the night, guiding his keys into the door. He would forget his name, but never his umbrella. The brain was full of mysteries. . . .)

He walked toward the park, absolutely panic-stricken now. Going west was all that he could think to do. Anna'd talked about how much she missed it over there—the café at Zabar's every morning with her friends, her favorite used bookstore on Broadway. Everybody Rudy passed he envied that they didn't have his problem. Even the roly-poly half-neck person whose whole job was to sort the paper from the plastics at 740 Madison—Rudy would've zapped himself into his body right that second. Taken his whole life on, the whole sad, luckless span of it, just to rid himself of the burden of the last few minutes, and the next few hours.

On 69th Street a cyclist almost ran him over. "Watch it, *fucker!*" Rudy called after him. You had to put these people in their place. Some web-developer-looking fuck from Sausalito or wherever, AirPods in, not even looking up. He couldn't stand these cyclists, their contempt for pedestrians. Their rude good health. They would save the planet and mow down all the people in the meantime.

As he was flipping him the bird he saw a figure one block down, standing in the middle of Fifth Avenue, swaying, staring into traffic, completely deranged-looking. Horns were blaring, drivers cursing at her. His body moved before his brain confirmed that it was really her, the two of them swerving past the bike lane, onto the curb, falling and rolling side to side over the sidewalk, someone on the corner yelling, "Woah!! . . . Oh!! . . . Look out!!," and for a second he was sure he'd killed her.

• • •

THEY PADLOCKED all the doors that night, front and back, the windows too. Anna retired after Nora drew a bath for her, completely oblivious that her vision quest this afternoon had even happened. Rudy had a couple scrapes where he had hit the pavement, but he'd somehow managed to muffle her impact.

"I'm sorry for this happening," Nora said to him, before she went to bed. "It's completely my fault. Thank you for taking care of it. Really—you probably saved her life."

Probably? He'd definitely saved her fuckin' life. And Jake couldn't even know to give him credit for it.

"You're welcome," he said. He wasn't gonna get anywhere by being shitty with her.

Around 10 p.m. the house was quiet. Sitting in his room he thought he'd jump out of his skin. The TV said NO SIGNAL, with a bunch of disconnected wires he couldn't figure out. There was some kind of a sex party going on next door, in the old hotel, two prostitutes a fat man and a bottle, but even that couldn't hold his attention for long. He wished he'd brought a bottle of his own with him. A cigarette, by God. . . .

He had dodged the bullet of the century earlier, but it was a lot more humbling than exhilarating. He was living on thin ice. Even the doorman job, beneath him as it was, wasn't a sure thing—word was the guy who he was filling in for would be getting his new liver any day now.

He realized how dependent he'd become on Jake's largesse, how his whole concept of the future had come to orbit around him . . . that hairy, roilsome little man, bursting with opinions. He'd been prepared if things went south today to blow up that relationship, move right along, another bit of earth scorched, same as always. But he really didn't want to have to. Not today, and not soon. Or ever, necessarily.

At eleven he noticed the smell of smoke coming through the window. The whole house was asleep, and no one in it smoked. He went into the kitchen. There were two sets of huge French doors with a balustrade outside. One of the doors was half-open, with someone's shoulder visible. An interloper. This would be the test of him. He wasn't about to drop the ball now. He grabbed a knife, and opened the door all the way.

"Woah! Woah!"

Nora was against the outside wall, smoking, in a mink coat, with a cocktail shaker and a massive, fuck-off-sized martini glass at her feet.

"Sorry, sorry—" Rudy said.

"Jesus Christ!" she said. "You *scared* me! I almost fell over the edge!"

"I'm really sorry. I didn't mean to interrupt. I was just paranoid and checking everything was okay out here, you—you go back to your thing."

"Hey—" she said as he was closing the door, "I never do this." Did she think he gave a shit? "Your secret's safe with me."

"Do you want one?" she asked.

He was dying for one. "Yes, actually," he said, putting down the knife.

"Close the door, though, please," she said as he came out. "All the way. I don't want the smell inside."

It wasn't so much a balcony as a suicide perch. Not much standing room. Nora was stone-silent for a whole five minutes, after giving him a light. Like she couldn't be bothered making conversation. Or had forgotten he was there, even.

Finally he asked, "Do you have some kind of a problem, ma'am?"

"No," she said. "I don't have a problem with you. I don't even know you."

She didn't look at him at all, just stood there smoking with that steely, ice-blue gaze of hers, her eyes fixed hard across the street. The moon was almost full.

After a minute she said, "I have a problem with my husband for getting us into situations where people like you are necessary."

"People like me?" he said.

"I don't mean that the way it sounds, I just mean . . . security."

"The robberies? Jake had no control over that."

"I know it's not about that," Nora said. "He's been paranoid for years. Sending the three of us to our summer house without him while he tends to business . . . while things *cool off* in the city? Whatever that means . . . Random guys named Spiros at my children's birthday parties. You know J.J. found a gun in his office desk once. No safety lock, in the same drawer where he keeps the Post-its. He went through a phase, J.J., he loved sticking Post-its on himself. That day . . . I think that day alone gave me some kind of nervous disorder. It definitely led me back to *this*." She gestured to her cigarette.

"I wasn't always like this. It's Jacob, it's the city, it's . . . maybe it's just me . . . I've begged to leave New York a hundred times. Some days I want to run for cover, just walking down the street.

140

I think pieces of the buildings are falling on my head. I go out to lunch with my girlfriends and I listen to them talk and I think, where is the . . . where is the wellspring? Where is this . . . *trough* of self-regard you're all drinking from? To go about your days, with your stupid, stupid, stupid bullshit, and be so goddamn—" She cut herself off. "You know what? Sorry, I'm sorry—I must sound insane right now."

"No, not at all," said Rudy. It was the first thing to come out of her mouth he could relate to in the slightest.

She poured herself another drink, and passed it to him, and they leaned against the ledge. She got sloppy as she talked more. She was all over the map.

"Jake was on the warpath to get him a wig, for a while. He was best friends for five minutes with some wig technician to the stars he met on vacation in LA. Six thousand dollars on some Dorothy Hamill–looking mushroom cap and press-on eyebrows. Of course he didn't wear it once . . . Poor baby. He's so sweet, isn't he?"

"He is," said Rudy.

"He's *so, soo* sweet. He's my perfect baby. But I worry about him constantly. Other kids can be such fucking assholes."

"Well, you're right," he said. "And you can't control them. But all this pomp and circumstance around him. This doom and gloom . . . it can't be good for him. He gets treated like some hemophiliac. He's healthy, right?"

"Yes, he is, thank God."

"So . . . so fuck it if he's bald. Or talks a little different. Of course if you insist on surrounding yourself with the most polished, highest-functioning people on planet Earth, he's gonna look like he's retarded. Not that he looks like he's—what I'm saying is, he's *not* retarded." That hadn't come out right.

"No, I understand what you're saying. I agree with you. I wanted to send him to a specialized school. His IQ is normal, better than normal, I just thought it would be better for him socially, being somewhere less intense. But Jake was adamant that him being in one of 'those places' would instill in him a *loser's mentality*, or something. And he, well . . . I think Jake wanted that Buckley pennant in his office, more than anything."

Rudy couldn't picture Jake as being quite that status-conscious. Though he guessed he was. He wanted that Park Avenue, Harvard-bound clout without ever giving up his right to call bullshit on it, as it suited him. There were worse hypocrisies in life, but still . . .

She told him all about herself. Growing up in Mahwah, New Jersey, in the boonies, her father gone, her mother needy, a string of deadbeat stepfathers who'd always held the hug too long. How her older brother Frank had died in a motorcycle wreck when he was sixteen, and she was twelve. How her second pregnancy had almost killed her, Jake working all the time those years, her stuck at home worried sick about the baby, way behind on all his milestones, eighteen months before he grasped a binky, a year before he ever smiled. Her attempts to get back out there hadn't come to much, though she'd just gotten her GED, she said, and was applying to some colleges to study clinical psychology.

She seemed to know a lot, about a lot, but she didn't really use it. And she was very, very beautiful, but she didn't seem to be enjoying it. Her beauty she wore awkwardly, almost scornfully, in the way some model types did. Like it wasn't really hers. Like it was just some valise full of stolen cash some man had given to her, told her to look after. She was an odd bird. Raw-nerved half the time, like Marley had described her, almost painfully genteel, buzzing through the house like some deranged Victorian heroine, puffing pillows, scowling at sconces, ready to burst into tears with one harsh word from the plumber, and then you got some gin in her and she'd be talking like some salty dame who really knew the score. It was hard to get a read on her. A man like Jake, with very little time, he'd probably stopped trying, years ago.

"You know, you seem to take great care of Anna," Rudy said.

"Except for the losing her for two hours part, you mean."

"It happens. But no, I know that that's no easy thing. Taking care of somebody, the dirty work especially, when they're not your flesh and blood."

"Anna's always been extremely kind to me," she said. "You hear about these nightmare mothers-in-law, but she's been totally laid-back and nonjudgmental about everything. It's just who she is. Or was . . . I don't know. She didn't even make a stink when I didn't convert. Whereas Melvin barely looked at me again. Except for at my tits, sometimes."

"Jake seems to revere his father."

"Melvin was severely overrated."

She lit another cigarette. She could really smoke, this lady. She couldn't have had too many outlets for stress release—Jake had mentioned how his heart pills gave him some libido problems.

"I guess I feel sentimental about her too, 'cause my parents are both dead. She's our last living link, you know? Are you close with your parents, Rudy?"

He hadn't been sure she knew his name. He shrugged. "My dad's in Queens," he said. "We're having a little bit of a tiff right now. But mostly we're okay. My mom went to rehab when I was six, never really came back. A hundred relapses, and now she's, yeah . . . God knows."

"Do you ever try to contact her?"

"We're friends on Facebook. Though she posts some pretty crazy shit these days. Like about how the Irish were slaves too. I think they might've gotten to her. The mind-snatchers, you know."

He'd last seen his mom eight years ago, at his St. Ignatius graduation. She'd been sober, at least for the duration, though it seemed like whatever pills they had her on had rerouted the oxygen from her brain into her face. All swollen like a beached whale, smiling but completely dotty. A thwarted, brittle woman, three beats behind the conversation, wearing a lei she probably

143

got at a Jimmy Buffett's or someplace, trying to be festive. She'd looked totally nuts. Seeing her that day, in his cap and gown, had been such a disappointment to him. It would've been less painful to think of her as some fallen supernova, too bright for the world, snuffed out, than another washup case just living out her term.

"Well," said Nora, "I'm not going to lecture you about how you'll regret it for the rest of your life if you don't make an effort with her, *but* . . . you'll regret it for the rest of your life if you don't make an effort with her. With both of them. Believe me. Before it's too late."

"Yeah, yeah . . . I'll do it later."

He'd been mired too long in all of that. The ties that bind. Now was the time to be out there, getting after things, not yakking away in the court of arbitration, going over the whole past. When it was time to pack it in, go home and talk it over, he would know. In the meantime forgiveness was of no use to him. It wouldn't solve the ego-panic, and it wouldn't pay the bills.

THEY GOT PUMMELED by snow Sunday morning. Nora brought up bagels and lox from a place on Lexington. They played backgammon and Chinese Checkers in the kitchen, Anna with her cup of tea, peaceful enough but vacant-eyed. It seemed like in just the last twenty-four hours she'd turned a corner, onto nowhere good.

Marley said she needed help with something for her school. She was auditioning to assistant-direct a production of *The Glass Menagerie*, and she asked everybody to run some lines for her, to practice.

"Do you guys do this kind of thing a lot?" Rudy asked her. They were in the living room, him rearranging furniture.

"What kind of thing?" she said.

"Just, put plays on in your living room?"

These uptown kids were a different make. Like the landed

gentry, with their drawing-room charades. He'd have been grunted off the face of the earth if he'd ever asked his dad or uncle to help with something like that.

"Oh, no, not really. Daddy doesn't have much patience for the arts. I think the end table would be better over there, actually."

"You got it."

Watching Marley do her thing, how clear her vision was, how determined she seemed to get the set just right, he hoped she wouldn't take one lick of his advice from yesterday about getting out there more. People who could focus, really focus, who cared enough to want to make things, should be encouraged to stay home and make them. Fuck going to some shitty party. Besides, you heard these cautionary tales about girls like her who bit off more than they could chew, went from staging plays with their stuffed animals to class pump overnight, to prove their worth, and all hell breaking loose. She should enjoy being a curious child for as long as life would let her. It was a good, good thing to be.

"Okay, so, we're gonna do the last scene," she said, handing out scripts to everyone. "Mom's gonna be the mom, Amanda. Basically you're like this fragile faded beauty who's a little bit phony and really stands on ceremony 'cause you hate your life. J.J., you be Jim, the gentleman caller, who—"

"Why can't Rudy be Jim?" said J.J.

"'Cause Rudy's gonna be Tom. He's clearly Tom."

"Why c-c-can't *you* be Tom?"

The poor kid was terrified of reading aloud. Rudy didn't know whether they were supposed to force him, throw him into the deep end, where he'd discover how the theater was the key to unlocking his self-expression or whatever, and the rest would be history. Not today.

"You know what," Rudy said, "J. J. can be the *assistant* assistant director. That's the most important job in the whole show."

"Oh yeah? What d-do I do?"

"Well, you sit there and you make sure everything's running

145

smooth. You've got your imaginary bullhorn there. And if anybody acts up, if your mom and me are goofing off and flubbing our lines, you get to crack the whip. You're the backbone of the whole production."

Rudy'd read the play in high school but he didn't remember it that much. They did the part with Jim and Laura on their date, then Amanda telling Tom off. Nora was stiff and lousy as an actress but she seemed to be having fun for once in her life, trying to keep herself from laughing, the kids excited just to have her upright. It was a kid's pretend-audition in her living room, anyway, not the time to try to prove your chops.

"Well, okay," said Marley, after the scene. She looked disappointed. "I think that's gonna need some serious work. But it's okay. It's . . . anyway. Now Tom's gonna do his closing monologue. That's you again, Rudy. It's really an emotional piece of writing so you have to really, like, sell it. Don't just read it. Try to put yourself in his shoes. Daddy said you were an actor?"

"I mean, not really," he said. "In high school, a little bit."

"Okay, well, just do the best you can then."

He wasn't about to make this about him. He hated that whole thing—actors and their acting. He remembered some guy who used to come into the bar, who'd flown a kite once in a commercial for genital warts medicine, talking everybody's ears off about his method. It was all so overearnest and embarrassing, acting. Unless you were already famous for it.

He did it real slowly, not hammy in the least. The wild young man set loose upon the world, haunted by memories of the sister he'd left behind. Talking to her as if from on a cloud, beyond the grave. . . . Rudy remembered thinking the whole play was overrated, another case of the emperor's new clothes. All that oohing and ahhing on the human condition, the American theater with its gallery of strivers, its hidebound men and raving women. They all seemed like archetypes, back in the day. Now they were all too believable to him. They were his parents.

146

"Then all at once my sister touches my shoulder and I turn around and look into her eyes . . . Laura. Laura. I tried so hard to leave you behind me—"

Nora ran out of the room just then, for some reason.

"I reach for a cigarette, I cross a street, I run to the movies or to a bar. I buy a drink. I speak to the nearest stranger . . ."

When he finished with the speech Marley said, "Wow . . . that was . . . that was *great*."

J. J. said, "What's w-wrong with Mom?"

RUDY FOUND HER down the hall a few minutes later in the room they called the library, crying on the couch. Jesus Christ, this woman. He knew after last night she hadn't had the easiest life, but they had pills for this kind of thing. She must've known about them, from her friends.

"What happened?" Rudy asked her. "I thought we were having a great time in there."

"Oh, oh," she said, "it's *nothing*."

"It's obviously not nothing."

He sat down on the end of the couch. It was less like a library in here than the champagne room at a gays-only ski resort—shearling rugs and turquoise wallpaper, acrylic vases shaped liked butts. The only books still in their shrink wrap, some coffee-table dum-dum fare: *Palm Beach Interiors* and *The French Country Tabletop: A Journey Through Style.*

"You just reminded me so much of"—she could barely get the words out she was so upset—"of Frank."

"Of who?"

"Of *Frank!*"

Her dead brother. "Oh," he said.

"You're both so . . . so—I'm sorry. I don't know what's wrong with me."

She hung her head on a pillow.

"You're all right," he said. He wished that she would finish her sentence. "You're gonna be all right." He didn't know if it was inappropriate or what to rub her shoulder. But he did.

A month ago Rudy would've chalked this kind of thing up to some *Eat Pray Love* rich lady midlife horseshit, impossibly irrelevant to him, trivial beyond belief, but now that he was up close he thought, well, he actually felt bad for her. She was really going through something, Nora. She'd said how she was turning forty later in the year and feeling out of sorts, questioning the future, and the past.

Where Rudy came from no one cried, or changed, or tried to, ever. Everyone was closed for business, your character all done and dusted by the time you left high school. Changeable only by your tragedies, and only for the worse. Not so with these high-class ladies. They were tender creatures, full of feelings. They listened when you talked. They put on plays just out of interest, and bought peonies just to have around. They took the time to think about their happiness. Well . . . they *had* the time, but Rudy didn't hate them for it. Not like he felt he ought to.

She raised her head, wiping her tears away. Her neck was long, like a beautiful swan's.

She was lovelier than ever with her face all red and swollen. You couldn't say just what the signal was—a certain breathlessness to her expression, or the way that she was staring at his mouth—but for a second he was pretty sure she wanted him to kiss her. He was almost positive about it. But you could never be too sure about that kind of thing these days.

Anna barged into the room just then, looking panicked.

"Hello?" she said. "Have you seen it?"

"Seen what?" Nora said.

"My lunch. I just had it."

"You had it? Or you're looking for it?" Rudy said.

"What? How do you mean?"

She stood there gawping at them for a second, then made a face like, *screw you guys*, and left, slamming the door behind her.

Nora said, "You don't think she thought we—"

"No, God no." The old woman could barely feel her own face anymore, let alone a thing like sexual tension.

JAKE CALLED HIM late that night, after the game. "How'd it go?" Rudy asked him.

"Oh, I don't know. The blue team won. I'm more a baseball person."

It was the first time Rudy hadn't had money on the Super Bowl in more than half his life. He'd forgotten about the game completely.

"But the weekend went fantastic," Jake said. "To say I'm relieved is an understatement."

The deal Jake had been working on had gone through apparently. He'd sold all of his medallion debt to a hedge fund or something. He was unencumbered now, his company safe from financial ruin, and free to pursue other avenues of business. Real estate. He'd even talked about running for mayor in 2021.

"My flight's delayed until tomorrow. They've got me at some airport Hilton. I don't even mind the food, I'm so relieved."

"That's great," said Rudy. "Take a load off. You deserve it."

"What about there?"

"Well, I don't think your fears were justified," said Rudy. "I think that our . . . friend, from up north, I think that was a one-off thing. Though I don't wanna speak too soon."

"Well, it never hurts to be safe. Anyway, it's a rave. They all love you. My daughter said my wife wants to adopt you."

"Oh yeah?" Hmmm. . . .

"They said you were greater and more helpful than I could possibly know. I owe you. And, well . . . I would love to talk about you coming to work for me in a more official capacity."

Please, thought Rudy. Yes. It was time to have that conversation. He was tired of feeling like an errand boy.

"Though maybe you've got better things to do." Not really. "I

149

swear, we'll all be saying we knew you when, someday. Standing on the sidelines at your movie premieres, begging you to acknowledge us."

"Oh come on. You've never even seen me act." It was embarrassing to have someone commend you on something you literally hadn't done at all. "I could be a total hack for all you know."

"Nora said you made her cry. Not that it takes much, nowadays. But you're a natural, I can tell. I've been meaning to call my friend Scott, at Universal, up. I'm sorry I keep forgetting."

"No, it's cool, it's cool . . . whenever you get around to it."

Rudy wasn't sure how that kind of thing was meant to work. The guy was practically the CEO of Universal. What was Jake gonna say to him, the guy who sorts my mail's a natural, I can tell? Still, he hoped Jake *would* end up calling him. Sometimes you needed to just board the train, get a Mommy or Daddy figure to get you in the room so you could take it from there. Otherwise you'd never be heard. Just be lost out there in the sea of wannabes.

"In the meantime, you take care," said Jake. "I'll talk to you when I get back."

"Safe flight."

In the morning he went back to his apartment to shower and shave before work, though something seemed amiss. Someone had been through over the weekend. There were boot marks on the bath mat and in the living room, big workmen's boots, and cabinets left open, Sobranies in the ashtray. He didn't even know they sold Sobranies west of Moscow. Jake had mentioned how people would be walking through sometimes, contractors, repairmen, but he hadn't said how they'd be making themselves right at home and not cleaning up after their shit. There was something more than incidental in the mess that had been made. There was something hostile to it.

He fixed himself an instant coffee, coal tar-strong, and threw an egg onto the range, hopping in the shower, working himself down from his hissy fit. He'd been spending too much time around the haves, to be feeling so proprietary. Or he'd just been traumatized by Kronman and his creeps. He was sure there was an explanation for everything. And it's not like renter's rights applied to him when he wasn't even renting. He was mooching, for the moment.

The weekend couldn't have gone any better—he was glad—and things were looking up. He was working hard, making good money, not blowing it on stupid shit. He wasn't even drinking all that much. Eating just one meal a day, two max, and healthy. No McDonald's, no junk ever.

Shaving in the mirror, naked to the waist, he had to stop a second to admire himself. He was back. He was a fucking beast. No wonder people wanted him around.

He dropped his towel. He hadn't so much as glanced at his cock all weekend for fear of soiling their Egyptian-cotton sheets. Now he came like a bronco, and in the seconds leading up to it he couldn't help but think of her . . . Nora. What a fucking bitch she acted like, but wasn't. It drove him nuts.

He leaned hard against the bathroom sink, catching his breath. So she wanted to adopt him now, huh? Okay, he thought . . . okay. He guessed that was one way of putting it.

NOELLE STARTED SCREAMING her head off in computer lab. At first Marley thought that something terrible had happened, like her mom had died—she skied a lot—but then Noelle said how she'd just gotten into Exeter and started jumping up and down and screaming and all her friends started jumping with her, hugging her and screaming too, and Annabel Wyckoff started crying 'cause she said she was so happy for Noelle but she'd miss her so, so much.

"Well obviously you're gonna come visit me, like, all the time," Noelle said.

"I mean, I'm *literally* gonna live there," Annabel said.

It was almost obscene, being that pretty, and having that many friends, who liked you *that* much, and the thought of Exeter, of boarding schools in general . . . ivied gates and bells in towers, and coxswains napping shirtless just across the quad. It was meant to be the best school in the country or something. A conveyor belt to Harvard. Marley couldn't even tell if she was jealous of Noelle or what, her future sounded so unreal.

She was definitely jealous of the going somewhere else for high school part. *That* she knew. Though not to Exeter, just to anyplace. Though they didn't even seem to make any normal high schools in Manhattan. The only ones you heard about had either squash courts and spring break trips to Crete for your archaeology elective, or there were knife fights in the locker rooms and kids all getting headaches from the lead-based paint, and if she even *suggested* public school Daddy'd be all, well, *maybe*

Stuyvesant, but there's no way she could get in. The test to go for ninth grade was already over, and even if she could try for tenth she'd need about ten thousand dollars' worth of tutoring to get her math in shape, which would kind of undermine the whole pretense of a meritocracy, and *then* of course she'd be taking the place of some totally deserving kid whose whole life and whole family's destiny might actually be transformed to go there, so maybe it *was* the right thing to keep sucking down her parents' money (she'd worked it out once, about two hundred bucks per hour of schooling once you accounted for the closures for the Jewish holidays) to be kept in squash courts that she didn't use, with well-bred friends she didn't have. It was hard to think of an alternative. . . . Daddy always said how it was so expensive being rich, but guys like him controlled things, didn't they? Rich dads? So why not make *not* being rich less shitty? For their *own* sake, if nobody else's.

One of the perks—so far it was the only perk—of eighth grade spring semester was you got to leave the building by yourself on Thursdays during morning break. Most of the time she went to the deli on 82nd and Madison with Noor Shawaf to get a Vitamin-Water or an egg-and-cheese if she'd slept too late to eat at home, but today—miracle—Dimitri texted her and asked her if she wanted to meet up in the park.

She'd reached out to him again like Rudy the doorman had told her to, and they'd ended up meeting for a coffee last week and talking the whole afternoon. Nothing *happened.* But she wanted it to, really badly, and she got a feeling like he might want it to too.

She was looking pretty good lately, she had to admit, since she'd turned fourteen, and upped her dose of Accutane. Plus she'd discovered this way of doing her eyeliner that made her eyes look wider and more almond-shaped, less like Daddy's beady ones. And she *had* actually kissed somebody once, if you can believe it, so she wasn't totally out of her depth there. Her family friend, Ross DeLupe. (Though that kiss was about as

154

erotically charged as getting your retainer fitted. No one was as bad at anything as Ross DeLupe was at kissing. The deaf could hear, the blind could see better than Ross DeLupe could kiss. Of course you could say how it was half Marley's fault—it took two to tango, or not tango—but no way was it her fault, not even half. He wouldn't even let her *try* to do it right, with his ferret tongue darting and swizzling around like that. How could anybody be so artless? Had he ever *seen* a French film? Didn't he *know* the canonical passions they were meant to be aspiring to?)

Dimitri was sitting on a bench at the park entrance near the Met on 79th Street, smoking a cigarette. He was wearing a leather jacket, which must not've been very warm—it was mid-February, and freezing out—but he didn't even flinch. He was really a cool person, with something thorny and pugnacious in him, not easily amused. He looked, he sat, he *breathed* like somebody who knew what kissing was about.

"Hey," she said, and sat down next to him.

"Hey," he said. "How's the school day."

"Oh, it's pretty lame. Is your online thing going okay?"

After a lot of wrangling between his parents over tuition it was decided he would finish his junior year taking classes online, through this video app thing—which sounded awesome; she wished *she* could find a way to do that.

"It is what it is," he said. "My mom wants me back at Lawrenceville for next year, but I keep telling her to cut her losses. She'll need every penny she can get just for groceries. And she's all, *But what about their college guidance,* when fuck that. Higher education's all a racket anyway. And as soon as I turn eighteen, I'm volunteering for the IDF."

"What's that?"

"The Israeli Defense Forces?"

"Oh." Did he mean, like, war? "Don't you have to be Israeli?" Marley said.

"No, lots of people volunteer as lone soldiers."

"Oh, okay . . . why though?"

"What do you mean, why? You're not pro-Israel?"

"I mean, I guess I just don't know enough about the conflict to have a really strong, informed opinion about it."

She hoped she didn't sound stupid. It was hard to be articulate about global affairs when her head was still exploding that she was having a real-life conversation with a sixteen-, almost seventeen-year-old boy during school hours. She wondered if she'd stink like his cigarette when she went back to school. She hoped so.

"Well, you *should* have an opinion, Marley," he said. "For such a smart person, you owe it to yourself to know what's going on. The world is fucked. Antisemitism is alive and well, and it's only getting worse. Those people who were murdered at that synagogue in Pittsburgh? When something like that happens, you have to pick a side."

"Yeah, you're right," she said. "I should know more about it, probably . . . I'm just more of a fiction person, I guess . . ."

"It's not your fault. It's how you were raised. Typical Jewish-American princess, bat mitzvah'ed at the Plaza. You can afford to be ambivalent, 'cause you've never felt unsafe, or persecuted. You've never had to give a second's thought to why Israel matters. Don't you know what our grandparents went through?"

"I mean, yeah . . ." she said. "But isn't feeling safer and less persecuted, for all people, kind of, like, the goal of history? I don't think my grandparents would *want* me to understand what antisemitism's like. And didn't Nicki Minaj perform at *your* bar mitzvah?"

She hoped he wouldn't think she was being fresh with him. She really wanted him to like her.

"That was then," he said. "Things have changed for my family, in a permanent way. And that was just my dad on his tacky American Dream shit, trying to impress people. Much good it did him, when he's a fucking laughingstock *now*."

He was really, really angry about his dad. At him, but also

for him. He was being hounded in the press, his every court appointment staked out by the *Post* and *Daily News*, a tabloid clown. He'd been involved in some car chase just last week with a city sheriff who'd been trying to serve him child support papers for Dimitri's little half sister. He had crashed his Chevy Tahoe into a traffic pole, and gotten concussed.

Daddy of course would say how Val deserved every bit of ridicule he was getting, how if there was one individual who had truly wrecked the taxi industry, who'd truly done evil, it was Valentin Zalebnik. But it was hard not to feel bad for him, the way Dimitri talked about his situation. Living in some safe house out on Staten Island, threatened by his contacts in the underworld. In his robe all day, drinking himself half to death, batting off his creditors, and awaiting trial for tax fraud. . . . Evil was a strong word for anybody, no matter *what* that person had done. And he had to have done *something* right, to end up with Dimitri for a son.

She'd never met anybody like him. He made every other young person she knew seem like a total lightweight in comparison. He made Benny seem like some cotton-headed nobody, living for his sneaker drops. He was really an intense guy, very principled and grave. He rolled his own cigarettes, and almost never checked his phone, and spoke Russian and Hebrew fluently, *and* English, and knew a ton of stuff, about Israel, and Eastern Europe, and New York in the '70s, and Emma Goldman, and Eldridge Cleaver, and all these anarchist writers and underground figures and intellectuals she'd never even heard of before. He read a ton, but not for school, and not in a lame bookish way. He made learning seem like a matter no less urgent than survival, the type of thing done in a fever of self-armament, by lanternlight, in trenches. And he made it seem like it was possible to have been raised in the tackiest environment on Earth, among knaves and whores and bottom-feeders, and Knicks City Dancers popping out of a cake at your dad's forty-fifth birthday

157

party, and to keep your head above it all. To take the fate of your soul as seriously as anybody. Basically he was hope for her, personified.

All of a sudden she felt stupid poking holes in his plans for the future, like a dumb naïve civilian, when what he was doing was extremely brave and different, and ought to be commended, really. *Way* more so than Exeter and Harvard. High-gloss robots like Noelle, scooting between institutions.

"I think it's really cool, what you want to do," she said. "It's just . . . I guess I'd miss you."

She couldn't tell if that was a really lame thing to say. They hadn't even kissed yet. But the thought of him over there in the desert, head shaved and deloused, cradling a Kalashnikov, made her want to wrap her arms and legs around him and not move for long enough to let him go.

"I'd miss you too, Marley," he said. "Honestly I would. I feel like I've known you my whole life. Which I guess I have. I just mean, there's something . . . really cool and different about you."

It was the dead of winter in New York, but it felt like the tropics all of a sudden. Pan flutes and banana leaves . . . everything humidified.

Had he really just said that? That she, Marley Cohen, was cool and different?

The way he approached her right then felt like the answer to the riddle that had plagued her for the last few months. Of what the hell to do with yourself when childhood's over. For a while now she'd been sloshing in the tunnel, gray and clogged, cast off from the safety of her cuteness, looking for an answer, and the way he put his arm around the bench behind her, and moved in . . . that just about cleared the matter up for good.

THAT NIGHT Daddy was on TV and Mom, J.J., and Grandma got a big bowl of popcorn to watch him. Not that Marley could eat, or even see straight, she was so cockeyed and exhilarated from what had happened to her earlier. She felt *so* happy it was almost a little bit unpleasant actually. Usually she had to use this therapeutic UV lamp thing every night for twenty minutes in the winter so she wouldn't get too blue, but tonight she wouldn't even need it. She couldn't even *take* it, she might die from all the dopamine.

The appearance was some kind of panel on NY1 about the taxi medallion crisis they were hosting at Hunter College, in front of students and the public. Ordinarily this kind of basement town hall setting would be a little bit beneath Daddy, but he said how he was taking more and more invitations like this to flex his public-speaking muscles and get his name and story out there. There was a councilwoman from Queens on the panel, and someone from the Taxi and Limousine Commission, and a cab driver, and Daddy. The moderator asked a question about the hedge fund that had been gobbling up all these medallions, saying how some cab drivers were worried about what it meant for them and their debt.

"Listen. Listen," Daddy said. It was so weird seeing him on TV. "You have to understand how this all began. You have to understand the reasoning behind this. This whole crisis began when a few bad actors, who shall remain nameless"—he meant Dimitri's dad, obviously—"took advantage of the city's lax attitude toward the market, and purposefully overpaid for medallions, and everyone else, the drivers on one side, like my friend Mr. Ibrahim here, and the credit unions and bankers like myself on the other, had to hold or issue increasingly unsustainable loans to keep up with these crazily overvalued prices. That's what happened. That's how the bubble grew. It was not a failure of the banks. The banks were only following the lead of those bad actors, who'd started treating the taxi market like their personal casinos. In the old days—and I'm almost embarrassed to admit this—I applied for a license to carry a handgun. Now, I'm not some tough guy who's nuts about guns. In case you couldn't tell from looking at me." He got a bunch of laughs for that. Though it wasn't *that* funny. "My second amendment rights, I could take 'em or leave 'em. I'm just a numbers guy from Long Island, but I'm five foot seven, with heart palpitations, and I needed extra protection just to sleep at night. Being leaned on left and right to broker completely outlandish deals, on threat of physical violence against my person. Against my family." Really? "That's how aggressive things had gotten. Well, fortunately, those days are over. The best thing for the drivers now is to be out from under the mercy of that way of doing business. No more piecemeal wheelers and dealers, no more fleet owners ripping off their drivers. No more desperadoes or intimidation tactics. You have one streamlined, unified company, Margate, controlling everything, with the deep pockets to be able to restructure loans in a more reasonable, forgiving fashion. You've got a big centralized player with bigger resources investing in newer, greener, more comfortable cabs, with better service. Tablets for the drivers to navigate better. It's the way of the future, this economy of scale. It's the only way to compete with Uber. Now, I know that change is hard. I understand that. And of course when most people hear the words 'hedge fund' they shiver in their boots, and I don't blame them. They think of some evil, faceless corporate entity that doesn't care about them or their families, when I assure you that couldn't be farther from the truth here. By going corporate,' we're actually doing the right thing. We're civilizing the Wild West. This *is* the best way to secure the future of the industry. Not some bailout with taxpayer money, like others on this panel have suggested. Because as much as I sympathize with the drivers, and I do, more than anyone, I also believe that hardworking New Yorkers have enough on their plates, without having to bail anyone else out for the city's regulatory failures, *or* for the excesses of those who got rich off exploiting them."

People clapped a lot.

"Those who got rich off *exploiting* them?" the councilwoman cut in. "Who got richer than *you*?"

"Ms. Sanchez," said the moderator.

"Not to mention two hundred thousand dollars in consulting fees from Margate. And he has the nerve to sit there and act like he and *his friend* Mr. Ibrahim are in the same predicament. Cheerleading for the future of the taxi industry, when he's been padding his lifeboat for years. How much faith do you really have, Mr. Cohen? Or does it not matter what happens to these people, now that you've got your money?"

"Jesus," Mom said. "*She's* got some nerve," though Mom was loving it.

"Ms. Sanchez," said the moderator. "This is a civil discussion, not a debate."

"With all due respect, miss," Daddy said, "I think you're one to throw stones. Personally, I think you care more about burnishing your populist image than actually helping people. Otherwise you wouldn't have screwed the Amazon deal. Demonizing industry and business to score political points while your constituents starve. I've been in the taxi business, fighting tooth and nail to help drivers put food on the table, for longer than you've been alive."

He always got the last word, Daddy. He *was* pretty good. A born politician, Mom said. He knew people could only hold one, maximum two thoughts in their head about a given topic or public figure at one time, so you had to really strike a chord with them. He had a way of making himself sound both pragmatic and humane, and making everyone else sound heartless to be one thing, or naive to be the other. The councilwoman, though she made some pretty valid-sounding points, mostly came off like a bit of a grandstanding gotcha artist, the TLC person like a dry, soulless bureaucrat, and Mr. Ibrahim the cab driver seemed like a nice man but he didn't say two words the whole night. Daddy clearly won the evening. He was beaming afterward, as they all clapped.

Marley guessed she should be proud of Daddy, on this new public-servant kick of his. He was excited about the future. And it was all a lot better than last year, when his company was hemorrhaging money, with no solution in sight, and he was running around like a marked man, taking midnight meetings, her sitting up at home thinking each new meeting was the one he might not come back from. But she wasn't, for some reason . . . proud of him. Not really.

She lay in bed later, scrolling through Dimitri's photos. Daddy would completely lose his mind when he found out about them dating. Not that that wasn't part (though just a very small part) of the appeal.

Dimitri didn't post much these days—he was too busy expanding his intellect—but in the ones he had posted a few months ago he looked so sexy she had to keep moving her pillow between her legs and squeezing and bearing down like she did to keep herself from peeing. She hadn't given much thought to actual sex, though obviously she understood the gist of it, and just the thought of masturbating embarrassed and confused her, so it was more about imagining him lying on top of her and kissing her and maybe humping her a little bit, while telling her that she was beautiful and how there was nobody else like her.

This annoying random guy, though, kept liking all her posts. The notifications kept popping up when she was trying to look at pictures of Dimitri. In the last two weeks he'd liked literally every single one of her photos, going back two years. It was really creepy.

In his bio it said his name was J. D. and he seemed to live in the country somewhere. There were photos of him sitting around with his cross-eyed friends, in Slipknot hoodies, rolling joints and drinking Mountain Dew. And then there were all these photos of a little girl, who was seriously adorable, but then the photos of her stopped. And then about twenty photos of more random stuff later there was another photo of the girl, the same age as in the previous one, and the caption said *Miss my baby girl I see ppl take their kids for granted and I just want to tell them dont I miss her evry second of evry day Skylar Daddy*

162

loves you he cnt wait to see your face again somday and there was an emoji of a broken heart and angels' wings.

Mom had told her to keep her Instagram account private to keep the creeps away, but then you couldn't really get a lot of followers that way. Unless you were a Noelle or Annabel type and were perceived as being worth the hassle. But for somebody of *Marley*'s social stature it seemed a little self-important and presumptuous of people's interest level to have a private account, so better to leave it open and just be careful. So that's what she'd been doing, and it hadn't been a problem so far.

A message popped up, from the J. D. person. *Wheres yr daddy*, it said.

That was pretty creepy. Guys in their thirties with a daddy fetish trolling the internet looking for young girls' accounts to follow. It was pretty uncouth. She wasn't gonna respond, but she also felt bad blocking or reporting him when something obviously terrible had happened to this poor guy's daughter. And he might just be a little bit fetal-alcohol or something not his fault. And there was only so much harm he could do from his farm in North Dakota or wherever. And also, frankly, she could use the likes.

THE BIG TALK the next week was that Noor Shawaf hadn't come to school for ten whole days. Marley'd texted her a while ago to see what was up but the message hadn't been delivered for some reason. Now everybody had their theories. Someone said she'd moved back to Syria, *or* that she'd gotten pregnant and been forced into marriage by her conservative Muslim parents, neither of which seemed very likely. Even Annabel, whom Marley wasn't sure had known that Noor existed and was named Noor, was talking about it.

"Well, I got the scoop," said Annabel during homeroom one Thursday, sitting down, making everybody wait for it. "Ms. Bloy told me. It sounds really sad. Her dad's, like, a cab driver or

163

something. And he lost his cab and has no money and her sister had to quit school to go work at a Dunkin' Donuts–Baskin Robbins, and they had to pull Noor out and send her to a public school near where she lives, in Queens."

"Oh," said Noelle.

"Oh," said Caroline.

You could hear their disappointment, that it wasn't any juicier than her just being poor.

"I thought she was on full scholarship, though," said Marley.

"I guess she got a C or something." It was hard to picture Noor getting a C. She was about the smartest, most conscientious student in the grade. "She was pretty stressed, I guess. They only let you stay on scholarship if you don't get below a B. Which seems pretty fucking unfair, if you ask me."

Talk about unfair. Marley got only Bs, except in English, and sometimes even below Bs in math. Noor had never even mentioned that her dad drove a cab. And Daddy'd made it seem like things were getting better for the drivers. No wonder Noor hadn't responded to the texts—they probably couldn't even pay the phone bill. They probably had her on one of those Consumer Cellular burner phones, the kind grandparents had for if they fell.

Marley couldn't even begin to imagine how depressing Noor's life was. Chess, dance, *and* soccer, and taking the bus to and from Randalls Island an hour each way on game days, more than that in traffic, and then getting on a train home, and *then* doing her homework, *and* getting all As. Until recently at least—...Marley did jazz dance once a week during the fall semester—that was her only extracurricular—and just getting out at 4:30 on those days really cut into her me-time, and the way the sun set early after daylight saving; like coming out of a movie theater when you hadn't known it would be dark, it really bummed her out. But Noor must live inside that feeling. Or not even, she was so used to it by now. Being spread so thin, and worked so hard.

Living way, way out, near Kennedy airport, past the mattress warehouses and the motor inns where people went to overdose on methamphetamines and hang themselves, their Honda Civics orphaned in the parking lots. Then coming all that way up to the East Side of Manhattan, through gilded doorways, into classrooms full of girls who must seem to Noor like the denizens of some distant, glittering, careless planet. Marley's isolation must be child's play in comparison. Not that realizing as much made her like school any better.

They had family dinner that night, like every Thursday, and Rudy the doorman came. He'd been around a lot lately. Daddy called him the J.J. whisperer. He was convinced that J.J.'s stutter had improved with Rudy around, which it actually might have. He *was* really playful and natural with J.J. in a way that Daddy for whatever reason couldn't bring himself to be, and a super nice guy. Though he seemed too old to still be hanging around as Daddy's lapdog, waiting for Daddy to say fetch, and trying to find his footing in life. By the time that *she* was twenty-six she'd probably be married, and a homeowner, and established if not downright influential in her field. It was twenty-goddamn-six. How much time could a person need?

"How was school today?" said Daddy.

"Well, my friend, Noor, I found out her dad, he's a cab driver, and, well, he lost his cab."

"Is that so," said Daddy. He kept looking over at Grandma, who hadn't touched her dinner, and instead was staring into space and doing this new thing of hers, this like buzzing-bumblebee noise.

"Don't you want to know his name?" said Marley. "It's Amir Shawaf."

"Well, babe, I don't know them all by name," said Daddy. "And I'm not really involved in that anymore."

"But why would he lose his cab right when things were meant to be getting better?"

"Why are revolutions bloody? They just are," Rudy shot her an apologetic look. "How was your audition, huh?" he said. "I'm on pins and needles waiting to hear about it."

"Oh, that . . . it was fine. I dunno . . ." she said.

The audition had come and gone and she hadn't even thought about it. Her school spirit was pretty low these days, and Dimitri had her thinking how her talents might be better used in some kind of actual public service, not just navel-gazing over crusty plays from sixty years ago.

"We're rooting for you, honey," Mom said. She couldn't understand why Mom was being so supportive and positive all of a sudden. Her and Daddy'd always treated Marley's interest in the arts like some kind of minor illness that would have to run its course. "What a cool thing to want to do. Between that and the Rubin internship, I think we've got the next Mike Nichols on our hands. When's that starting anyway, Jake?"

It actually turned out to be a good thing about the internship, probably, that she wasn't going to Cuba, 'cause this way she could be in the city with Dimitri to soak up as much time as possible with him before his shipping out. Not that he was likely to leave for Israel for another year or so. But the specter of war put a lot of pressure on the here and now.

"Oh, that . . . that's off," said Daddy.

"What?" said Marley.

"Why?" said Mom.

"Something's changed," said Daddy.

"What do you mean? What's changed? When?" She'd missed literally every other deadline to do any other worthwhile thing in the city, "What am I supposed to do instead?"

"I don't know. Be a lifeguard. You'll figure something out."

"What happened, though?"

"It's none of your business what happened."

"Jake," said Mom.

166

He was so evasive it was unbelievable. She never even wanted to do that dumb brown-nosing internship anyway, but the way he went from hyping something up to dismissing it entirely, so offhandedly, was about the phoniest, sketchiest thing imaginable. He was a born liar. She could just picture him back in the day peddling his snake-oil no-down-payment loans to penniless drivers, then when they suddenly owed him eighteen thousand dollars by the weekend saying, *Well . . . something's changed.*

"If you must know," Daddy said, "he was forced to resign. I don't even want to dignify the conversation any further, it's so unfair what he's been put through. Some intern saying he endangered her mental health. God forbid. All this mental health crap, I swear . . ."

"I know," said Marley, "why can't all these mentally ill people just, like, get over themselves, right?"

"Are you being sarcastic? 'Cause I don't like that, Marley. I don't like that sarcasm one bit. That's low. That's glib, okay? It's beneath you. If you have something to say, you express it straight on. And where are all of these quips and hot takes in history class, huh? In biology class? Miss Participation Needs Improvement?"

She just rolled her eyes.

"Obviously I agree that mental health things—*issues*—should be—what's the term they use—destigmatized," he said. "That anyone with a major psychological problem should get the help they need. And that actual abuse should be prosecuted to the highest extent of the law. But sometimes these young women are taking it too far. Talking about their *mental health* and their *anxiety* and their *trauma* the way old folks talk about their bunions. When it's not your bunions. It's you, your character. It's what you're *made* of. And maybe you're just made of flimsy stuff. Or is that some cause célèbre now too. We're meant to be doing charity walks for them. The basket-case-itis club. All I know is, no boss of *mine* every mollycoddled *me*."

Everyone was quiet for a while, eating in awkward silence. Except for Grandma and her buzzing noise. Even Rudy looked despondent, for some reason.

"I'm sorry the internship didn't work out," said Daddy finally, "but *you'll* get over it."

Later she looked the producer guy up and it turned out he'd groped one of his assistants—*allegedly*, Daddy would have her emphasize—and verbally harassed two others, and they'd brought a lawsuit against him and now he had to step down from his position at Universal and his own theater production company to save face. Marley was all for due process, but there was no way there wasn't fire where there was smoke with this guy. He'd been notorious. And Daddy'd talked about him like he was some beleaguered martyr, and those women had just lacked a hearty temperament for things. Like Daddy knew their lives better than *they* did.

She should hardly be surprised about the whole thing. He'd always seemed to run in some extremely smarmy circles, Daddy. Everything incestuous, everybody knowing everybody. A mid-town shadow world of profiteers and social climbers—guys with ties to taxi medallions, real estate, politics, Russia, money laundering. Donald Trump. Daddy'd always said *don't google me* like the internet would spontaneously combust if she so much as typed his name. But now she knew that he was full of crap.

She went into his office. She hadn't stepped foot in here in what felt like years. Mom and Daddy would be out for hours, though.

This place had seemed so mythical to her when she was little—brown leather chairs and signed sports memorabilia, and pictures of her dad with Rudy Giuliani, and with Pop-Pop and Patrick Ewing at a Knicks game in the '90s. There were press clippings all over the walls, from the *Times* and *Forbes* and the *Observer* and *Bloomberg Businessweek*, from before Daddy'd soured completely on the liberal media.

One piece she remembered, him in this feature they did on him in this business magazine that had since gone out of print. There was a picture of her and Mom and Daddy, before J.J. came along, that she used to think was so, so cool. She'd thought it meant that she was famous. Four years old, sitting on Daddy's desk in his old office on Madison, holding a taxi-shaped piggy bank, smiling with big curly hair. Mom looked super young and beautiful. Daddy stood behind them, ten years younger, with the skyline out the window, arms crossed and a kind of cocky annual-report smile on his face like, "Success! The Big Apple, baby! Get a load of *this*!"

She didn't know why looking at the picture made her sad. It all seemed prelapsarian or something. Like pictures of people who'd since died, their doom somehow inscribed on their smiling faces. Not that anyone had *died*, thank God, it's just . . . they'd all changed so much. She remembered how Daddy'd been super annoyed the journalist had Mom's name down as "Norma" instead of "Nora" ("Norma Jean of Mahwah. Jesus Christ. They make her sound like a hillbilly."), though Norma actually *was* Mom's name—Mom's mom had idolized Marilyn Monroe, but then Mom changed it, legally, to Nora, which she thought sounded more refined. Anyway, Daddy'd found the rest of the article flattering enough to have it framed.

In the article he mentioned he was on the board of something called We Care, Inc., a nonprofit. He'd never mentioned it again, and when she looked it up it seemed like the company had been dissolved, for some reason. She couldn't find out much about it, but apparently it used to operate something called a cluster site, and apparently these cluster site things were really bad. They were started under Mayor Giuliani for handling the spillover from homeless shelters, by paying private landlords to put people up in their own buildings, mostly in the Bronx, sometimes at three, four times what the apartments were worth, with no oversight at all. People living in squalor and misery while these landlords made a killing, some of the buildings completely falling apart. It sounded like a horrible racket.

She found lots of court cases involving Daddy's bank too, and legal mumbo jumbo that she couldn't understand, and paywalls for court documents. The only ones that she could access were for cases that had been dismissed, or that Daddy's side had won.

She went from feeling like some movie-montage Nancy Drew, about to zero in on something big, to feeling totally dispirited, and a little bit disloyal, frankly. What was she after anyway, some way of blackmailing her own father? To what end? Daddy was right that anyone could accuse anyone of anything—grown-ups sued each other all the time, sometimes over really stupid things, like some very fat person she'd read about suing Lay's 'cause they'd choked on a potato chip—and he always said how conflict was the cost not just of doing business, but of drawing breath. It was true there were some pretty litigious crybabies out there, which didn't mean there wasn't some awful truth too, somewhere in the past, to answer for. Just that the forces of bluster and untruth and idle talk and innuendo were bigger and more powerful than any one person ought to bother making sense of, nowadays. It must've been some headache for him, honestly, putting out so many fires over the years. And he couldn't have been the one who'd started *all* of them.

Mom had said it was a time of change for everybody, a time for hanging in there. How Daddy was hurting a lot about what was happening to Grandma's brain, more than anyone could see, and feeling really powerless, and working overtime to try to control the things he could. . . . Marley thought Mom ought to turn her aspiring-psychology-student acumen on *herself* one of these days, but she might've had a point there. Maybe you had to have mercy on people. Maybe even the merciless ones.

• • •

DIMITRI INVITED HER to his cousin's wedding the first weekend in March. It was at some social club his dad's friend owned on Coney Island Avenue, in Brighton Beach. She could tell that he was nervous about going, which was really cute. She'd never seen him anything but totally composed and chill. (*She* felt pretty nervous too, setting foot on Val Zalebnik's turf—there were probably people in his crew who didn't care much for her father. Dimitri reassured her, though, saying how his dad would never recognize her, she'd grown up so much, plus he had this thing where he couldn't tell girls apart that easily unless he was their dad or sleeping with them, and even then not always.)

"When was the last time you saw your dad?" she asked him.

He had an Uber take them out there from the East Side, his hand draped across her thigh in the backseat, him in a suit and tie she for some reason kept wanting to tear off with her teeth. He looked good.

"God," Dimitri said, "three months ago? Maybe longer. I hate seeing him these days. But it's the only way I get to see my sister."

He had a four-year-old half sister from his dad's third marriage he was super protective of. Now Valentin was already on his fourth wife, and his relationship with the little girl's mom was even *more* acrimonious than with Dimitri's mom, if that was possible.

"I'm not gonna let those awful people fuck her up," he said. He was *such* a good big brother.

It took almost an hour to get there, but Marley didn't mind the drive at all, looking out the window at the city. She'd only been to Brooklyn twice, one time to this famous pizza place where the crust gave her horrendous diarrhea, but it was totally worth it, and once to visit the cemetery in Sheepshead Bay where Grandma's mom and dad were buried.

They drove through someplace called Borough Park and there was a group of Hasidim walking down the street, the men with their fur hats, the boys and girls in clumps of three and four, a woman with a baby stroller running after her little boy with the mitten he had dropped, her wig flopping in the wind . . . the sight of them beguiled her. Their dark clothes, like a permanent

171

funeral, how impervious their sense of ceremony. It was like some kind of glitch in the projector, like some chimera from bygone Kraków, so out of place among the modern streets. She had never seen Orthodox Jews in New York City before.

Mom and Daddy as a rule didn't care much for religion. They were a couple of spiritual dilettantes mostly; God was just a nice idea, selectively indulged in, all the rites and rituals a chance for them to hobnob, and mostly Marley didn't really care or feel that strongly either way. But sometimes getting all these presents for both Hanukkah *and* Christmas she felt like she was cheating. Like some greater tithe was owed of them, or they'd be paying double someday.

She wondered what the kids were talking about, the girls about her age, arms linked, all in cloddy shoes and navy leggings, the boys in yarmulkes and curls, bursting at their seams with puberty. Of course she didn't envy those kids at all—they were missing out on so much, on the whole world, really—but neither did she pity them as much as other people might've. Maybe their proscription was just a more extreme and formal version of everybody else's, and at least when they grew up they'd have each other, and a blueprint for their lives, for how to act, and how to help, and who to be. Whereas *she* had neither freedom, really, nor a clue.

The social club was called Vasilisa and it looked like Caesars Palace in Las Vegas, with a circular driveway and a fountain with King Triton shooting water from his trident. Apparently the head of the Russian mafia used to have an office in the back, the headquarters of his prostitution ring and gas-bootlegging scheme. Dimitri said the Russian mob still existed in New York but it was less out-of-a-movie dastardly, their hustles tamer now, more twenty-first-century. Defrauding Medicaid and things like that. They still killed people sometimes but not as often, or as violently, and not whole families.

Inside was like fake St. Petersburg, with gold-leafed columns

172

and purple velvet drapes with ermine trim against the walls. It could've been three hundred people gathered in the main hall, women in stilettos and fur coats, and grim-faced men in shark-skin suits and leather jackets and tables overflowing with vodka urns and candelabras and buckets full of caviar on ice. Dimitri didn't let go of her hand for one second. He introduced her to his cousins and his little sister, and his new stepmom, who was like a scowling not-that-pretty version of the Minka Kelly–looking orphan woman who had come to their apartment that one time. Marley wondered what had happened to that woman. She hoped nothing bad.

At one of the tables near the omelet station she recognized one of Daddy's friends, this publicist guy he knew. Very much a Manhattan character, like a sore thumb in his understated Zegna suit, busy shouting on his cell phone, probably trying to get some Saudi strongman off the sanctions list, or whatever people like him did for a living.

Finally they approached Valentin, who had a seven-foot-tall bodyguard standing near him, intercepting visitors. "Tarzan, hey," said Dimitri to the guard, and waved him off.

"Dad," he said, "this is my girlfriend." (*That* was crazy. They totally hadn't had that conversation yet. Not that she was complaining.) Valentin didn't seem to notice that she hadn't said her name, just looked her up and down and said, "What's a girl like that doing with a schmuck like you, huh? You better treat her good," and gave them both a big bear hug. "Please, sit, have a drink. It's nice to meet you, sweetheart."

She'd remembered Val always being super-duper friendly, and now was no exception. There was something endearing about him, buffoon-like, the way his ears stuck out, how his eyes were half an inch too close together. Dimitri said he'd had a really rough childhood growing up in Russia, malnourished in the womb and never smiled at as a boy, and he'd told this story about how one time as a kid Val had made a baby doll out of

173

logs and empty pickle jars and his own dad had beat him to a pulp for being wanton with the firewood and reusables. That he had any capacity for levity at all was kind of a miracle.

"He seems so nice," said Marley, after Val had left them to go make the rounds. For someone Daddy had described as friendless, he seemed to have an awful lot of friends.

"Well, he's not as bad as they say," Dimitri said. "I know he's done some bad things, but you have to understand the Soviet mentality. The only way to survive there was to cheat and lie. And people here might stand in judgment of that, saying they'd know better, but they're flattering themselves. Their knowing any better's just a luxury of birth."

"Wow, that's so true."

He was *so* deep, with such a dark and epic view of human nature.

After the ceremony they had champagne and snifters full of lemongrass vodka and Dimitri led her out onto the dance floor. It was like a different world in here, blackly resplendent, full of vigor and loud voices, and twelve-year-olds drinking schnapps out in the open, and couples fighting and other couples all but making babies under the disco lights. They made people on Park Avenue seem like a pallid, bloodless, sorry crowd, ignorant about what life was for.

She was having a great time. What had she been thinking, that they'd be poisoning her stroganoff 'cause she was Jacob Cohen's daughter? Dimitri'd said how the Russian mob wasn't like that anymore, and it was true she looked nothing like she used to the last time Val had seen her . . . some Friday night a year or so ago, tip-toeing through the kitchen where he and Daddy sat up talking, come to fix herself a hot fudge sundae, an ashen little twerp in her poodle-print pajamas, no boobs and no plans either. Who she was now, in comparison to that, it was night and day.

A while later Dimitri was in the bathroom and Val came walking toward her, smiling. He seemed a little looser than before, his face redder, the pupils expanding in his eyeballs. The Russian band was singing a heavily accented version of "Conga" by Gloria Estefan.

Marley couldn't tell if he was drunk—she hadn't been to many parties where there was drinking involved, and Daddy obviously didn't drink, and Mom, when she did drink, which was more and more these days, come to think of it, got a little cutting and sardonic but she rarely lost her composure.

He came right up to her and did the double-kiss thing people did in France—he really was remarkably jolly, considering all his legal troubles—and put his hands around her waist, quite low, and then he whispered in her ear, "You've got your mother's legs, you know that?" She almost choked. "Long and lean. Very nice. But the nose, the eyes. Those're all your dad's. The eyes especially. Rat eyes."

He backed up again, his hands lingering on her haunches.

"Is everything okay here?" Dimitri said.

"I'm just talking to your little friend."

"Dad, Dad . . ." Dimitri shook his head. "Don't."

"We were like brothers, him and me. Like brothers."

"Dad, you're drunk."

"He held the chuppah at my wedding. When your grandpa Melvin died, I held him in my arms and he wept like a little boy. And what was all that for, huh? That loyalty, that friendship? Everything he has was because I had the balls to get it for him."

"Dad!"

"Not just all his money. I gave him his balls. He couldn't look a goddamn waitress in the eye before I taught him how to."

"Dad . . . we're gonna go."

"No . . . no. Don't go. Don't go. Hey, it's a party. I'm sorry. Listen, I'm sorry."

"It's okay," said Marley. She didn't know what else to say.

"Just make sure he knows that I'm not done for yet, huh," Valentin said. "He knows about me. I'm a fighter. I'm a mother-fuckin' slugger!" and he started shadowboxing in place, jumping up and down, more playfully than anything, and then he said, "I gave him everything. And what did he do? He ptttth. He fucked me. And now she has the fuckin' nerve to come here, while my kids are forced to live off scraps. Some ugly little rat-faced whore from—"

Then Dimitri swung at him and hit him on the jaw and Valentin fell backward into a table, and she clucked and flapped her arms, saying things like "Woah!" and "Stop that," feeling womanish and ineffectual, and then she ran to the bathroom 'cause she felt like she maybe needed to throw up.

"MARLEY, MARLEY." Dimitri came running in after her. He was holding some ice from the caviar station to his hand. "I am so *incredibly* sorry about that."

She could hardly get a breath in. She kept thinking, *Sticks and stones. Sticks and stones.* Her mind raced to think of all the violence in the world, of people mugged and tear-gassed and dragged out of their homes, of what it must take for them to calm their nerves and carry on with living, and that back there—that was *nothing* in comparison. Those were words. Just words. A hand a half an inch too low.

"I'm so sorry," Dimitri said. "I should've never run the risk of that. I just wanted you here, 'cause I didn't want to deal with these crazy fucked-up people by myself. I'm sorry. I'm *so* sorry, Marley."

He cupped his hands around her face and wiped her tears away, very tenderly, and started kissing her hands. "I hope you can forgive me," he said.

Was he kidding? Of course she would forgive him. The way he'd come to her defense like that, and what his dad had said, about how *she* was taking food out of *his* mouth, *he* should be the one forgiving *her*.

He kissed her deeply on the mouth then and moved her up

against the sink and there were canisters of Aqua Net and a Diamonds by Liz Taylor bottle that went crashing off the counter as he grinded up against her. Her head was spinning.

Jesus Christ. For the longest time she'd felt like *such* a pipsqueak nobody with nothing going on and now it was too much. Too much. Hanging out in the former US headquarters for the Russian mob, being yelled at and threatened and called an ugly rat-faced whore by a drunk disgraced taxi mogul, then kissed passionately in the bathroom by his son with his fist swelling in her honor and his fingers running up her thighs under her dress.

Then his fingers got up higher and they were on top of her underwear and he looked at her a second, half like in scrutiny, half asking for permission, and then he pulled the band of her undies down and he slipped one finger from his good hand down and up inside her and his face softened and his eyes got all foggy and he said, "Oh god, Marley, oh Jesus fucking Christ," and his face was swollen with this crazy cockeyed lust, and he said, "Oh god . . . oh *god* that pussy," and he bit his lip and he took his finger back out and he put it in his mouth like a chef tasting his sauce and at first she was so, *so* embarrassed and grossed out she wanted to run out of the room, or throw up in his mouth, or slap him, or just go home and curl up in her bedroom and go on living in her daydreams for the rest of time and she'd be *fine* with that, 'cause if the legs that he was touching now were the same legs that Valentin said were long and lean and very nice she would rather not have legs at all, just dissolve back into prepubescent nullity forever, but then he put his finger back inside her and she kind of swooned and fell back further onto the sink, and she felt this molten lava lamp–type feeling rising up inside her belly, and she knew there was no stopping and she didn't want to either.

Later, looking in the mirror in the elevator, she barely recognized herself. Her face had been kissed raw, her hair all messy, with hickeys starting to show themselves up and down her neck. Her pupils were like pins from all the Georgian wine and vodka.

She gave herself a good, long stare. Who on Earth would call her ugly? Granted she wasn't some natural-born *Hadid* or one of those girls. But neither were *they*. It was nothing a little tune-up, when she was older, couldn't fix. . . .

When she got back up to the apartment Mom and Daddy were sitting in the living room, looking very grave.

Her heart stopped. "Oh my God. Is Grandma dead?"

"Where the hell were you?" Daddy said.

"I told you. I had Daniela's party. Is Grandma okay?"

"Don't lie to me," said Daddy. "Don't even try to lie. You think I don't know people who were there?" Oh God. That horrible PR guy'd probably told him. "You *cannot* see him again. Okay? I forbid it."

"Mom, can you please—"

"Sweetie, honestly," Mom said. "I know you're probably feeling a lot of emotions, and you really like him, or you *think* you do, but you can't be seeing that boy anymore. Valentin's a very dangerous person."

Mom had always hated Val. Always calling him a reputational hazard, begging Daddy to cut ties. A ham-fisted fleet owner from Russia in an ill-chosen suit, that all didn't jibe with her image of Park Avenue ascendance. Norma Jean had higher aspirations for herself. What a fake, pretending her concern was about their safety, when Daddy was just as much a criminal, and she was *married* to him.

"You can't force me not to see him," Marley said.

"Of course we can!" said Daddy. Now he sounded *really* mad. "What do you think this is? We can take away your cell phone, and your allowance, and your opportunities, and everything you've ever owned. Everything you have, the air in your damn *lungs* is borrowed, Marley."

Back in her room she felt so breathless and berserk she didn't know what to do. Her very consciousness was like a house on fire she needed to jump out of. She could swallow all her Accutane at once but then she might not wake up, which would mean never seeing Dimitri again, which would be horrible, but even disregarding him a second she sensed that life was broadly worth sticking around for, if only for the movies and the food, so that was out.

After a while she took a punishingly hot twenty-five-minute shower and that calmed her down a bit. She could *not* believe that anything that had happened today had really happened. Not just the bad stuff, but the good stuff too. . . . How on the car ride back Dimitri lay on top of her with her underwear pulled down around her knees saying *mmm mm baby, mmmm mmmm yeah* and even as she squirmed and shuddered to feel so exposed and flung so fast into her womanhood she also wanted him to not stop doing it, to not stop touching her and crushing her with kisses. She just needed to talk to him. They would find a way to see each other, no matter what.

When she unlocked her phone that weird guy from the mountains had messaged her again saying *I need to talk 2 u just hear me out its importnt.*

What the hell did this guy want? Who did he think she was that she had anything to do with him?

One of his photos caught her eye then that she hadn't noticed before. It was a picture of the outside of a squat brick building with a green-and-white street sign, dated November 2015, and the caption said:

Finally found shelter thru the lottery this place is fucked yo but itll be alright they say if u can make it here you can make it anywhere nyc here we goooo

The picture wasn't taken in the country. It was in the Bronx. It was one of those rat traps Daddy's nonprofit used to run.

She messaged the guy back immediately:

hey, she wrote.

if you wanna talk im here

179

LANDLORD BURIED BRONX TOT TRAGEDY: EXCLUSIVE

MARCH 15, 2019

A city landlord arranged a payment to a shelter occupant as part of an agreement to prevent him from publicly discussing a tragic incident in 2015, according to people familiar with the matter. Jeremy McLean, 34, contacted the *News* to describe a fatal radiator explosion at his former Bronx apartment building. His daughter, Skylar Paone-McLean, aged 3, was napping when a radiator valve exploded in her bedroom in December 2015, killing her.

Though the incident made headlines at the time, the anguished parents alleged they were offered money not to talk to media outlets or pursue a lawsuit against the owners or the Department of Homeless Services. They declined to disclose the amount of the payoff or the identity of the person who approached them, citing privacy concerns.

The apartment building, in Soundview, is a mixed-use facility for housing homeless families as part of the city's controversial cluster program. The program has come under fire for lack of regulation, with its more than three thousand units ranking consistently among the Department of Housing Preservation and Development's watchlist for hazardous conditions. The city government wouldn't publicize the sites' addresses or their owners' identities, but a list of names obtained via a Freedom of Information request shows that a relatively small number of landlords account for a vast majority of code violations.

In 2015, Mr. McLean and his then wife Jessica Paone put their life in Parishville, New York, in St. Lawrence County, behind them to make a fresh start in the city. By his own accounts, Mr. McLean, a US army veteran who served in Iraq, struggled with opioid addiction and had multiple run-ins with the law, often bristling at the strictures of small-town life.

"I heard how in the Big Apple, they, you know, took care of their people," he said, citing the relative ease of accessing methadone treatment in the city.

In July of that year the family of three showed up at the city's homeless intake center in Queens, and after several months of unsuccessful applications were approved to move into the building at 2100 Soundview Avenue. Mr. McLean, an aspiring tattoo artist, had gotten sober and found work painting houses, while Ms. Paone was applying for a license to work as a nail care technician. Then, on December 18, their lives took an unfathomable turn. Ms. Paone was out buying groceries and Mr. McLean playing guitar with a personal amplifier when he noticed steam pouring under his daughter's bedroom door. The girl was rushed to the hospital, but was pronounced dead on arrival.

In the year before the incident, the building showed half a dozen code violations for vermin and missing window guards, though all of the violations were subsequently cleared. A spokesperson for the Department of Housing referred to the apartment in which the girl died as "perfectly habitable," and noted the building did not appear on the public advocate's watchlist of worst buildings. He referred to the incident with the radiator as an "absolute freak accident."

The building was operated by a nonprofit, We Care, Inc., that appears to have been dissolved in the wake of the tragedy. Though the building has changed owners multiple times over the years, with the owners' identities obscured by a series of limited liability companies, the News was exclusively able to trace its ownership as of December 2015 to Jacob Cohen, a prominent businessman and taxi-industry executive from the Upper East Side.

Mr. McLean has since moved back upstate. A news story from late last year, in which a young man, Darrell Wade, 13, was killed in an elevator accident at a different cluster site, in Brooklyn, prompted Mr. McLean to come forward.

"I just thought, I can't stay silent when maybe my talking about this more could've stopped this kind of thing from happening again," he said.

According to one non-homeless resident, Julissa Martinez, 43, conditions in the Soundview building have deteriorated even further since the ownership changed hands.

"It used to be a fine place to live, 'til they converted it to clusters and drove it into the ground," said Ms. Martinez, a nurse.

Of all the problems of living in a dilapidated building, their former neighbor says she's most bothered by the memories of what happened that day.

"We called her Elsa 'cause she looked just like her, from *Frozen*," she said of Skylar, referring to the Disney animated movie. "She was a sweet, beautiful little girl. It's just heartbreaking. I can't think about it. This place . . . I think it's haunted."

HER NAME WAS Libby something. She lived down the block in the penthouse at 710 her dad had bought for her. She was around his age, maybe a little older, pushing thirty. She'd walked past the building with her schnauzer about a month ago and they'd started talking and one thing had led to another on his lunch break. It wasn't love—far from it—but it was something, and it felt like a good release valve for him to stop obsessing over his boss's wife.

She was a little bit condescending to him, Libby, and definitely a spoiled brat, and not strictly good-looking either, with one of those La Toya Jackson–looking hack jobs on her nose, like a perfect whittled little snout, too small and delicate for the rest of her face. The sex was off the charts, though. Rudy couldn't figure out just why. Maybe 'cause he'd hated her immediately . . . strutting down the street that day, in her boss-bitch finest, thigh-high boots from Balmain Paris, pouting self-consciously . . . your typical born consumer, a sheep in wolf's clothing. It was a thrill to get beneath all that, to get someone so smug and glossy into such human positions. It made him feel like a king, like the city was his, and it was teeming inexhaustibly with sexual opportunities. Like beneath the streetside masquerade was just a crazy-ass volcano of loneliness and need, a million bluffs just waiting to be called . . . not to sound too presumptuous about it.

"What are you up to today?" he asked her, zipping up his pants. She was sitting on the bed in her robe. They tended to

183

meet up in the mornings at her place, never dinner, and never overnight.

"Why do you ask?" she said, like he'd been implying they spend it holding hands. Definitely fucking not. He'd just been making conversation. "Crazy day as always. I have a lunch. Then meetings all afternoon with our new buyers from Bergdorf's. Then drinks for my friend's engagement down in Meatpacking."

She ran her own line of high-end bed linens and sweaters or something. Slapped some eco-conscious, fake-woke shit on 'em, to hopefully offset all the child labor in Brazil involved.

"What about you?" she said, with that same smirk. "Holding the fort?"

"No, I told you. I'm on this new thing."

She seemed to keep forgetting that he had a real job now. Like she didn't want him ruining her long-held fantasy of fucking someone from the underclass.

"Oh . . . right," she said. "Good for you."

He leaned down to where she was sitting to kiss her goodbye, just to be friendly, and she wagged her finger in his face, like, *We don't do that.*

Fine, whatever. She seemed to have some notion in her head that she was a very special and enthralling woman and he was slowly falling in love with her. No ma'am . . . no way. The power was all his. He might even break it off soon, just because. Give her something real to pout about.

His uncle called him on his way out the door. Rudy hadn't talked to him or his father in forever.

"Long time," said Mike. "How you been doing?"

"I'm good, I'm good," said Rudy. He couldn't imagine what he'd be calling about.

"We were wondering if we'd be seeing you for St. Pat's this weekend. It's the eightieth, you know."

He'd completely forgotten that that was coming up. The bar had opened on St. Patrick's Day in 1939, and Dad had been planning a big anniversary shindig for the better part of the last year.

Pulling out all the stops. Green and orange balloons. Some deputy to the deputy police sergeant set to give a speech. Corned beef and cabbage all around. Sad.

"If Dad wants me there, he can invite me himself," said Rudy.

"He thought you wouldn't want to talk to him. He thinks you've iced him out for good."

"Oh come on. I think that's being a little dramatic."

"Is it? It's been almost three months, Rudy. What do you think, you're gonna get that time back? He's your father."

Mike really knew how to lay it on. "I've been busy. How's he doing anyway?"

"Between us, not so good. The landlord's upping the rent. They're talking about putting some commuter passageway in again, and if the landlord don't settle for the city's offer, they'll go eminent domain with it. So we're back on the chopping block."

They'd had a few scares and fake-outs like this over the years. But it was inevitable that one of them would be the final blow. "How's he taking it?" said Rudy.

"Well, he's devastated. Between that and some health problems—"

"Health problems? What health problems?"

"Nothing serious. Some lung stuff."

"Oh, just some lung stuff . . ."

"He's just feeling a little bit fragile lately. He had to quit smoking. You know Jimmy and his smokes. He's rudderless without 'em. It's like he's lost his mojo. These doctors, I don't know . . . I swear the heartache of quitting has been worse for him than anything else." Sounded like another entry in the Coyle family book of alternative medicine. "Maybe now's as good a time as any to take the place off his back honestly. It'll be hard at first. But maybe it's for the best."

"How can you be so fatalistic about it?" Rudy said. "This is, like, the family's history going back four generations."

"Since when were *you* a martyr for the place?"

"I'm not, it's just . . . it's the type of thing, when you see it every day you bitch about it. But the thought of it just being gone forever, it's . . . I feel like that would really kill him. What the hell would he live on anyway?"

"You know your father will always be taken care of. It might not be the Ritz, but he'll always have a place to stay."

The way Mike said that, even though it was meant to be helpful, made Rudy feel sick. The thought of Dad growing older, dribbling his oats, some bachelor invalid living in his brother's attic, rolled out for christenings and family parties. Rudy had had plenty of uncharitable thoughts about the man, but the thought of *that*. . . .

He realized that he wasn't mad at him at all anymore. It felt like twenty years ago he'd been stuck at Liffey's, feeling like Dad's foot was on his neck. When Dad was just some guy, in his smelly little bar, in his stupid hat, and he'd be in the ground a whole lot sooner than Rudy. He remembered thinking it was so pathetic the way Dad clung to relevance, when what was the alternative? Just rolling over and dying? Just conceding to Father Time and Mother Commerce everything he'd ever known and worked for? Everybody had the right to have an ego, and a little bit of self-pride, no matter how lame or misguided or retrograde it seemed from the outside. Every single person had that right. Who was Rudy to say otherwise?

"Just say you'll come on Sunday," Mike said. "It'll be a party. We can have a drink, talk in person."

The thought of going back to Liffey's wasn't so terrible now. Rudy knew he wasn't stuck there, now that he'd been proven right in his lifelong hunch that he was far, far too good for the place.

"Okay. Sure. I'll try to be there."

"How's everything with the building job anyway?"

"It's good. I used it like you said, as a stepping stone. I'm working for one of the residents personally now. Onto brighter things."

"That's great."

Jake's hiring him officially couldn't have come more in the

nick of time. The co-op board had axed the whole door staff just days after Rudy'd given notice, when Ron the super got caught by Bruce and Ethel Ratner's plant-sitter in their penthouse apartment, while they were away in Jackson Hole, wearing Ethel's diamond necklace. Ron had been the one behind the jewel thefts, apparently, though he insisted he was just trying them on this one time, and Rudy was inclined to believe him. Guilty or not he felt awful for the guy. Slaving away like Quasimodo all those years, in the bowels of the cathedral, paid in peanuts, living in shame for his proclivities. He was probably gonna go to prison now and not be able to pay for his wife's surgery, let alone his own, if that's where he wanted to take things . . . a sad, strange end for Ron the super.

"My boss, he says he knows you actually," said Rudy. "Or knew you. Jacob Cohen."

"Doesn't really ring a bell," said Mike.

"Really? You sure? Jacob Cohen. He said you were involved in some nonprofit thing, for the homeless, a couple years ago."

"Well, I'm sure there was a Cohen in *that* scam. Half of them are Cohens, aren't they?"

"Half of who?" Jews . . . he meant Jews. Mike was sometimes like that.

"It was a long time ago I was involved with that. I don't remember. Anyways, I'll see you soon, Rude."

Maybe he could talk to Jake about the bar. Get him to help with rent, or pull some kind of string. Help him get the building landmarked. He was the type of person who made problems like that go away. He'd made the whole Kronman thing just disappear into thin air. It was just about finding the right moment to ask him.

THE RESTAURANT he was meeting Jake at, Enzo's, was an institution and a racket, white tablecloths and Michael Bublé on the speaker, forty dollars for a penne alla vodka that tasted the

187

exact same as at a place called Vito's Macaroni Grill in Maspeth. But people around here seemed not to notice, or not care. It was barely eleven and filling up.

Jake was stuck in traffic somewhere, and so was the potential donor they were meeting, which was just as well, to give Rudy a second to read up on them. They were meant to meet somebody named Rose Sinclair, a businesswoman from the Upper East Side with a lot of friends and cronies in the art and philanthropic worlds.

This was part of Rudy's new gig as outreach coordinator for Jake's mayoral campaign, among his less official titles—he had a salary, a business card, the works. It was a trip. The card especially. He could run his finger over that embossment job all day and never get sick of it. The election was still two years away, but Jake said he'd been burned for throwing his hat in the City Council ring too late, and now was the time to start networking and building support so that by showtime he'd have every power player and community organizer in the five boroughs singing the gospel of Jacob Cohen. He was running as an independent, a maverick self-made millionaire, a problem-solver above the petty battle lines of party ideology, whose leadership would signal a much-needed return to the data-driven, no-nonsense style of Bloomberg after a flailing, flaccid eight years mired in hypocrisy and hollow moralizing . . . Rudy had the whole spiel down. He couldn't even tell if he believed it anymore, he'd run through it so many times. Maybe he believed it. Sure he did.

He honestly enjoyed the schmoozing part of things, wining and dining people. He'd been impressed by his own chops there, just to learn he had them. It was like tending bar, but the people across the table didn't make you very sad for them, and there was actual money and influence on the table. Surprisingly the question of his background and credentials hadn't come up once so far. No one seemed to care about that all that much as it turned out. The stuffed-shirt saps slaving away on their degrees, their internships, their positions on the whatever-the-hell task force for public policy boogie-woogie—it was just a kiss-ass bunch of syllables. In one ear and out the other. Charm and people smarts went the distance in this world after all. And he hadn't even had to go into a sinkhole of debt to get them. Not officially at least.

He looked the woman up. Rose Elizabeth Sinclair was her name on her LinkedIn. Rudy'd just assumed she was seventy or older from her name. But he'd been wrong.

In she walked as if on cue, spotting him across the room, approaching his table with a shit-eating grin. Libby.

"What are *you* doing here?" she said.

"I have a lunch here," Rudy said.

"So do I."

"Yeah . . . it's with me."

She looked highly amused, sitting down.

"So," she said, taking off her gloves, "you really *are* going places."

"Unfortunately, Mr. Cohen's running late. He sends his apologies. Could I interest you in an appetizer?" He grabbed the menu up from in front of her and almost knocked her water glass onto her handbag. "I heard the clams are good."

He hoped his eyelid wasn't twitching like it sometimes did when he got nervous. He could feel the confidence draining out of him. Stiff as hell. No game. No game.

"Could I tell you a little bit about his platform while we wait? Mr. Cohen will be running as an independent, a maverick, someone above the petty battle lines of party ideology, a much-needed return to the data-driven—"

He didn't know why he was so nervous around her all of a sudden—they'd been naked together less than three hours ago. But there was something in the way she was looking at him. Like a cock trying to play piano. It threw him off. And it'd be awkward as hell having to explain to Jake when he got here how he'd fucked a potential donor, when Jake had already gone way out on a limb involving a career bartender-turned-FedEx-signer-offer in high-level campaign transactions.

"Now, if you *are* interested in supporting Mr. Cohen's campaign, it may be in our best interest to cease . . . relations . . . which I think might qualify as fraternizing."

"Wow," she said. "He can talk. That must be what they pay you the big bucks for."

She was an extremely snotty person.

"I don't really care about his platform," she said. "This is just something my dad made me do as a favor to get this Cohen guy off his case. He keeps approaching him in the sauna at his gym, asking if he knows any well-connected young people who would want to get involved in his campaign. Dad says he's like a cockroach that he can't get rid of."

He wanted to dump that glass of water on her head, talking about Jake that way.

"Well," he said, "*would* you want to get involved?"

"No, of course not."

"Oh . . . well, that's disappointing."

"Yeah . . . I'm gonna, like, go? I've got meetings."

She stood up and started going through her purse.

"Is there anything I can do to make you reconsider?" Rudy felt completely panicked. Like a vacuum cleaner salesman, behind on his commission, trying to keep the front door from slamming in his face. "If you're interested I can send along some literature for you to review—"

She put her hand up, like, *just stop talking,* then bent over and started writing out a check and handed it to him. It was for ten thousand dollars. Way more than the maximum legally allowed donation to a candidate. She took a long sip on the straw of his Diet Coke in a wannabe-sexy way. Her head was like a horse's in broad daylight.

"You'll have to earn that later, you know," she said, then

walked out. Rudy felt like a big dumb stupid whore. Though at least he knew what he was worth now.

Jake came in right as she was leaving. "What," he said, "she's not here yet?"

"She left," said Rudy.

"Why? What happened?" Rudy handed him the check. "Oh. My god. Atta boy!"

"It's bigger than the max allowed donation."

"Oh, well, I'm sure it won't be a problem. There's a B of A down the street. We'll grab a bite and then we'll go. I'm starving. I've had the morning of my life, let me tell you." He stuffed an entire bread roll in his mouth before even sitting down.

"Everything all right?" said Rudy.

"Val's flipped," he said, though you could barely make the words out through his chewing. "He's agreed to testify for the Mueller people."

"Why?" said Rudy. "Him? What the hell does that have to do with him?"

"I guess they've got nothing. No surprise there. They're giving the barrel one last scrape. And *he's* dangling a carrot. There was some billionaire from Moscow he went in on a failed construction project with a few years ago, who also bought some buildings in Trump Tower. They think there's some connection. Which if there was and he told the truth about it he'd be dead within a week."

"Really?"

"This could not get more ridiculous. He's just playing it up to save himself. He must be feeling good today, though. The tackiest, most ignorant schlub on the planet, can barely spell his own name, thinking he's some prized government witness. What a joke. It was a very aggressive move, I have to say. I'd honestly not've expected a play like this from him and his Podunk legal team. His testimony will mean nothing real for the investigation, but he'll get off for all his financial crimes with a slap on the wrist, a disbarment, and avoid prison completely. Then he'll get the witness fever, which is where the trouble really starts."

"You've got nothing to hide, though," Rudy said. More in hope than certainty.

"It doesn't matter. They just ran some exposé about the human toll of the taxi crisis. Some nobody from *The New York Times*, thinks he's the next Jacob Riis, doing a photo-essay on the drivers and their suffering. Give me a break. The Southern District's set to launch a probe into predatory lending in the taxi industry in response, with Val's cooperation, mostly so the mayor can pretend to care. Heads will roll. Plus the head of the TLC has her eye on City Hall and wants to make sure my campaign's dead on arrival. If the city bureaucrats want to throw the book at Maverick to make themselves look better, that's exactly what will happen. We'll be the scapegoats. When the conviction machine wants you, it's going to get you, plain and simple. And it gets even better—that dirtbag Valentin's son is dating my daughter. Did you know about this?"

"Oh, no, I didn't." He hadn't realized that's who that was. "I knew she liked somebody, but . . ."

Marley'd been walking through the lobby with valentine hearts shooting out of her head, thanking Rudy for encouraging her to reach out to the kid, saying how right he'd been about the male psyche. It might've been his last shift she'd snuck out of the apartment on his watch to spend the night at this kid's place, begging Rudy not to tell her parents. Which of course he wouldn't—far be it for him to keep young hearts apart. He just sure as hell hoped Jake wouldn't ever get wind of that.

"I don't like this," Jake said. "Not at all. It's a setup. Val's just doing this to screw me. Taking advantage of a naive young girl, probably so he can get her in some compromising position and use it to blackmail me."

"With all due respect, I think you've got it wrong. I think you're being paranoid. The way she talked about it, I don't know . . . I think they're just two lonely kids who dig each other."

"Lonely?" There was anger in his voice all of a sudden. "What do you mean *lonely? How* could she be lonely?"

Rudy seemed to have struck a nerve. Implying that for all Jake's money and hard work a child of his could dare to be unhappy.

"Okay, maybe not lonely," Rudy said. "Maybe that was the wrong word. What I meant was, I don't think this is about you. But if you make it about you, take some kind of a stand, well, I think that could backfire in a serious way."

"Maybe you're right . . . though it might already be too late."

He let out a sigh like Old Man River. He sounded fucking stressed. But he was a fighter. He had weathered worse storms. Now definitely wasn't the time to ask for his advice about the bar, though.

"I'm so tired, Rudy," he said. "I'm so tired. But you know what? This could all go south, the money, the reputation, everything, so long as she—" His lip started to quiver. "She hates me. She's started . . . she's started calling me Dad."

"I don't get it."

"Instead of . . ." He was full-on shedding tears now. " . . . *Daddy.*"

"Oh. Oh yeah. That's rough."

"She hates my guts. She thinks *I'm* what's wrong with the world. My own daughter—"

"I know it's hard," said Rudy, patting him on the arm. "But if it makes you feel any better, and it should, it's the oldest story in the book, that generational divide. We've all been a part of it, one side or the other. It's the circle of life, it's . . ."

Jake had told him a few times how he gave such good advice, and Rudy felt a lot of pressure to keep it up. It was a lot of work, sometimes, casting around for a fresh, streetwise perspective.

" . . . It's the circle of life. And people nowadays think Gen Z is sanctimonious. When the boomers, when *they* were young? My God."

"How old do you think I *am*, Rudy?"

"Oh, I don't mean you, I just . . . what I'm saying is, maybe it's every generation's job to hate their elders, in a way. Maybe that's what it takes to move the needle forward. It's the cost of progress. Like, you've got to break a few eggs to make an omelet, you know?"

Jake wiped his tears away. "That's a load of crap," he said. "Wait 'til *you're* the egg. Wait 'til *you're* the—you'll rage that anybody in their teens or twenties would dare tell you who you are, or what your life's been like, or what your motivations are, when they don't have a clue. And it's easy enough for *you* to say it'll all work out fine in the end, to spew your little theory on the pendulum of social history, when you've got the rest of your life to fall down and get back up. When you've got no reputation of your own, 'cause you've never had to do your own bidding."

"Woah—okay." Is *that* what he thought? That Rudy was some kind of hanger-on? Rudy'd asked him about twenty times if he wanted him to start paying rent already, and Jake had just deflected, saying not to worry about it. "Are you pissed at me or something?"

"I don't know why that came out so nasty," Jake said. "I'm sorry." He blew his nose into his napkin, loud and abrupt, like a car horn. The people at the next table turned their heads. "I didn't mean it like that. I'm just . . . I'm all worked up today. I'm all wound up. You know I love you."

It was only natural Jake should be lashing out a bit, these days, and at the ones he trusted most. Rudy ought to steel his nerves, and buckle up. No use being oversensitive.

"It's all good, it's all good. I get it," Rudy said. "Love you too." He couldn't have gone back to doorman duty if he'd tried.

SOMETIMES HE PICKED UP J. J. from school and took him to Central Park. He didn't mind being a bit of a mentor to him. He was such a sweet kid, and he hardly ever made a peep, plus it was important for Rudy to show his face with the family, stay in deep, now that he was no longer in the building daily. Plus there was no one else to do it—Anna was completely off her rocker now, Marley in full teenage-rebel mode, Jake busy putting out fires, and J. J. at an age he didn't want to be around his mom that much. Which made one of them. . . . Rudy looked forward to seeing Nora all day. She was on his mind so often it was a little bit embarrassing.

He took him to climb rocks along the east edge of the park, or to the playground on 72nd Street off Fifth Avenue. He was a little old for that playground, or any playground, and sometimes they got weird looks from the other kids and nannies, a gangly kid with no hair and his minder of unknown relation, smoking just outside the gate, but who gave a shit. Let 'em look. So what if he liked to push his backpack in the swings. People were such hypocrites anyway. Fall all over themselves coochie-cooing at a two-year-old, then give the same kid hairy eyes for daring to grow a few years older and still take up space and oxygen. Like cuteness was the tax you had to pay for living.

J. J. needed to get his kicks in now, build up some physical confidence, before the world got in there and made him hate himself. He was more than likely in for one mean adolescence, only nine years old and the bullies starting in on him. And the way his father treated him wasn't gonna help.

Jake had once jumped, straight-up "ah!," and dropped his coffee cup—it had shattered on the floor—when J. J. walked into the room unannounced. He seemed to view his son less as a person than an apparition, some haunted-mirror version of himself he wanted as quickly as possible to get away from. But he was just a kid. Not the human albatross or frailty personified, just J. J., and you had to be yourself around him, and let him be himself. It was very simple, really.

Anyway, hanging out with him was a good excuse to see Nora afterward.

"How'd he do?" she said. She was standing at the apartment door. Rudy had just dropped him off.

"His water bottle's in there," he said, and handed her his backpack.

195

"Thanks so much. How was the park today?"

"Jesus, he's a mountain goat. I'm huffing and puffing like an old man just trying to keep up with him."

"Thank you so much for doing this, Rudy. It means a ton to him. And to me."

"It's nothing. Everything good with you?"

"Yes, actually. I just found out I got into a program, at Columbia."

"Hey! That's fantastic. Ivy Leaguer. Holy smokes, Nora!"

"Well, it's the school of continuing education. But hopefully I'll be able to get my degree and go back to work. I mean, not back to work. *To work.*"

"Well, raising two great kids is plenty work, if you ask me."

Jesus Christ he was a sycophant. "You must be over the moon."

"Yes, I'm excited. It's great."

"That's great."

"Yeah . . ."

They just stared into each other's eyes for like twenty seconds. He didn't even want to fuck her that much anymore, necessarily. His love had hardened into something chaste and noble. He just wanted to cup her face in his hands and tell her everything was gonna be okay.

"Anyway—I'll be seeing you," she said.

"Yeah, yeah, I'll be seeing you too, Nora."

He didn't care if she only liked him 'cause she hated her husband, or 'cause he reminded her of her dead brother, or if the only liked her 'cause she was totally, completely, murdered-for-so-much-as-touching-her off-limits to him. He knew most crushes left to fester had less to do with the other person than your own shit . . . hang-ups, visions, delusions of grandeur. Some old song of yourself you were trying to remember, or forget . . . nothing you could build a life on. But just knowing he was even capable of wanting someone that much . . . it kept him lean and lively, his blood high and on edge. His passion ticked inside him like a bomb. It lent a sweet hurt to the days.

THE IDES OF MARCH, 8:30 a.m. Rudy stepped onto First Avenue. He liked watching the day start up, stores opening. People rolling into work, pained but dogged. He couldn't believe the years of his life he'd wasted as a night owl, never waking up before eleven, thinking there was something French and brassy in his indolence. He'd been flattering himself.

Today he was happy for the sunshine and a clear head and a good night's sleep. It was meant to be hitting sixty later on, and he had high hopes for the warmer months. . . . Hustling in the city, making house calls to the Cohens's pad out east every weekend . . . gimlets by the pool with Nora, splashing around with the kids while Jake got called into town on some last-minute business. . . . It could be good.

He was going to meet Jake and his publicist downtown now for an interview Jake had agreed to with the *Daily News*. As a rule he was very anti-media, Jake, so it had taken some convincing to get him to sit down with the reporter, engineer some good press for himself to get ahead of any damage from a possible indictment. Rudy'd met the publicist a couple times, just your average man-shaped maggot. He'd worked for Eliot Spitzer. R. Kelly. Valentin Zalebnik too. The pantheon of miscreants. Just hiring him felt like copping to the worst kind of depravity. Jake said he was the best in the business, though, diamond-sharp, Stanford-educated, how he'd worked for the NSA or as a spy for the Turkish government or something before entering PR . . . real credentials. Rudy couldn't tell if that was a subtle dig at him or what. Probably not. Jake wasn't the type to bother with subtle.

Rudy went to his usual kiosk on 49th Street. "I'll get my Winstons, please," he told the guy.

There was a picture on the front page of one of the papers that caught his eye. The headline said "Heartbroken Parents Played by Landlord: Exclusive." There was a picture of a family, a little

197

girl smiling, the mom and dad in skullcaps. Inside there was a whole long story about how while living in temporary housing in the Bronx, a few years ago, a radiator had exploded and scalded the kid to death . . . awful. Apparently someone from the non-profit that ran the shelter had reached out to offer the parents hush money to keep them from talking about it or suing. Now they'd had a change of heart for whatever reason. Running out of the hush money might've done it. Not to be cynical about human greed where a child's death was involved.

Rudy recognized the father from someplace, though he couldn't for the life of him figure out where. Jeremy McLean was his name. Of Parishville, New York, way upstate. . . . It was the country cousin who'd come to the front desk a couple months ago, convinced that he had personal business with Jake. The article had mentioned Jake by name. The nonprofit must've been the thing he and Uncle Mike had been involved in. *Mike* had called it a scam, and Mike was a big boy, with a strong stomach for that sort of thing. Even the name reeked of malfeasance. We Care, Inc.? They may as well have called it Get That Money, Inc.

He called Jake three times in a row. No answer. The story'd been on newsstands for three hours, and Jake was never shy about interrupting his sleep. Why the hell hadn't he called him?

THEY WERE MEETING in the back of a nine-hundred-dollar-a-month private club and workspace in Soho, Crosby House, where the publicist was a member. Like Dracula's castle for the urban rich . . . a place to fill up, purge the sunlight between meetings. There was a sitting room with leather couches and a whiskey bar and purple curtains that come nightfall might be seductively swank but in daylight just looked menacing, like the anteroom to date rapes. The reporter was sitting on a stool on the other end of the room looking over her notes, Jake in the corner with his eyes closed, rubbing his temples, while the publicist pep-talked his ear off. He looked beside himself.

"Jake, hi," said Rudy. Rudy wasn't exactly sure how to be of use here, but Jake seemed to be taking more and more stock just in having a posse around him.

He stood up and gave Rudy a hug. "Hope you've enjoyed the ride, kid," he said. "We're dead." What had been promised as a light schmoozing piece about the future of his company was more than likely going to be a grilling with this morning's news. They'd sent a different reporter at the last minute. "I'm about to walk the gangplank here."

"It'll be fine," the publicist said. He didn't acknowledge Rudy at all. Felix Bracha was his name. They'd come from breakfast together, he and Jake. "Just say what we talked about. You did nothing wrong. Okay? You are not a fucking radiator repairman. You are not a fucking plumber. You are Jacob Fucking Cohen. Okay?"

He might've been the slickest bastard who ever lived. The supreme operator, so much a product of the here and now it was obscene. Wickedly sophisticated, with his media jargon and his Apple Watch and his Brioni loafers, his marathons twice a year, Brooklyn half, Manhattan full. He made Rudy want to go live on a hill somewhere in Texas with only dial-up internet and raise sheep and grow extremely fat and never have to see or deal with anyone like this type-A status-crazed scandalmongering fuck ever again. Slim chance of that, though.

They all sat down. The reporter started running the tape.

"I wanted to address something contained in a news story from this morning," she said. She couldn't have been more than thirty, Poindexter glasses, dad jeans on purpose. She probably had a shrine to Bernie Sanders on her refrigerator door. She was gonna rip Jake to shreds.

"According to the article, in 2015, you were the owner of a mixed-use building at 2100 Soundview Avenue, is that correct?"

Jake bristled, leaning back in his chair. "Yes, yes, that's correct," he said.

"The building has a history of code violations and complaints, squalid conditions—"

"Of course the conditions were squalid," Jake cut in. "You're living in a one-bedroom apartment with six kids, leaving your pizza boxes out for months, you're going to get mice. You're going to get roaches. You don't need a fancy middle school diploma to figure this stuff out."

Jesus Christ, Jake . . . the whole idea was to sound in touch with the people. Not like a spiteful millionaire who thought the poor deserved it.

"I'm sorry if that sounded—I just mean—these were otherwise able-bodied people who'd initially been secured housing under the guise of an emergency. Emergencies do happen, people get knocked down, and they need temporary help. It could happen to anyone. But there are people living in some of these buildings for four, five years at a time, people with no work ethic, no sense of personal hygiene, who would sooner spend what money they *do* have on Candy Crush than condoms. If the cluster sites are squalid, it's not exclusively the landlords' fault."

"But an exploding radiator?" she said. "No amount of cleanliness or eagerness on the tenants' part could have prevented something like that. You, on the other hand, as the owner, might have performed the proper inspections."

"We did, though. We did. You said yourself, I mean, the article did, my building was not on any watchlist. All our violations were cleared in a timely manner. It was practically a model building. And someone did inspect the radiators, in January 2015. You can look it up if you're so thorough. That their assessment was clearly wrong or, I don't know, they missed something is and will remain one of the great regrets of my life, but it was not my doing. I was managing ten properties at the time, not cluster sites, various apartment buildings, not to mention an entire bank at the height of the medallion crisis. It was not in my purview, personally, to supervise the radiators. But of course when everything went down *I* was the one who was first to take responsibility. You think the other guys involved in this were personally meeting with victims' families to *apologize*?"

"Well, but of *course* you should've been the one to take responsibility. It was *your* building."

"And I immediately sold it, and dissolved my part in the non-profit. I knew the whole system was unsavory, and I didn't want to be a part of it anymore. I wasn't trying to negotiate for some astronomical payout for the building either, like some of these guys, who've sold their clusters to the city for a fortune. They made off with one hundred, two hundred million when the first dissolutions happened."

"And you got, what?" she said.

"Well, about twenty for the Soundview building. Which was reflective of its market rate."

"Twenty million. That was big of you, to take a hit like that."

"I think your sarcasm's misplaced and frankly very unprofessional. Some of the people involved in cluster sites, you have no idea the corruption. The Podolskys? They just got *one hundred and seventy-three million* from the city for a crumbling apartment complex in the Bronx worth half of that. All because their lawyer raises funds for the mayor. Mr. progressive-agenda, my-Black-son the mayor. Why don't you write an article about *that*, if you're so interested in muckraking?"

He was playing it all wrong. The aggrieved landlord, whatabouting every which way . . . not at all the charming, open guy Rudy knew and loved.

"Okay, we're getting off topic now . . ."

"*You're* getting off topic. I'm here to talk about the future. What I'm saying is, I'm saying I got out, and without unjust reward. The family, the victims, got a crazy sum that of course wasn't enough 'cause it just went straight into the father's arm. I learned what a losing enterprise it was, my whole involvement in it. I'm sorry it wasn't before the worst thing possible happened."

"And the crazy sum you mentioned?" the reporter said. "That was hush money, essentially. And you're admitting you were the one to offer it. Why not just settle out of court?"

"I don't settle lawsuits. If you settle lawsuits, everybody sues you. Besides it was important that the tragedy not receive undue publicity or be on the public record. And permanently damage people's businesses and reputations for a fluke? A one-time freak accident? To do what, bring that girl back?"

"A freak accident."

"Freak accidents do happen. I don't know what they taught you at the college they just sprang you from, but in the real world not everything's systemic. Not everything's nefarious."

"And the misery and debt and suicide incurred by Maverick's loan system? Were those freak accidents? Aberrations? I just mean . . . it's incredible how much this stuff follows you around, Mr. Cohen, if we're getting personal."

"You're incredibly unprofessional, you know that? So much for journalistic neutrality. We're done here. We're done. I'm done with her. This is stupid. She's just out to skewer me."

He stood up to leave. Rudy and Felix followed him into the hallway. Rudy felt like he was going blind it was so dark in this place. Why was it so dark? What were they trying to hide?

"You've got to finish the interview," Felix said. "If you walk out, you can kiss your campaign goodbye."

"Jake, he's right," said Rudy. "If you walk out, that's the story. She writes the story for you. You've got to make her see things from your perspective. You've got to be yourself. But you've got to calm down. Have some water," he said. Jake had a couple sips.

"Do you need a snack?"

"No, no, I had eggs before."

They went back into the room.

"Can we move forward, please?" the reporter said, clearly livid.

"Yes, of course," said Rudy. "Sorry about that." Jake sat back down.

"One other thing," she said, "about your properties in Willets Point, in Queens . . ."

"What is this? What is this?" Jake said. He started chuckling, fake good-naturedly. "I stole a Mike and Ikes from an A&P on Long Island when I was twelve, are you gonna bring that up too?"

She just stared at him and said, "Um . . . no."

So she was a pretty tough customer, this woman. Jake could still recover, though.

"Mr. Cohen," she went on, "you were part of a lobbying effort to prevent the Willets Point Community Board from pursuing legal action against the city. They were in the process of suing the city for neglect—insufficient roadwork, insufficient sanitation services—and you managed to get the lawsuit thrown out. This is a community you owned property in. Presumably you'd be just as invested in its upkeep as anyone who worked there."

"Of course I was. Why wouldn't I be?"

"There were some that claimed that individuals who bought property in the area around 2008, anticipating its redevelopment, had a vested interest in maintaining the blight. That without the city being able to condemn the area, the redevelopment would be stymied, and the investors couldn't make good on the millions they predicted coming their way."

"I didn't buy a judge, if that's what you're implying. We did nothing illegal. No one actually lives in Willets Point anyway. The community board is about three people. There was no reason for an improvement to services. The judge threw the case out of his own accord. And again, I have no interests there anymore . . . I've sold my properties."

Rudy hadn't realized that he'd sold the garage. He wondered what would become of all those guys now, Rodrigo and them.

They talked for another painful hour. Their discussion of the taxi loans was a drag and a draw. Jake kept punting, punting, deflecting blame, Felix interrupting, saying how the loans had been made in good faith, under pressure from the fleet owners and desperate drivers. It was convincing enough, and hard to prove ill intentions with the lending. There was no smoking gun there. But the whole interview left a bad taste, like a harbinger of things to come. It felt like practice for the stand.

On the way out, near the elevators, Jake started going off on Felix.

"Great idea. Great fucking idea," he said. "You led me right into an ambush there. So much for managing that interaction. I should've never agreed to this in the first place!"

Jake never cursed. He must have really been lit. But Rudy couldn't help but be a little bit glad, to watch this jackass getting put in his place.

"It's going to be fine," said Felix. "Trust me. I couldn't have predicted she'd be such an inexperienced hack, but I'll get it taken care of."

"*You're* the hack, Felix. You can consider this relationship finished. I'll find somebody else. You won't see a penny of your retainer either."

"Whatever you say, Jake," he said, grinning like a crocodile. He got into the elevator, going up. He probably had a flogging to attend to elsewhere in the building, like in that *Hostel* movie.

"And you can tell Felix Jr. there's no way I'm writing him a recommendation to Columbia," Jake said.

Before the door closed Felix said, "Frankly, Jake, coming from you, it would only hurt his chances."

THEY DROVE UPTOWN together, in the back of a town car, in enraged silence. Rudy was a little bit scared to talk, or roll the window down, or even breathe.

Halfway uptown he noticed Jake was softly crying. Twice in as many days with the tears. He wondered if it was some kind of a male menopause thing.

"When I got that call, about that girl," Jake said, "*that* . . . that was the worst moment of my life."

"It's a horrible, horrible tragedy," said Rudy.

"It still makes me sick when I think about it. When I said I was going to see the parents, one of my associates at We Care told me not to use my real name. They were obsessed with keeping their interests obscured. If I was going to show my face, he said, at least don't tell them my real name. I told them my name, I showed them my face, thinking, these people have lost their child, this is the only halfway-conscionable thing to do. And look where it got me. Stalked, hounded, and maligned. I should've never been such a mensch. You give some people an inch, they take a mile . . . "

"It's true . . . "

"I just can't imagine why this whole thing got out, Rudy. I thought it was behind me. And right when all this stuff with Val is happening. I should've known it would come out sooner or later. I just didn't think it would happen so soon. Before we even got off the ground."

"Until you get indicted, and even if you do, this is all just innuendo. Right?" said Rudy. "The election's still two years away. Think about how hopeless things felt a year ago at this time. Your company was in the dumps. Watching your every move thinking you'd be popped off by one of Valentin's goons. And all that you've accomplished since then. The groundwork you've laid for the future. This is all just a part of the roller-coaster ride."

Jake didn't respond, just kept staring out the window, Rudy scrambling for an inspiring word.

"Think about how Trump must've felt a month before the election. A week, even. With that tape? All the liberal rags salivating at his downfall. But they were wrong."

He sounded like the toady of the century right now, but he knew it was what Jake needed to hear. And besides Rudy genuinely believed it, that the last twenty-four hours were just a detour.

"That's true," Jake said. "Anyway, what did you want to talk to me about?"

205

"Oh, you've got a lot on your plate. It can wait."

"Just say it. Please. I'd like to be distracted by someone else's problems for a change."

This wasn't gonna go well. Jake was in a horrible mood. He wouldn't be able to hear him. But Rudy didn't want to come off as a dawdler either.

"Well, they're talking about taking over my dad's bar—"

"Take the money and run, I say. He'll make a killing," Jake said.

"That's the thing. He doesn't own the building. He won't make a penny. He'll lose his income, his security. And he's that type of person if he stopped working; he'd be dead within a week, you know? He's been going there every day for fifty years."

Jake seemed like under other circumstances he'd be just the guy to talk to about this sort of thing. He was highly sentimental about dad stuff. Also about old New York. The way he talked about the apartment building, the Beaux Arts masterworks, all that.

"So we were thinking about maybe trying to get it landmarked. I was wondering if you knew anything about that."

"Well, you can't landmark a building you don't own," Jake said. "Second, they can't all be landmarks."

"How do you mean?"

"If you want landmark status to mean something, you have to respect that not every older building is a landmark. Our building? Of course. But a pool and darts bar on, where is it, 33rd Street?"

"34th."

"Oh."

"I don't know how landmark-worthy that would be."

"Penn Station's in need of a real reboot. That's a lot of very prime office and retail space. Better something productive there than a watering hole." Geez. The teetotaler rears his ugly head. "I don't mean to sound harsh. I know this is your family. But, well, when you're saying you want to preserve something forever, forever's a long time. And a bar? Forever? Why?"

206

"Well, 'cause it's historic," Rudy said.

"Why? 'Cause Spencer Tracy passed out once in the back?"

"Well, yeah, but that's not why. It's about ordinary people who came there. Come there. They've been doing so for eighty years. That's worth preserving, isn't it?"

"Why exactly? Really think about it, why. Divorcing yourself for a moment from personal sentiment, why is it worth preserving any more than, say, a defunct *historic* pillowcase factory? I'm sorry, it's just, I'm tired of these preservationists, breathing down my neck. They've been a real pain in my you-know-what, frankly, at my places up in Inwood. Always on their high horse posing as advocates for ordinary people. When a lot of times it's just the opposite. When a lot of times, who are they really? They're white NIMBYs, all in a dither over their river views." Rudy doubted that was true, especially in Inwood. "They've made development a dirty word. The big scary white man coming in with his scythe to raise the rents, to displace the natives, when in fact—"

Jesus Christ. This guy was like a fucking stick-a-quarter-in-him, run-his-mouth machine. Rudy was getting *so* sick of all the little speeches. He'd started zoning out sometimes. Within reason. . . .

"—And look at the streets downtown that Jane Jacobs, little miss hero of the people, once stood up to protect as the real, authentic, accessible New York. She succeeded, and now it's hand cream shops and fifteen-dollar macarons. Ordinary people, my eye. I'm starting to think people just like to complain. It's just part of the rinse cycle. They *love* to sing the chorus of 'There goes the neighborhood.' 'There goes our heritage,' when what city do they think they're living in? Madcap development *is* this city's heritage. Neighborhoods are born and die. Businesses relocate. It's all about change, and it always has been, and the complainers have always been on the wrong side of our history. People in the nineteenth century, crying over Peter Stuyvesant's precious pear tree—"

Man, Rudy hadn't had a pear in . . . God, it might've been five, ten years by now. He wasn't . . . he wasn't . . . he wasn't sure he'd seen a pear. For some reason that made him totally depressed. He loved pears.

"Rudy? Are you listening to me, Rudy? You brought this up."

"Of course, yeah, it's just . . . I just think, they've got enough buildings. They need more? Housing yes. Buildings? They got buildings in the sky with no one in 'em fifty-one weeks of the year. You need a building, use one of those."

"Oh yes, the eat-the-rich school of economic philosophy. That's real mature. That's a really sophisticated, complex, realistic, well-informed view of things. Do you know what it takes to make a city great, Rudy?"

"I don't know . . ." He couldn't tell what he was getting at. "Its people?"

"Its people, of course, its people. But they've got people everywhere. The people who made New York great? Truly great? They weren't just any people. They were people like Astor. And Carnegie. And Havemeyer. And I'm sorry, but Ratner and Schwarzman too. But that's not fashionable to admit these days. No, sir. The people would rather kvetch and bitch and moan about big business. They keep this up, just you wait . . . it'll be Detroit on the Hudson."

Rudy didn't even know where to begin with that. The first night they'd met Jake'd talked about those power players like he was relieved and proud not to be one of them. Now he was talking like Ozymandias or something, destroyer of worlds.

"Jake, Jake . . . I'm not talking about the Astors here," said Rudy. "I'm not talking about some . . . some civic-minded gent in 1860 who bankrolled Central Park. Bless that guy, that's great, whatever. I'm talking about some shitheel in a tracksuit—you mentioned these guys yourself—setting up shell companies so he can bury his blood money here. Probably made it selling guns to the clampdown. Contributes nothing to the culture, gives nothing back, barely pays taxes, doesn't even fucking live here, building an escape route on American soil in case Putin wakes up one morning, misses his bowel movement, decides he's on the kill list, and doing it all at New Yorkers' expense. Those people are a cancer, and you've said so yourself. But honestly—I wasn't looking to get into that. I'm not trying to talk about the whole history of the city and the people versus the money and whatever. I don't really care about that. This is just one person I'm talking about, and he's my dad."

Jake exhaled. "Okay," he said. "I understand. I get a little carried away with these things."

They were quiet for a minute as they pulled off of the FDR.

"We've had our shit over the years, you know?" said Rudy. "I haven't always been son of the year, but I worry about him. I just want to keep some ground under his feet. You know about that, don't you?"

Rudy'd seen the books. He'd read the allegations in one lawsuit that had been thrown out. How Jake had had his own father on some ten-thousand-dollar-a-month consultancy retainer in his twilight years, coming right out of the investors' fund. Looked a whole lot like embezzlement. Seemed like old man Melvin wasn't doing much consulting at that point. Nora said how he could barely wipe himself toward the end.

"What do you mean exactly?" Jake said.

"I just mean, you know, a son, he'd do anything to look out for his old man."

Rudy wasn't threatening anything. He didn't play dirty like that. He wouldn't even know how to, in all honesty. But, well, it was worth reminding Jake he wasn't dealing with no dope. That NSA or not, Rudy had his eyes and ears wide open too.

"Yes, well, yes, of course. He's your father. I'll see what I can do for him. It's a crazy, crazy time, Rudy, but I'll see what I can do."

Jake offered to have the driver drop him off near his apartment, but Rudy preferred to walk instead. It was a beautiful day. Colder than they'd said it'd be, but nice.

Libby called him on his way. She'd texted earlier to see if he

209

wanted to come over during her lunch break. Thinking she had him pegged, some bridge-and-tunnel boob, some beefcake ignoramus for her to buy to feel empowered. Fuck that. Girls like her had enough power. He never wanted to see her again.

He pulled his coat up, and rejected her call. It felt good. It's not like if he spurned her she could get her money back. Her check had cleared already.

10

LIFFEY'S WAS SO RAMMED Sunday he could barely get in the door. It was always a corker of a day, St. Pat's, starting at dawn. College kids in shamrock glasses and Mardi Gras beads, and retired cops and firemen come from the parade on Fifth Avenue. There was a sergeant from the Fighting 69th, in his brass-buttoned finest and shillelagh, already snoozing on the bar from his morning toast of Jameson's.

"Rudy! Rudy! Hey, Rudy!"

Some old faces called him over, raising glasses to him. The unholy trinity were right where he'd left them, three bumps on a log. They looked even worse than he remembered. Cobwebbed in their bar chairs.

"The prodigal son returns!"

Gary slapped him on the back, genuinely moved to see him. Rudy felt like some former dark horse at his high school reunion, rolling up, shiny with success, less vindicated than humbled to see how shitty and unblessed everyone else's lives had turned out.

"What's up? What's new? Everybody doin' good?" he said.

"Great," said Gary. "My wife and I got back together."

"He tends to lead with that, these days," said Hector.

"Hey, well, that's great news. News worth leading with," said Rudy.

"Someone get this kid a drink. ASAP."

Rudy hadn't gotten drunk, properly drunk, in weeks. Months, maybe. He'd been feeling all superior about it, but by now it was starting to feel a little bit unhealthy honestly. He felt like he was made of rubber bands some days, too springy and efficient to be real. All this pure, unmodulated consciousness . . . it was good, but it wasn't *right*. He was pretty sure that humans had been wired to stupefy themselves. Not every day, not even every week, necessarily. But once in a while you had to knock yourself around a little. Get your bell rung. It was how the blood reset itself.

"Thinking of moving near her folks in Redding, actually," said Gary.

"New York's for the scrap heap. It's all criminals and free-loaders on one hand, and tech fucks and oligarchs on the other. It's all—"

"You? Leave New York? Is that even allowed?" said Rudy.

"I knew a woman from my building," Elaine said, and grabbed Rudy's arm, bringing her face right up to his—he'd forgotten how she did that—"she was a taster for one of those guys. You probably thought they didn't have those anymore, right? Tasters? You probably thought that was some kind of a Julius-Claudius sort of a thing. But no, no. This fellow thought someone had it in for him apparently. A Saudi fellow. And this woman was so desperate she would risk eating *ricin* just to eat at all. She'd had uranium poisoning as a girl, from a nuclear reactor spill, in her village, and everyone else got eye cancer but she . . . she got these superpowers. No fooling, Rudy. She could digest anything. Whole spoons just passed right through her. She could deadlift three hundred pounds like she was lifting bags of chicken feathers. But I told her, Katya, this is no way to make a living, this is stupid, you're a nice, smart, nice young lady, and you're gonna die. Do yourself a favor, join the circus at least. And you know what? She did. Died, I mean. Nothing food-related. She fell off a boat, like Natalie Wood. Off South Beach. I'm pretty sure she knew some things the Saudis didn't want her knowing . . ."

"Anyway," said Gary, and raised his glass. "To the last hurrah. New York is dead."

"No way," said Hector. "People have been saying that forever. They get off on it. It's some kind of doomsday fantasy thing. An old lady gets mugged, New York's dead. I had a bad day, New York's dead. Go grow a beard and climb a tree or whatever you need to do in Pennsylvania or wherever the fuck, but we'll still be here, working. Not tying ourselves in knots wondering if New York's dead."

The deputy police who was meant to speak had fallen through, and they'd rustled up a last-minute replacement for him, a Joyce scholar turned poet from Dublin who was now chair of Irish studies at NYU . . . Rudy couldn't imagine how that had happened . . . it seemed like an odd choice. High-tone, given the crowd.

He took the mic, some Tom Wolfe–looking sprite in a three-piece suit and carnation in his lapel, gay as a blade. "Today," he said—the microphone screeched. "Today—"

"We can't hear you!" Gary shouted. Less to be helpful than obnoxious. You could hear him fine.

Dad fiddled with the microphone and handed it back to him.

He'd put on weight, Dad, a whole mess of it. All those Cadbury Roses he was chomping on to curb his nicotine cravings, probably. He always loved those. Rudy felt a surge of affection for his father so sudden and unwelcome he thought he might burst into tears. He took a swig of rye to drown the instinct.

"Today we celebrate the legacy of Joseph Coyle, who founded Liffey's bar eighty years ago today. He had come all the way from County Cavan as a young man, and grew up with his country and his city. One of millions of Irish men and women who came to New York Harbor fleeing poverty and war, wretched and reviled, on coffin ships, and were propelled sometimes in the space of a single generation to safe keeping, acceptance, and even the highest ladders of success."

A few people said "Wooooh!" and "Yeah!!" and one woman said "Give it *uuu*-uupp!"

"But it's important on a day like this not to let nostalgia fool us, not to flatter ourselves too much for the courage of our forebears. Today is a day for celebration, but it mustn't be all Danny Boy and bogus cheer. We are living through times as disheartening as any I've witnessed in my life, in a bitterly divided nation Joseph Coyle would scarcely have recognized as the America he loved. Today the president's men wear kelly green, and tout the bravery of their immigrant ancestors, while the children of the dispossessed are left to soil themselves in cages, and the—"

A rumble of boos moved through the crowd. Though not for the kids being put in cages necessarily. Maybe for this guy having the nerve to bring it up. It wasn't clear.

"Erra—let us remember that the success of the Irish in America wasn't manifestly destined, that our story wasn't one of our tenacious—" He signaled for the hecklers to quiet down. "—Our tenacious character borne out of its own will, but a combination of good timing, lack of melanin, and sheer strength in numbers that from Tammany to Ted Kennedy paved the way for us to show it. I am a proud Irish American, and I call on my fellows now to remember the great tradition of social activism that got us to where we are today. Edmund Burke once said, erra— Edmund Burke once said that the only thing necessary for the triumph of evil is for good men to do nothing. And make no mistake, that there is evil in our country."

Another set of boos and jeering. They were like carnival people. . . . And him with the Edmund Burke. What did he think this was, some coffeehouse from the Enlightenment? There was a large-chested girl next to Rudy trying not to fall over, in a tank top that said I PUT THE DD IN ST. PADDY'S.

"The future of our democracy grows darker, the ranks of the powerless and targeted more numerous each day. Misinformation reigns, and everywhere disdain for reality wraps itself in the false flag of independent thought. So let us not roll up the ladder now, and retreat into complacency and boorishness. The future of the world is full of challenges for which, without good sense and empathy for others, the luck of the Irish will surely be no match."

It was dead silent as he handed the mic back. Silent with a note of hostile. He'd seriously bummed everybody out.

Dad said, "Okay there, lad, okay," and patted him on the back. "Thanks, thank you for that. Some applause, please, wouldn't kill you." There were a few ragged claps. "This is a man with more degrees than some of you have teeth. I'm looking at you, Gerald."

Everybody laughed.

"But anyways, less talking now, more drinking, I'd say." There were cheers and whoops at that. "I wanna thank everyone for being here and I hope you have a great time and a Happy St. Patrick's Day. Here's to celebrating eighty more here."

They'd be lucky to get even one. But that didn't matter for the moment. In a second the music was back on, and the drinks were flowing, the voices loud and joyful. Self-reflection banished, meekness scorned, at least for as long as they could will it.

"DAD," SAID RUDY, and walked up and hugged him. "It's good to see you. You look good." He looked like a tub. "You okay?"

"It means a hell of a lot to see you, son." He had a new crop of veins in his face. His eyeballs were almost rheumy.

"Hey, well. I wouldn't miss it for the world. You march earlier?"

"'Til I'm dead."

Dad took his rituals seriously, especially the parade. They always used to walk together when Rudy was a kid. Mid-March in New York was basically still winter, but in his memories it was always springtime, the sky always that stupid, splendid blue. Opening Day blue. Dad carrying him on his shoulders when he was too small to see over the crowd, waving the flags for County Cavan and Mayo. It hadn't ever occurred to Rudy to think of his father as a single parent, in the statistical sense, but of course that's what he was. Tooling around town with his kid while trying to keep tabs on his morbid alky of a common-law wife, busting his ass to pay the bills and keep up with the shortfall from Rudy's scholarship to Catholic school. It must've been a lot.

"I hope we can find some time to, you know, talk," said Rudy. "About what? It's all water under the bridge. Just come around sometimes. Don't be a stranger like you've been."

"I will. I mean, I won't. Be a stranger."

Meanwhile Uncle Mike looked like the dead man walking. Full of troubles. He looked like he hadn't shaved in three whole days.

"What the hell happened to *you?*" said Rudy. "Rough morning?"

"We need to talk."

He dragged Rudy by the shoulder to the far end of the bar and sat him down. There were boxing gloves in the corner that once belonged to Sonny Liston. You took Dad's word for it, at least.

"It's about this shelter thing, that your boss was involved in." Rudy's stomach lurched. As much as it behooved him to know where the bodies were buried with Jake's businesses, that whole thing was too grim to even talk about.

"Why'd you deny knowing Jake, by the way?" he said.

"I don't know him. I met him maybe once. This whole thing was so secretive, Rudy, it was like some kind of cult. But I knew he owned that building at Soundview."

Once he started talking Rudy couldn't get him to stop. He'd never heard his uncle ask to talk or ask for help in any way. The flintiness, the hard-ass condescension he so resented in the man, he'd pay no small sum to have it back.

"There were something like twenty people on the board of this nonprofit," Mike said. "Taxi guys, real estate. One of them was a developer I knew, apartment buildings. I met him on a few of my construction sites over the years, we became friendly. And he made us an offer. He was threatening to use nonunion labor for his projects if some of us didn't fall in line. That's years of work, Rudy. Not just for me. My whole union. Food on hundreds of tables. So we did what we had to do to help him out. Rushing contracts through, greasing the wheels a little, signing off on inspection certificates—"

"Falsifying them, you mean."

"It was always for minor things, rodents, issues with the fridges or the toilets backing up. Anything serious we did our best to see to in person."

"You did your best."

"It was like Whac-a-Mole, the way some of these people lived, Rudy. Food on the floor. Shit on the floor. You couldn't address one complaint before another would pop up."

"Well, maybe if their toilets worked there wouldn't be shit on the floor."

"Will you quit it? You think anyone wanted something like what happened to happen?"

Rudy'd always wondered how Mike made such a good living on a pipefitter's salary. Sure he was high up in his union, and there were probably all sorts of kickbacks going on behind the scenes, bid-rigging and things, but he'd crept from decent earner into comfortably middle class the last few years. Rudy'd chalked the ostentation up to his wife's horrible fresh-off-the-boat taste in things, the kind of joy-starved, single-minded woman who thought Swarovski-crystal napkin rings were the best life had to offer, and was prepared to withhold intercourse to get them. But the money for all her tacky crap had to be coming from somewhere.

"I was familiar with the building," Mike went on, "but I never stepped foot in it, and when I heard about that explosion a few years ago I didn't even put two and two together, and it just sort of went away. The family never sued. The nonprofit got dissolved when one of them went to prison for something unrelated, tax fraud. But I'm worried if they sue the landlord now the paper trail will lead to me."

217

"Why would it?"

"'Cause that inspection, of the radiator, my signature is on it."

"Jesus, Mike."

"I don't know what happened. I honestly don't know. I swear to God, on my daughters' lives, I didn't sign it. The office at We Care was committing all kinds of fraud. I swear after a while they had a boilerplate they were just forging signatures on. I'm sick to death about it, Rudy. I don't know what to do."

The legal fees alone would bury him. And there was no way to exonerate himself of that one lie but to admit he'd had a hand in a hundred lesser ones. Rudy's little cousins visiting their dad in prison . . . losing the bar would be the least of the family's problems.

"I don't even know what I'm asking you to do," said Mike. "I just needed to talk to somebody. Your father—he wouldn't understand. I don't want to lay this shit on him now. He's stressed enough as is."

"No, no, I'm glad you told me," Rudy racked his brain for a reassuring word. "Jake, he says those cluster site guys are the scum of the earth. I'll bet he has worse dirt on them than even you. I'm sure forging signatures is just the tip of the iceberg."

"What do you mean, those guys? He's one of them, Rudy."

Of course he wasn't. One of them. Jake had his issues, his unsavory connections, but deep down he was a class act. And he wouldn't throw any blood relation of Rudy's under the bus if there were any other workable solution. Like smearing someone powerful and crooked who deserved it. He loved that kind of thing.

Worse came to worst he could even maybe—*maybe*—be convinced to eat the costs. Prison was nothing for guys like Jake. Like summer camp with bars. Kosher food, paint-by-numbers, a little me-time away from the city. Rudy taking over operations for a spell. . . . He'd still be a very rich and powerful man, a millionaire many times over, on the other side. Transferred to house arrest within nine months, testing the range of his ankle monitor at his favorite Italian spot off Lexington. And who knew, maybe a little jail time would up his street cred in the mayor's race. Crazier things had turned out to be true.

Oh, who was Rudy kidding. . . . It was lose-lose. Jake would never plead guilty in a million years. There was no way anyone emerged unscathed from this, and frankly it was so ugly, Rudy wasn't sure anyone deserved to.

"We're gonna sort it out," he said to Mike. "Just, in the meantime, you know, hang in there. Don't kill yourself or anything."

"Jesus, why would you even say that?"

"Nothing, it's just, you know, that kind of thing happens sometimes. Get stuck in a tough spot, some people choose to disappear." Mike pretended to be all proud and macho and a good upstanding Catholic, but it was too often the rock-steady ones with the purest streak of nihilism running through them. "Don't forget you've got a family. You've got kids."

"Oh, I don't need to be reminded. I can't even look them in the eye lately I'm so sick. Cece . . . little Ceara . . . Little Cece's the exact same age as that girl woulda been."

All of a sudden all the chatter and good cheer felt totally beside the point. Smiling faces, good times. Gary down the bar on another drunken rant of his, going on and on and on about how PC wokeness was draining the red blood from American society. Which was such a load of horseshit anyway. There was plenty of red blood left. Rudy'd seen two homeless guys outside the McDonald's on the way here beating the crap out of each other over a twenty they'd both spotted on the street at the same time. In the papers, war and rape and misery. Kids murdered in their classrooms, and steamed to death inside their homes. The world would drown in all the red blood that was left. And so what if some soft-handed university types wanted to spend their time drafting a petition to make, like, a yogurt commercial more inclusive. So fuckin' what. God bless those people.

219

It's not like they stood a chance in hell against the hustlers and the bottom-feeders anyway. Motherless, motherless hustlers. Motherless killers.

He walked out for a smoke to clear his head and saw he had three missed calls from Jake. It'd been too loud in there to hear his phone. He called him back.

"Jake, what's up?"

It was Nora's voice on the other end.

"You should come here if you can," she said.

She sounded beautiful and sad, like she'd been crying. So the old woman had kicked it. It had just been a matter of time. She'd had a good, long life, Anna. She'd seemed like a wonderful person.

"It's Marley," she said. "She's had an accident."

He hopped a subway uptown right away, willing himself sober. He felt bad for ghosting all of them but it's not like he had any choice, and besides it felt in keeping with the spirit of the day. An Irish exit.

11

THE SECOND he got to the waiting room J. J. ran into his arms and climbed on top of him.

"Woah, woah, hey," said Rudy, "hey—easy—what's up." He was sobbing like crazy, almost convulsing he was so upset. Rudy tried to put him down but he wouldn't budge, Jake and Nora looking on.

He had met them at the hospital, New York–Presbyterian, in the emergency wing. Marley'd told her parents she was doing yearbook at school when she'd been hanging out at some kid's house in Brooklyn, took some bad ecstasy and started hyperventilating and heating up. Talk about going from zero to sixty in no time, overcorrecting for her purity. Now they had her hooked up to all kinds of tubes, the doctors disappearing, running tests. Her parents were beside themselves. Somebody had mentioned kidney failure.

"Son, son," Jake said limply, "son, come on. That's enough. Let the man sit down now."

There was a March Madness game on the overhead TV no one was watching. Oil paintings of '80s billionaires glowering above the archway, some dead grandee named Alfred T. Zuckerman and his wife Doris, pompous and beneficent.

"I'm gonna sit down now, okay?" said Rudy. "But you can sit with me." He could feel the kid's head nodding against his shoulder.

They both sat down and J. J. put his hand in his. It was a little much. Rudy gave his hand a few pats and removed it from his own. "What do you think . . . you wanna play Pet Rescue on my phone?" J.J. nodded, wiping big fat tears away.

So the kid was pretty attached to him. Under other circumstances Rudy might have been flattered, proud to show off their relationship, but something in the way Jake was looking at the two of them, he didn't seem too thrilled about it.

"Thanks for coming," Nora said. "We ran over here so quickly we forgot half our stuff."

"Did you get the thing?" Jake said.

Rudy'd had to run to the apartment on his way uptown to pick up some of J.J.'s pills and Jake's briefcase, a few changes of clothes. He'd been just drunk enough for a little riffle through Jake's office while he was at it. He didn't even know what he was looking for, really—Jake wasn't the type to have evidence, damning or otherwise, just lying around. There were lockboxes in his shoe closet you could only get in with a crowbar. Or the passcode. But they weren't quite on those terms. Yet. He had walked out none the wiser.

"Yeah, yeah, here it is," said Rudy, and handed the bag over. "Everything's in there."

"Thanks," Jake said, without looking up.

The kid Marley'd been dating, Valentin's son, was sitting there, exiled to the dunce chairs on the other side of the waiting room. Clearly persona non grata with the family. Marley had talked about him like some brooding intellectual–freedom fighter–sexual legend of his time. He looked like a little bitch was what he looked like . . . gross Sicilian-grandma mustache, stupid sneakers. He looked like he was twelve years old. It was incredible what vivid overpraise a teenage girl's mind was capable of.

At least he'd had the personal maturity to bring her to the hospital and call her parents. That must have taken some guts. Rudy had known horror stories of kids twiddling their thumbs, afraid to get in trouble, while one of them lay frothing at the mouth. It had happened to one kid in his middle school, Johnny

O'Day, from one too many turns on whip-its. He was still in a wheelchair, Johnny, last anybody'd heard.

"On a Sunday, a Sunday, in the middle of the day, taking pills," said Jake to no one in particular, shaking his head.

"I told you, she didn't take a pill," the boyfriend said. "It was dissolved in a juice."

"Oh a juice. A juice. How very wholesome of her. And what pray tell was she doing with this *juice*?"

"Well, what do you think? She was trying to get messed up."

"Messed up."

"She's been under a lot of stress lately."

"A lot of stress? Okay. Stress."

Was Jake just gonna repeat everything the kid said, twice?

"Yeah, stress. With school, and her grandma basically dying right in front of her. And stress with you guys. She says you guys hate each other and you fight all the time."

Jake looked about ready to slap him across the face.

"Jake," said Nora, "Don't. Just stop."

He took tiny sips on his Dasani, deep breaths, and composed himself. "It's the lies I can't stand, Nora, the facility with lying. It's chilling. In a kid her age . . ."

"Who do you think she learned it from?" the boyfriend said. This kid really had some balls on him.

"Excuse me?"

"What did you expect? You're out to lunch her whole child-hood, working, disappearing to some gangster's yacht for half the summers she's a kid, leaving her to be raised by an old woman. Throwing money at everyone and every problem. Then she makes one mistake or acts the tiniest bit ungrateful and you go nuclear on setting boundaries. Trying to make up for being totally checked out by obsessing over shit that doesn't matter, her clothes, what she eats, her summer internship. Her friends. Treating her brother like some basement baby 'cause he's not what you expected him to be."

"Don't you dare even *mention* him—"

"Someone ought to. For the way you've been parenting, you deserve for her to be ten times worse. You deserve some brainless little slut posting her ass all over TikTok. And she's not. That she's curious and kind and has two thoughts in her head is totally remarkable and awesome, but it's no credit to *you* guys. So don't think it is. You don't deserve her for a daughter."

"Are you hearing this, Nora?" Jake said. "Are you hearing this? What the hell does *this* kid know to criticize *our* parenting?"

"I know, I know," the kid said, "because my parents did the same with me. You think 'cause they've got Russian accents and wear polyester pants that you're doing better by your kids? You're just the same. You're not any better. You've just got better taste. You're all a bunch of parasites."

Rudy was almost jealous. He reminded him a little of his younger, bolder self. Those were the days, when you could run your mouth like that with zero consequences, trying indignation on for size. Everything you did and said back then was like playing with house money.

"There's no love lost between me and your father, trust me," Jake said, "but if you knew the things he'd sacrificed for you, to give you a good life, you would hang your head in shame to talk that way. It would break Val's heart. You have no idea the things you take for granted. You'll know when you're older, though. *If* you live that long, with that smart mouth of yours. Grown-ups make mistakes. People have to throw their weight around to make big things happen."

"What are you talking about, big things? Big things . . . You guys have always talked about yourselves like you're Walt Disney or some shit. Like you're American visionaries. Like the world's a better place 'cause you and my dad had the bold imagination to speculate on taxi loans. You don't make *shit*. You just gamble on other people's backs. You didn't give us *shit*. What did you give us? A tarnished name to live down, a bunch of blood money. You don't make *anything*. And even if you did make something

224

it wouldn't be worth it from your kids' perspectives. 'Cause we didn't want the best of everything. We didn't want Park Avenue. We just wanted you around."

He got up and walked to the door.

"Where the hell are you going?" Jake said. "Are you leaving?"

"No, I'm going to smoke a cigarette. And I might go get a sandwich too. I wouldn't leave her with you people."

This kid was fucking great. No wonder she was into him.

Jake sat there, gobsmacked by the boy's impertinence. Nora looked pale and ashamed and said, "I told you we should've never raised them in the city."

"That's very helpful, Nora, thanks," said Jake. "Thanks for that. That's . . . thanks."

THE DOCTOR CAME in after an hour with the news that there was no news. They thanked him for the update, Jake begrudgingly. He was young and handsome and nice as could be, from Pakistan, one of those luminously decent, lawfully accomplished people Jake would've resented the shit out of if his daughter's life wasn't plainly in his hands.

"Ridiculous," he said, after the doctor left. "It's almost ten. Two hours without a word. Finally come in and nothing."

"What do you want him to do, Jake? Make something up?" said Nora.

"At least acknowledge the lag. For all the money I've donated here you'd think we'd be getting better treatment. Or at least be offered a nicer place to wait."

"It's not our room at the Four Seasons. It's not our table at Boulud. We're not getting comped for the inconvenience. It's life and death. It's our only daughter's breath."

"Oh Christ, life and death. Life and death. Miss Life and Death whenever it suits her. Driving your only daughter practically to tears 'cause she dared to have her monthly on your favorite couch cushion one time. Where was your perspective then, hmm?"

Nora just rolled her eyes.

There was a clementine somebody had brought up from the Au Bon Pain in the lobby and Jake took it and sat down with it, fuming as he peeled it. Rudy watched him, half-drunk still and fascinated. There was something almost farcical in the sight of somebody like him, so knee-deep in his life, so over-leveraged money-wise, morals-wise, doing something as simple and inno-cent as peeling a clementine. It was like seeing him naked, or on the can. You felt you ought to leave the room.

Even having spent so many hours with him over the last few months, Rudy realized he hadn't the slightest clue who Jacob Cohen was really. What he thought about when he was all alone. What really made him tick, under the hood. . . . He didn't drink. He barely fucked. He only seemed to want nice things 'cause the WASPs had them first. Maybe that's all it came down to with him . . . the golf caddy's revenge. Making the little people bow down at his feet forever, all 'cause some fuck in boat shoes had condescended to him once the summer he was seventeen.

An hour later Rudy managed to get his arm back from where J. J. had fallen asleep on it. The boyfriend was back upstairs, reading *The Gulag Archipelago*, for pleasure, Rudy bet, Nora and J. J. sound asleep.

He found Jake by the vending machines in the hallway, punching one to try to get his snack out.

"This damn thing—"

"Do you want me to go downstairs, get you something?" Rudy said. "They've got soups and things."

"No, no, why would I want *soup?*"

He was in a worse mood than Rudy'd ever seen him in. And Rudy in that post-drunk crabby phase, his whistle parted from its wetness too abruptly. He just wanted to go the fuck home, sleep it off. Leave Jake to his hissy fit. His work tonight was done. They could talk about the Mike thing once Marley was awake.

"Or if there's anything else—"

"We should talk."

"Sure, of course," said Rudy. "What's up."

"I'm getting calls from Larry Sinclair, asking for his daughter's money back. Did something happen? Something I should know about . . ."

"No, of course not. What did he say?"

Who Rudy fucked or ceased to fuck was none of Jake's business. They had laws protecting employees with that kind of thing. Didn't they? Rudy didn't actually know. He just couldn't believe she'd have the nerve to ask for the money back.

"Cause I can't have his daughter blabbing to her social set that my campaign is being aided by a clown. Or a predator. I can't have that, Rudy. Are you sure nothing untoward happened?"

"I mean, frankly, I think cashing a check for three times the legal amount would be considered untoward by some people. She probably got hip."

"That rule only applies to election years, as I explained to her."

"Are you sure about that?"

"Are you questioning my ethics, Rudy? She wouldn't have even noticed if you hadn't given her cause to quibble. That money's nothing to her. I had to give it back. It was humiliating."

"Well, okay, I'm sorry that that happened. But frankly she's a total cow. You don't want to be indebted to someone like that anyway."

"You have no idea how any of this works, do you?"

"Are you pissed or something, Jake? 'Cause if you're pissed, why'd you call me here tonight, on a Sunday, to sit around a hospital room with your family?"

"I didn't call you. Nora did. I don't know what kind of school-girl fetish she's got going on, wanting a tall man around in her hour of need, but don't flatter yourself in imagining it's personal." He punched the machine again, a wallop this time. Some Lorna Doones came tumbling down. "And that was before my mother's caregiver said she saw you in my office."

"Excuse me?"

"You heard me."

Rudy's heart bucked. He could've sworn there was nobody in the apartment. "I have no idea what you're talking about." Unless he'd been way drunker than he'd realized, which, it wouldn't be the first time. . . .

"Keep digging the hole, but you've been caught. She wouldn't lie. She's an extremely upstanding woman, Imelda."

Jake turned and went back into the waiting room, Rudy following him. This was escalating way too quick. He had to walk it back, calm him down.

"Listen, I can explain," said Rudy. "There's a lot going on right now. Your daughter's in the hospital. But she's gonna be okay. You know I'm not a thief." He wished Nora would wake up soon, put a word in for him. "I'm practically running your campaign, and—"

"Running my campaign? What makes you think you're running my campaign, Rudy?"

"I mean . . . what about outreach coordinator?"

"What did you want me to put on the business card, personal lackey?"

It was quiet for a minute.

"I've been doing you a favor, Rudy," Jake went on. "It was a vote of confidence. To be perfectly frank, I've felt sorry for you. When I met you I thought, here's a nice kid, pissing his life away, nice way about him, though. Potential. Obviously has had some kind of rotten luck to be white and in that job of his. I thought you could use a little boost. I like giving people little boosts. But, honestly, honestly, I can tell you're not cut out for it. It's not last call at Paddy O'Grady's Saloon, Rudy. People don't want to chat. They want results. They want substantive conversations. You're either too familiar with them, as has become all too apparent, or when you try to talk the lingo it feels studied. Like you're overcompensating. Maybe you thought you'd just clean up your act, cut back on your toots and read a couple books and it would all work out, but that's not how it goes unfortunately. Certain boats, you miss them, and that's that. I'm sorry. Going forward, I'm going to need someone with a more professional background. More professional credentials."

Rudy thought back on all the work he'd done for him. All the rides he'd been along for. Here he'd been thinking he was second-in-command when in Jake's mind it was take your kid to work day. *Nice kid . . . nice way about him.*

"Don't look crestfallen. What I was *going* to do," said Jake, "*was*—and might still, if you're lucky—I was going to offer to pay for you to go to security guard school. Though now I see you breaking and entering I'm not so sure that's such a good fit either."

"Security guard school?" Did he think he was retarded?

"It's a great living, private security. Special events security. It could be just the thing for somebody like you. Lots of actors meet their agents that way, you know."

"Is that so."

"That Ricky McSomething did. You know him?" He was just making shit up now. It was almost pathological. "You could meet a lot of interesting people that way. Use it as a stepping stone."

"Yeah, yeah," Rudy said. "Interesting people. Another bunch of smarmy fucks to tell me what potential I have."

"Well, you'll never get anywhere with *that* ungracious attitude. You should go, though. I think this has all gotten way too close for comfort." He sat down. "It's unseemly, honestly, carrying on the way you two do."

So that's what it came down to. Trying to make him feel like some fucking maladroit mall cop in training 'cause he was jealous of him, 'cause he knew he had the moves. Meanwhile Rudy'd been a saint with Nora. A saint. He may as *well* have been fucking her.

"... A grown man, holding hands with him," said Jake. "Going on walks together. Feeding ducklings. It's peculiar."

For real? "You really wanna go there? You think *I'm* some kind of—you should thank your lucky stars someone will give the little creep the time of day!"

Nora was awake. Rudy flinched to see her sitting up, staring into space, expressionless. Not a peep out of her for however long she'd been aware of them talking.

"You really ought to go now," Jake said.

"Okay, that wasn't nice. I didn't mean to call him that. Just hear me out about this one thing and I'll go. It's about that building certificate, with my uncle—"

"What'd he tell you? That he's innocent in this? His union is as crooked as they come, Rudy."

"Honestly? You're probably right. I'm sure he's cooked a few books in his time. But this is different. This is about being responsible for a little girl's death. You're always saying how much you hate innuendo, right. Guilt by association. How just 'cause someone's made mistakes doesn't mean they don't deserve a chance to defend themselves on a case-by-case basis. Or does that presumption of innocence only apply to you?"

"Okay, settle down, your point's been made."

"He says somebody forged his signature on that inspection. If we could prove it, you'd both be able to clear your names."

"He probably signed a hundred certificates for work he never did. And he'll never prove it was a forgery."

"Why not? He's positive he didn't sign it. I believe him. You can hire a handwriting analyst, or somebody."

"Oh, right, 'cause *they're* not on the take too."

"What do you mean?"

"It's the highest bidder's say-so. We had some drivers bring a forgery case against Maverick, years ago, saying how we'd signed refinancing agreements without their knowing. We laughed them out of the room."

"Say that again?"

230

"Say what?"

"You're saying you once bribed an expert to deny a forgery. You were forging drivers' signatures."

"What? No. That's ridiculous." He was lying. "You're just twisting my words . . ."

"You should be in prison."

"That's ridiculous." He threw his raincoat over his knee, imperious. "It's not like they could read the contracts anyway. Besides, the statute of limitations is already up."

It was worse than Rudy'd imagined it could be. Not a series of misunderstandings and misfortunes. Plain chicanery.

"I've only ever done my job," said Jake. "Nobody was complaining when skies were blue, mind you."

"Jesus Christ. My job. It's like Eichmann in Jerusalem with you fuckers. It's *I didn't do it, I was just doing my job*. You think *I'm bad, wait 'til you meet this guy. I'm just trying to keep up* . . . When poor people complain about the system they're just being crybabies, but when a man of means's ass is on the line all of a sudden his environment's to blame."

"You're way out of your depth there, Rudy. Way out. Talking like that . . . read two Wikipedia articles in your life and you think you're some kind of philosopher. I've got news for you. No one cares what you think about anything, okay? You're nobody. And so no, no, I'm not interested in brokering some kind of death pact with your plumber uncle. I'll be fine, thank you," he said.

Rudy had no doubt. Even if he went to jail, which he wouldn't, he'd be fine. It was like he'd paid his quota in self-doubt as a much younger man, and now you could put him through the wringer or put him on the stand—you could even take his money away—but hellfire wouldn't change him. He'd be bloviating 'til the end of time, peddling his influence forever. Telling the hounds of Hades they had real bright futures, just sign here on the dotted line.

"And don't forget, don't forget—" he said, "I'm the only thing

231

standing between you and a royal go-around by Edgar Kronman's lawyers. So watch your tongue, okay? Your back too, from now on."

Nora was still staring into space. Rudy tried to catch her eye. She looked like the brittlest biddy in the world sitting there, so small and sallow under the hospital lights, clutching a blanket around herself, one hand fingering her eighteen-carat diamond cross. She was starting to show her age, some Ruth Madoff-looking ruin of a trophy blonde. You could snap her in two.

He went over to rustle J. J. to say goodbye to him, and she waved him off.

"Please," she whispered, still avoiding looking at him. "Don't wake him."

He wondered if she actually gave a shit how her husband had made his money . . . probably not. Or if she did, it made no difference. She'd go on living, appeased by gin and cashmere, praying that some memory of poverty would save her soul. . . . Who was she kidding.

It was raining when he got outside. He felt like Jack the Ripper walking home, so psychotically unnerved he could slice a face for looking at him wrong. He saw a beer sign in a puddle, like a searchlight in the night, and stepped into the place it came from.

There was a long dark bar with some checkered tables in the back. St. Patrick's Day stragglers, holding out for one last drop. He always used to work the Sunday night shift. They were haunted, those shifts. Showing up for them had felt like entering the catacombs. Endless, endless dark. Sunday nights brought all kinds out to brawl—the werewolves howling at the moon, no sense of time or self-respect, the normals on their final futile stand against the working week.

He sat at the bar and drank himself to clarity. He'd had tunnel vision with all this. Taking Jake's word for it that he was mayor material, some pharaoh of New York. What a joke. It'd be a twelfth-place showing if he was very lucky. Maybe he'd get a couple fuckyou votes from the ignoramuses, the MAGA lawn-sign crew from Staten Island, all too happy to send the city's policies to hell 'cause they kinda sorta dug his style. But no one else would take him seriously. He was just a little cockroach like that Sinclair guy had said, scuttling around in the pockets of more gracious, more established men, no limit to the backdoor schemes and monkeyshines he would involve himself in. Rudy probably only knew the half of it.

There was a group of guys in vests and khakis watching the Michigan game and drinking responsibly and talking about Deutsche Bank. All these clean-nosed, gym-before-work, only-booze-on-weekends types, heads held high in the land of the living. Guys with lives and poli-sci credentials and fiancées with credentials too, and shitty legs, if Rudy had to guess. God knew who deserved the shitty legs. . . . Rudy would spend the whole morning in bed if he wanted, phone off, see if Jake had the balls to call on him or force him out. There'd be a standoff if there had to be. It would be the Alamo of 49th Street.

He was nobody's keeper. He was nobody's yes-man. He was a no-man from now on. He was young and strong and smart and good at things, and he could read a room since he'd first stepped into one.

(But what was it *worth*, that kind of thing. What was it *worth*, if you had nothing to deliver.)

A small faded woman with fuzzy hair was sitting next to him. He'd been buying her drinks for how long he couldn't tell. "You're in school, honey?" she said, leaning over her milk and vodka.

Geena was her name. Or Gina. Geena, Gina. Probably early fifties. She had a wounded air about her that made her very sexy to him.

"You in school?" she said.

They had to stick together, him and Gina. Grotty old-time characters like them. Real-ass New Yorkers.

233

"No, no, Peace Corps," Rudy said. "Ecuador."

"Oh, wow . . . wow."

"I'm back home for my mother's birthday."

"Oh, well, isn't that sweet . . . she's a very lucky woman to have you as a son."

One of the blue team scored a goal and one of the Deutsche Bank guys went, "Boooooooom," his Adam's apple bobbing.

"I've gotta say, the Peace Corps," Rudy said, "it's by far the most enriching, eye-opening experience of my life."

"What's that?" said Gina.

"It's enriching's what I said. You wanna go somewhere?" He had some money. He wished he had some heroin. They could both go die in a midtown Marriott.

"Oh well, I've got my fella here tonight actually." She eyed a big meathead-looking person in the corner, Ed Hardy hoodie, hunched over, sucking on his straw. He looked like the kind of guy who made a living owning-managing massage parlors in Jersey City, making Chinese ladies cry. He nodded. "But he doesn't mind sometimes to watch. If you're okay with that kind of thing."

"Yeah, sure, whatever. I don't really give a shit. Just let me take a piss first."

In the bathroom he kept forgetting what his problem was, though he was very sure he had one. His thoughts skidded not unpleasantly, like boats half-moored. He pissed sitting down for something different. When he got back to the bar his pants were wet, and the person he'd been talking to was gone. His phone and wallet too. He guessed he must've been in there for some time.

He dragged his ass back home a little after 3 a.m. His mind went in and out, pinwheeling. Tying one on had been a rotten idea. He just needed to sleep some and tomorrow he would figure the rest out. It had been too long a day to think straight now.

A memory came to him, of this guy, Joe Something—an old customer had given him a book about him once, and Rudy'd actually read it, for some reason. Out of boredom more than anything on one of his graveyard shifts, years back.

Anyway this Joe guy'd been a real New York character, a bum during the Depression, a graphomaniac, who wrote things down compulsively. And he walked around for years recording conversations everywhere he went, Black, white, young and old, on subways and in speakeasies, under bridges and in barbershops, shoeshines and accountants and mothers at the playground, just wandering around the city with his pen and his rucksack full of papers, saying this is gonna be huge, this is gonna be the defining chronicle of modern life, of the city and its people as they really are. Just wait and see. And he lucks into a meeting with the head of Scribner or something, on his streetwise charms, the way you sometimes could in those days, and then it turns out how his notebooks, these pages and pages he'd been carrying around for years, were nonsense. Half the pages blank, the other half like in that movie—the name escaped him now, what the fuck was the name of it, the "All work and no play" bit. He'd been writing the same sentence over and over again, some random shit about his childhood, rewriting and rewriting it, trying to get it right. His so-called chronicle of modern life . . . no more than the chicken-scratch of his neurosis.

When Rudy'd read about him he'd thought, poor crazy fucker, and never thought of it again. Now he knew he and that bum, they were one and the same. Hanging around, talking a big game, waiting for the city to deliver him his masterpiece. An empty vessel, like the women had said. So much overheard and nothing listened to, or learned. A lotta hype for nothing. A lotta empty pages. It was ashes to ashes for everybody, in the end. But for some unlucky people, it was ashes in the middle too.

He turned the lights on over the kitchen, back upstairs in the apartment. There was a burrito in the freezer there somewhere, a beans and cheese number he ought to force himself to eat or he'd feel like hell tomorrow.

"Turn this off."

235

Rudy looked up from the microwave.

"Turn this light off," someone said, though Rudy couldn't see him. "Go stand over here." The voice had a thick accent, Eastern European. Middle Eastern. "Near this window."

Rudy obeyed.

Had Jake actually sent somebody here to clear him out, just now? With his daughter in the hospital? *That* was tacky. Jake was as vindictive as they came, of course, but not like that. The worst thing Rudy'd learned tonight was not that Jake would jeopardize or threaten him, but that he might not even deem him worth the effort.

"What's this all about?" said Rudy.

He could make out there were two of them, in the middle of the room. One tall, one short, like George and Lennie. They started talking in Russian. Not quite Russian. Serbo-Croatian or something. He had no clue what the fuck was going on.

"What's this all about?" he said again.

"Shut up," one said.

His consciousness was like a wormhole. Like a movie screen with the letterboards, the picture getting smaller. He was trying very hard to stay awake and upright. Even fear might not be strong enough to power him.

Outside the floor-to-ceiling windows First Avenue was dead, a lone cab cruising in the rain. There were a few lights on across the river. A tugboat moving down the water, stern lights blinking, bearing cargo through Hell Gate.

The men kept talking. It could have been for forty seconds or four hours. It could have been for his whole life. He thought he heard them say Valentin.

"Valentin?" Rudy said. "Is that like Valentin Zalebnik? Do you . . . did Val send you?" They kept on talking. What the fuck were they *talking* about? "Hello, excuse me? What's this about?" he said. "Whatever this is, let's talk it through."

Rudy'd never been anyplace too far from home—Ireland,

once, when he was seven—and maybe now he never would, but this must be what it was like sometimes, coming here. The brick wall of words, and no way in. Not a syllable's foothold. People deciding the fate of your soul in a language you couldn't understand, and they weren't gonna give you any time to learn.

"Valentin's as good as dead man," said the little one finally.

"You betray your friends, you're good as dead. He's rat. Are you rat?"

"No, no, I'm not rat," said Rudy. "I swear it. I'm not rat. I'm honestly not anything. I just sleep here sometimes. I don't know shit about anything. And I don't have any friends. I'll just get my shit and I'll get out of your guys' way."

He started walking toward the bedroom when he heard the click.

"Shit. Shit. You're serious with that?"

Jesus Christ. Rudy couldn't help but laugh a little bit. Not that it was all that *funny*, it was just. . . .

"C'mon, man! A gun? That's just *tacky*. What *is* this?"

The taller one stood up, Rudy inching backward toward the window.

"Okay, okay," said Rudy. "Let's think this through. There must be some kind of a mistake here."

In the moonlight you could just make out the tall one's face. There was something almost clinical about his ugliness, like he might have had that big-bones syndrome that Abe Lincoln had. His mug might be the final insult, the last face certain people saw before their Harlem River graves.

"Okay," said Rudy. "Okay. Let's talk this out. I see you there. You've got your gun. Your Armani Exchange windbreaker. Okay. You're tough. You've come a long way from whatever shithole in your former Soviet Republic. Good for you. But I've got news for you. You're small-time over here. Whoever sent you doesn't care about you at *all*, okay? You think *they* care if you spend your life in prison for their dirty work? Wake up, man. This is your *life*.

237

Isn't there anything else you wanna *do* with it? Isn't there—"

He felt his organs jolt. Lacerating pain. He slumped against the window, clutching his side.

There was no use trying to call for help. The neighbors wouldn't hear him. He wasn't sure he had any. Sometimes at night he heard a violin, but had no clue where it was coming from. These high-end modern buildings were like ghost towns in the sky.

He had a vision of himself flung headlong through the glass. Dead before he hit the ground. The Russian mob had pulled that kind of thing before—he'd read about it—businessmen who'd run afoul of their Eastern associates, impaled outside their Marylebone apartments. Men who knew too much, bled out in their English gardens, Scotland Yard too chickenshit to even touch it. Ruling it a suicide, and moving right along. (And would people be surprised, to hear the news? Would they say, *But Rudy loved his life.*)

He used to think that kind of thing could never happen in America. But as the big one's boot came down on him he thought, *Any old thing could.*

12

TREES WERE BLOOMING on the Henry Hudson Parkway, but it didn't feel like springtime. They were taking Grandma to a home this morning, then looking at some houses up near there, in Westchester. It had been a losing battle trying to care for her in the apartment since she'd stopped eating entirely, even her favorite chicken noodle soup, and her limbs were like match-sticks she was losing so much weight.

"Anyone need something for the road?" Mom said. She was behind the wheel of the Mercedes. "There's that drive-thru McDonald's. It's in Thornwood, I think."

"Sure, sounds fine," said Daddy. "Is there anything the kids can eat?"

"Well, a few McFlurrys shouldn't do much harm," said Mom, and winked at her and J. J. in the rearview.

Since when did Mom wink. Or know what a McFlurry was. They'd never let them have McDonald's in their lives.

Marley guessed they were being nicer and more laid-back since they'd come to whatever agreement about their future. They hadn't dropped the d-word officially but it was pretty clear that was the direction things were heading in, Daddy staying on in the city for work and Mom commuting to Columbia a couple days a week from wherever their new house would be.

Daddy kept saying they were "downsizing" and "simplifying assets" like it was all completely voluntary and part of a real plan, but she was pretty sure the co-op board had forced them out of their building after one too many headlines related to the taxi probe, plus Buckley'd asked J. J. to leave 'cause his stutter had taken a turn for the worse, and if that hadn't been enough Daddy'd gone completely psycho in the meeting to discuss his future, really throwing his weight around 'cause he'd renovated the whole gym, and much gratitude he was getting for it, and he'd threatened to "ruin" one of the administrators or something if he didn't give him his donation back. The administrator'd explained how they couldn't return charitable gifts per se but offered to arrange to sell him back the Bowflexes, which apparently were all Daddy's donation had been good for anyway, and it turned out how of all the dads in J.J.'s class he was only like the thirteenth-biggest donor, his however many tens of thousands being child's play in comparison to the other guys, who for what it was worth, the administrator added, were real gentleman philanthropists, not just tit-for-tat artists and bullies (which Marley doubted was completely true), plus their sons, you know, could speak (which was probably true), and how a Buckley education wasn't merely a commodity to be bought and sold and bartered for by any *petit bourgeois*'s huckster off the pickle boat, at which point Daddy just stormed out. She heard Mom say on the phone to her friend Candace that the incident "took the cake" in terms of most humiliating moments of their marriage, of which there was "damn stiff competition," and Daddy seemed a little chastened after that.

As for her, she felt like hell. Or like some broken wayward girl in a nighttime teenage soap opera, whose whole family in the pilot's just moved to a sleepy postindustrial town up north while she recovers from some unnamed scandal in the city. Dimitri had been pretty justified in ghosting her, of course—his dad kept getting threats against his life for testifying for the Mueller thing, and his mom had found a pipe bomb in a flowerpot outside their house in Staten Island—but they hadn't even gotten to say goodbye at all. She'd just gotten a text out of nowhere Tuesday night that she was leaving in the morning and he couldn't say where to. Not even that he'd miss her or that he'd love her forever or anything.

She thought where he could be right now. . . . Scottsdale or someplace. Yucca trees and roadside diners, violet sunsets in the desert. Living out his life under a whole new name probably, and thinking of her sometimes, then less and less, then not at all, and finally never again. When she'd texted back to say goodbye and maybe needle for some reassurances—that of course he'd miss her too, and that her giving him her (technical) virginity hadn't been in vain—she'd gotten no reply. His number wasn't in service.

Mom said she'd get over it someday, that broken hearts always healed eventually, and that people *did* just disappear sometimes, hard as it was to accept. Speaking of which, when Marley'd asked Daddy where Rudy the doorman had gone he got all cagey and said he'd abruptly moved to LA to take an acting job. Which was sad for J. J. obviously but great for Rudy. She was super happy for the guy. At least *someone* was thriving.

THE SIGN SAID Elysium Hills Luxury Eldercare and you drove up a long hill to get to the main property, like at an English country manor. There were orderlies on golf carts and rose bushes and sprinklers and an artificial lake with swans. It was a pretty plush environment to grow old in, she guessed, but that couldn't take the sting out of the death and madness on the premises.

It really was a beautiful day, though—everybody kept saying that, but it was true—those ten minutes of springtime in this part of the world before the summer funk came in the air, the sun so high and mild it lent an epic flavor to events, like something big was close at hand.

Daddy looked beside himself as they drove up the hill. Taking deep breaths, closing his eyes, like he was walking to the guillotine. He'd grown a beard the last few weeks—he'd never had a beard before. He looked like some religious mystic, or like Jean Valjean.

He seemed a bit more solemn and less squirrelly overall lately, Daddy, and there was less running away to take phone calls. Though maybe there were fewer calls to take.

She couldn't believe herself that she'd been plotting to expose him the way she had . . . her own father. She'd had all these fantasies of leaking that story about that poor girl in the Bronx, really showing him what she was made of, and how he shouldn't mess with her or try to control her ever again, then watching him be horrified at her duplicity and guile, and then she'd give this whole big speech about how *he* had made her that way. *He* had created this monster. But then the story came out on its own before she even got around to it. The second he'd decided to run for mayor it was like the dirty-laundry-airing machine just started up full blast, and every halfway-questionable thing he'd ever been involved in came to light. Maybe he deserved for it to happen, maybe not. But she was glad she hadn't tattled. She couldn't deal with guilt and lies in addition to the sadness. She'd take plain old heartache any day.

Benny and his siblings and Aunt Brenda and Uncle Brandon and Uncle Meyer were all there waiting at the top of the hill with Grandma. Just the sight of all their silhouettes made Marley's stomach wobble, and she pulled her sunglasses down over her face.

Sometimes these days she felt so totally allergic to people, just the thought of saying hi and making small talk for even twenty-five seconds made her want to run away screaming like her head was on fire. What was with that? She'd heard all these celebrities and models talk about their social anxiety and how they wanted to use their platforms to help normalize it, but this, whatever it was, it didn't really seem like what they were talking about really. It didn't really feel like a clinical thing, like the brain's natural fight-or-flight response to being hounded by a paparazzo on your way to get a Frappuccino or whatever, so much as a deep, unprompted loathing for the performativity of human speech, and a radical desire to just be *done* with it somehow, without being mean or rude about it, or hurting anybody's feelings. She wished somebody would normalize *that.*

Grandma had come separately with Meyer. She wore her finest, brightest pantsuit, vintage Chanel the color of apricots. She looked great, though she didn't seem to understand what she was doing here. Her eyes were misty.

Mom and Daddy kissed Aunt Brenda and then Daddy hugged Grandma, and he started crying, and Uncle Brandon patted him on the back and said, "It's hard. It's a hard day, Jake. It's okay, buddy." Aunt Brenda said Marley, how *are you* sweetie, holding her shoulders between clammy hands. Marley knew Aunt Brenda meant well but she was over being treated with kid gloves since her little brush with death. It's not like she'd been trying to *kill* herself with the ecstasy thing. Someone had told her it was juice.

Benny finally came up to her. He was wearing Vans, and his hair had a little emo-looking flip in the front.

"Hey!" he said.

"Hey . . ." she said.

"How *are* you?"

He was so bright-eyed and bushy-tailed and positive sometimes she couldn't deal with it. Not right now. Also, he seemed different. He seemed . . . well, he seemed gay. Which was totally fine obviously, both for, like, the world, and for her personally—he was her cousin anyway—but how in God's name had she never noticed it before?

While the grown-ups were getting Grandma registered and moved in they sat on a picnic table out front, J.J. and her younger cousins running around in the grass.

"What's with the sunglasses," said Benny. She thought they really suited her. Black wayfarers.

245

"What do you mean? It's sunny. There's nothing *with* the sunglasses."

"Okay . . ."

They didn't say much for a few minutes. He was picking at some tall grass.

"So, I heard you had some epic love affair and almost died," he said.

Had his voice and manner changed completely, or had she just been fucking blind before?

"Yeah, I guess so," she said. She didn't really feel like confiding in him. Maybe if he hadn't totally abandoned her she wouldn't have needed to go off the deep end just to keep life interesting.

"Well, I'm really glad you didn't. Die."

"Thanks."

"I think you'll really like it if you move here. I promise. I think you'll be surprised. Some of the girls in our grade at school are really cool."

"What about the boys?"

"Well, some of them are kinda basic. But no, they're cool too." He'd probably swapped being JV quarterback Mr. America for being resident gay BFF-enabler to some awful group of suburban bitches who each had their own Range Rover.

"I feel like you like everybody, Benny, and everybody likes you," she said.

"Is that meant to be an insult?"

"No." Kinda.

"What's your problem, Marley?"

"Excuse me?"

"I just mean . . . you think you're the only person who's ever had your heart broken?"

"I mean, in this particular way? Honestly? Kind of."

"Well, you're not."

"He *literally* disappeared, Benny."

"Well, he was there, for a while. So you're lucky, Marley."

His eyes looked wet all of a sudden. Maybe she should be a little nicer to him. Who knew what he'd been going through. Just 'cause they had rom-coms now with gay people in them didn't mean it had been easy for him, or that he wasn't super, super lonely.

"You're right," she said. "I'm sorry."

"It's okay," he said.

She felt sad to think of how she used to think of him. How simple that had been. A crush like that was a country of its own, population one. Like a magic kingdom in your mind, and you could live in it for years. She guessed she couldn't rely on being hopelessly infatuated with him anymore to entertain herself. She would have to do the harder thing, and be his friend.

"What are you gonna do this summer?" he said.

"Oh, God, don't ask. Everything fell through. I might babysit just to make some money. What about you?"

"Well, I might be a lifeguard up here at the club. I think they're looking for other people our age, if you're interested. Technically you need a license, but it takes, like, twelve seconds to get one."

"Hmm, sounds cool," she said. "Also suspicious." Benny laughed.

The grown-ups came out then and said they were all going to go somewhere nearby for lunch. A nice place, with outdoor seating, and a great Cobb salad, about ten minutes' drive.

"How's that sound, Anna?" Mom said.

"What's that?" said Grandma.

"Lunch. How does lunch sound? With your whole family? Nice?"

"Oh. Nice, very nice."

Marley'd definitely ruined her appetite with the McFlurry earlier, but it might be okay to check out the town, and talk to Benny more.

While they were all loading back into the cars a massive black Escalade pulled into the driveway down the hill. A few men in dark suits got out, and talked amongst themselves. Then they started walking up the hill in her and her family's direction. One of them was wearing aviators like a federal agent in a movie.

"Are you Jacob Melvin Cohen?" the one in aviators asked.

"Who's asking?" Daddy said.

They told Daddy he was under arrest for a bunch of things and words and they did the whole "You have the right to remain silent" business, which . . . they obviously didn't know Daddy. It was the most absurd moment of any of their lives.

Mom looked like she was going to faint, crossing herself, Aunt Brenda going, "Oh, oh God. Oh God."

"Well, this, *this* is classy," Daddy said. "You really know how to pick a moment, fellas."

The words he said half-heartedly, like talking back was merely what was expected of him. They were putting him in handcuffs.

"When my poor mother's being put in a home. In front of my kids, my whole family—"

He looked right at her as they put him in the car. He didn't put up any fight. He didn't even look that angry. He just looked tired, and small. She tried to run and hug him but the agent put his hand out and said, "Miss, miss, stand back please, miss."

Everyone was pale, agog, their faces draining. It was only Uncle Meyer who registered no shock, just standing there a foot behind the group, lapping up the show.

She wanted to walk up to him and slap his ugly face. All smug in his purity, bemused by Daddy's desperation, when he couldn't have understood his desperation if he'd tried. He'd never had anything worth being desperate over. What did *he* have to protect? A one-eyed calico he shared a walk-up with on West 87th Street. His smelly old books. A sculptress ex-girlfriend named Suki who'd moved all the way to Japan to get away from his sad, bad-breath-breathing ass.

She knew her dad had done bad things. But she *was* his daughter, and she loved him. She didn't know if it was worse to smash and grab at things and say at least you did something in your life, or to sit back and tread lightly on the world and bore everyone to tears. Old men loved to tell her it was one sin or the other, idleness or greed, but she knew they were just lying to themselves. There were other ways of doing it.

After the car pulled away everybody rushed to Grandma's side, patting her and comforting her, like they were worried she would keel over and die from the sheer shock of it all. But she just waved serenely as the car went down the hill and said—loud as her old voice would let her—"Jacob, don't be long now! Your lunch is almost ready."

TAXI TYCOON NABBED IN BRIBERY SCHEME

APRIL 20, 2019

The CEO of the embattled Maverick Financial Corp. was charged Friday with accepting bribes from taxi fleet owners and an unnamed media company.

Maverick was one of the biggest lenders of taxi medallion loans before pivoting its business to consumer loans in 2016, a move that some say left thousands of drivers in the lurch, and may have even driven some to suicide. The arrest is the latest crackdown on an exploitative industry in which lenders treated inflated medallion values as their personal piggy banks.

Federal authorities charged Jacob M. Cohen with two counts of conspiracy to commit bribery, and one count of bribery of a financial institution officer.

According to the indictment, Cohen, 46, accepted gifts and favors from other taxi moguls in exchange for refinancing up to $200 million in loans on sweetheart terms. Separately, he accepted luxury vacations, including trips to Paris and the Super Bowl, by an unidentified media company in exchange for buying up more advertising, and violated his own company's anti-bribery statutes by not disclosing the getaways to Maverick's board of directors.

The trouble for his company doesn't stop there. A separate complaint filed in federal district court in Manhattan by the US Securities and Exchange Commission alleged that Cohen engaged in fraudulent schemes to reverse his company's dwindling stock fortunes as the growing competition from ridesharing companies sent medallion prices plummeting. According to the charges, Cohen hired a public relations firm to anonymously tout Maverick stocks on various websites, a violation of the anti-touting provision of the federal securities laws. In a statement, Maverick said it planned to "vigorously defend" itself against the SEC's claims.

For decades Mr. Cohen wielded enormous power in the taxi industry. At its height, his company handled more than $3 billion in loans and thousands of medallions. A prolific donor to campaigns on both sides of the aisle, the politically connected Mr. Cohen was said to have been mulling his own bid for mayor in 2021.

The bribery charges against him carry a maximum sentence of thirty years in prison. He was released on $1 million bond.

13

"YOU OPENING TODAY?" said Dad.

Rudy fixed them coffees and some toast. Formica, lace curtains in the kitchen. It smelled like Fancy Feast, though the cat had died some years ago.

"Yeah, I've gotta leave at ten, though," he said. "I've got an audition before."

Dad's Saturday paper was open on the table. "You see about that investigation?" he said. "Not guilty." He said it with a kind of pride, like, *that'll show 'em.*

"Yeah," said Rudy, sitting down. "I'm sure a lot of people are very disappointed."

"Well, screw those people. He's our president. I don't agree with everything he's ever done, and I don't like that grabbing women by their privates either, but he's our president and we're gonna have to live with him."

Dad started hacking crazily again. The doctor kept saying it would get better. But it was getting worse. He sounded terrible. The whole house seemed to shake with it, at night.

"He was—" Again with the hacking.

"Dad, Dad," Rudy said. "Hold the thought, okay? Don't get yourself worked up. The pontificating, it just makes it worse."

After a full minute the spell passed.

Dad gathered his breath and said, "He was investigated fair and square. And now it's time for all of us, as a country, to move on."

Yeah, yeah, thought Rudy, the same fair and square investigation you were calling a baseless witch hunt when it looked like it might go the other way. Whatever. Rudy didn't care. The news was full of smoke and mirrors, sham occurrences. He read the weather report, looked at the hotties on Page Six.

"Don't forget, tomorrow's Easter . . . we're going to your uncle's. Mass before at ten. And I don't want you rolling in half an hour late, smelling like last night's ashtray."

"I'll be there. I'll bring some hot cross buns."

On page twelve of the paper was an item Rudy almost missed. He nearly spilled his coffee, reading it.

Rudy went over it three times in a row but still he couldn't square it, how after all of that—forging signatures, forcing hundreds of drivers to sign over their futures on false pretenses, an international money laundering conspiracy—Jake would get nabbed for what appeared to be some small-fry financial improprieties, taking Knicks tickets out of the company fund, accepting limo rides and spa trips from 1010 Wins. Rudy guessed the people in charge had to take whatever they could get on him. He didn't know what would upset Jake more, being indicted or consigned to page twelve news.

HE WAS PRETTY MUCH recovered from the pistol-whipping, though his jaw still clicked when it was cold out. It turned out the apartment was another shady deal of Jake's, bought on behalf of some Russian aluminum tycoon Valentin had introduced him to. Jake helping this guy sidestep the sanctions on him in exchange for the use of his yacht, funneling his dirty rubles through the lease arrangement in whoever's name it was who would be dumb enough to think that Jake would do them a straight favor.

Once word got out that Val was blabbing to the feds this Russian guy had panicked, sent his enforcers to go stake the place out, find out what Rudy knew, assuming it was everything. Jake for all his paranoia hadn't seen it coming. He'd been nice as could be afterward, though, over-the-top contrite, paying all of Rudy's hospital bills, and plying him with teddy bears from the downstairs gift shop, and hamburgers from J. G. Melon's, offering to put him up at the Carlyle after he got discharged. A big fat raise too, like he'd forgotten that he'd ever fired him. He'd even offered to buy the bar, which was hardest to say no to—it would solve a lot of problems. But Rudy had to. Say no. He hadn't even mentioned it to Dad.

What was Dad gonna do holding on to it? Reporting for duty day after day, wheeling his oxygen tank through the 42nd Street subway station . . . those elevators never worked. And Jake hadn't done too much to recommend himself as a landlord— he would wait a couple years then sell it out from under them when the price was right. It was over. They should let it die. Send the precious artifacts of culture to the American Irish Historical Society, donate the rest to an Applebee's someplace. All that Rudy'd asked for was to make the thing with Uncle Mike go away. Which Jake had. For good this time, he promised. Rudy didn't want to know the details.

He wanted nothing more to do with Jacob Cohen. No hard feelings, but nothing else. No more favors, no more golden opportunities. No more spin, and bluster, and shady business, and kissing ass, all this not-work fakery that was extraneous to actual work. . . . He wanted to just . . . work . . . doing what, he wasn't sure yet. Maybe something with kids. Speech therapy or something. He'd been taking night classes at the Borough of Manhattan Community College, though he tried to avoid telling people that.

"Anyway," said Dad, "I might not see you later."

He hobbled over to the counter, fiddling with something. When he turned around he had a cupcake on a plate. Rainbow sprinkles, and a candle in it.

255

"Dad—Dad—" said Rudy, "what the fuck is that." Where the hell had Dad gotten hold of a cupcake? He barely left the house except to work. "You didn't have to do that."

"Of course I did," said Dad. "Who knows where we could be this time next year."

It was his twenty-seventh birthday. It was funny how the goalposts changed. From lights, camera, action one month to just keeping you and yours alive and out of jail and debt the next. Maybe someday he could hope for something big again. But he wasn't gonna hold his breath.

"You've got to celebrate the good things while you can, son." Dad put the plate down on the table and lit the candle. Rudy watched it burn.

"It was a good, good day, Rudy," said Dad, "the day you came."

GETTING TO THE CITY was a big pain in the ass. The bus to the N train, almost an hour one way. The sights and textures out his window offended and degraded him.

He'd gotten some nice messages so far, though. He should be grateful for them, people reaching out, but he couldn't help being in a snit. You never heard from who you wanted.

He'd gotten one from Allison, which was a big surprise. All that agonizing over her when she hadn't so much as crossed his mind in months. He was glad she didn't hate him, though. His friend Matty called him up while he was walking to the train.

"Hey Rudy, Rudy, wassup? It's your birthday, man!"

"Yeah, yeah," said Rudy. He was surprised Matty'd remembered.

"I always remembered your birthday. 4/20, boy. I remember thinking it was so chill 4/20 was your birthday. Like, right on. A chill birthday for a chill dude."

"Yeah . . . I guess it's pretty chill." It was also Hitler's birthday, Columbine. The accursed associations felt more pertinent these days. Plus he never smoked anymore, it made him crazy. "So how you doin'."

"Well, not so good. My fiancée, she broke it off," said Matty. "I've been pretty down in the dumps to be honest with you . . . But I'm feeling like, screw the negativity, you know? Gotta live for today. So I quit my job to pursue my dream of stand-up comedy. I'm having a show later tonight, actually, and was wondering if you wanted to come. It's like an open mic kind of thing."

"Oh, great."

Open mic nights were the worst. And Matty was maybe the least talented person Rudy had ever met. His lack of talent just . . . beamed out of him, like a shmuck force field.

"I should warn you, though—I've put on a little weight. I thought it was better to tell you now so I don't have to watch you notice it later and it bum me out."

"Oh, well, that happens. Don't worry about it."

"It's a club in the village. I'll text you the address. Nine tonight. Though I'm not sure when I'll go on exactly. It depends how many people show up, and their set lengths, you know. Last time there was this slam poetry lady took forever."

"Oh."

"Also, just so you know, I think they have, like, a four-drink minimum."

"Well, so do I."

"Oh. That's funny. That's great. I hope I see you later, man."

"For sure." He definitely wouldn't go.

He studied his lines on the train. The reading today was for a totally terrible sitcom about three dum-dum white guys in the city in their twenties, plus their neighbor who's a twelve-year-old Black girl chess prodigy, and they were looking for a Jersey boy, over-the-hill jock type to play one of the roommates. Okay, thought Rudy. He could name that tune. He was trying not to be so uppity about these things, but goddamn if it wasn't embarrassing when even the lowest-hanging fruit was out of

257

reach. He'd been to a few auditions in the last month, always the same scene, all the hopefuls gathered on the upper floors of a crumbling office building on Eighth Avenue, gorging on the free provisions, half of them starry-eyed, the other half visibly depressed, like this one last chance was all that stood between them and packing it in, going back to Oklahoma and hanging themselves in their parents' garages.

The train groaned as it crossed the water. It rocked and rattled underground.

He looked around the car. Everybody looked a little lighter on their feet today, like the loads of winter had been cast off for good. He wished he felt it too. That easing up. Sometimes the weight of the present moment hung down on him so heavy, like some kind of crust, or carapace—his life, this set of thoughts and habits and memories and obligations he wanted just to snap his fingers and be rid of, without having to die of course. He wondered if it wasn't something chemical with him. Though maybe it was just the times.

He'd always been a sucker for nostalgia. There'd been no escaping it, growing up in Liffey's bar . . . the lore of the past was in his blood. The lore of how the neighborhood once was, what a dollar could once get you. How the Irish used to rule New York.

There'd been a photograph behind the cash register he'd been obsessed with as a kid, Penn Station, 1947. Almost painful to him in its loftiness, the casual grace of things back then. The cut of people's overcoats, the shadowfall of arches in the old main concourse. Shopkeeps, men in fedoras buying chocolates for their wives. Workmen with their lunch pails, walking through the Parthenon.

It was false thinking, of course. They were all just people, back then, just like him. And their times were no great comfort to them probably. They weren't walking around, pumped out of their minds that it was 1947. Certainly not the Blacks and the women. They were all just people, full of tics and hang-ups, and stupid thoughts, and tense shit with their families, and bodies to tend to—itches to scratch, pisses to take—going home to lie in bed, alone in the dark, maybe having trouble sleeping. Bummed out on their birthdays, fearing for the future. It had always been that way for people. Just hours, minutes, and seconds, weighing heavily on every human head. There had never been no cure for it.

A woman got on at 49th Street with her son. They sat across from him a couple bodies down on the only seats left open now. The car had filled up as it neared Manhattan.

It took him the whole rest of the ride to 34th to place her—she looked exactly like a woman he had kicked out of the bar one time, however long ago. Same dark hair, same heart-shaped face. Five years younger since quitting the skag.

She looked up and caught him staring at her, and instead of looking creeped out, which she had every right to be, she smiled. The kid was playing peekaboo.

It couldn't have been her. No way. That girl was probably dead by now. If not in body then in spirit, back by Greyhound bus to Erie County or someplace, some dreary little mill town, never to step foot down here again. Another person chewed up and spat out by the city. It couldn't have been her. . . . What were the chances of a thing like that.

The train sped up as it approached the station, smashing, hurtling through the tunnel, his reception coming back. A flood of messages, ads and ads, the automated crud. The usual bother-ations. *Hand-Picked Styles For You, Rudy. Redeem Your Birth-day Credit Now! Free Shipping Ends at Midnight.* The news of the world, the endless dripfeed. But there was something else too, actually for him, and the letters of her name were clean and per-fect in his eyes. It was Tara, writing to wish him happy birthday, and thank God, thank fucking God for *that.*